SEALED AT THE ALTAR

Bone Frog Brotherhood Book 2

SHARON HAMILTON

Print Edition

SHARON HAMILTON'S BOOK LIST

SEAL BROTHERHOOD SERIES

Accidental SEAL (Book 1)
Fallen SEAL Legacy (Book 2)
SEAL Under Covers (Book 3)
SEAL The Deal (Book 4)
Cruisin' For A SEAL (Book 5)
SEAL My Destiny (Book 6)
SEAL Of My Heart (Book 7)
Fredo's Dream (Book 8)
SEAL My Love (Book 9)
SEAL Brotherhood Box Set 1 (Accidental SEAL & Prequel)
SEAL Brotherhood Box Set 2 (Fallen SEAL & Prequel)
Ultimate SEAL Collection Vol. 1 (Books 1-4 / 2 Prequels)
Ultimate SEAL Collection Vol. 2 (Books 5-7)

BAD BOYS OF SEAL TEAM 3 SERIES

SEAL's Promise (Book 1)
SEAL My Home (Book 2)
SEAL's Code (Book 3)
Big Bad Boys Bundle (Books 1-3 of Bad Boys)

BAND OF BACHELORS SERIES

Lucas (Book 1)
Alex (Book 2)
Jake (Book 3)
Jake 2 (Book 4)
Big Band of Bachelors Bundle

TRUE BLUE SEALS SERIES

True Navy Blue (prequel to Zak)
Zak (Includes novella above)

NASHVILLE SEAL SERIES

Nashville SEAL (Book 1)
Nashville SEAL: Jameson (Books 1 & 2 combined)

SILVER SEALS
SEAL Love's Legacy

SLEEPER SEALS
Bachelor SEAL

STAND ALONE SEALS
SEAL's Goal: The Beautiful Game

Love Me Tender, Love You Hard

BONE FROG BROTHERHOOD SERIES
New Year's SEAL Dream (Book 1)

SEALed At The Altar (Book 2)

SEALed Forever (Book 3)

SEAL's Rescue (Book 4)

PARADISE SERIES
Paradise: In Search of Love

STANDALONE NOVELLAS
SEAL You In My Dreams (Magnolias and Moonshine)

SEAL Of Time (Trident Legacy)

FALL FROM GRACE SERIES (PARANORMAL)
Gideon: Heavenly Fall

GOLDEN VAMPIRES OF TUSCANY SERIES (PARANORMAL)
Honeymoon Bite (Book 1)

Mortal Bite (Book 2)

Christmas Bite (Book 3)

Midnight Bite (Book 4 Coming Summer 2019)

THE GUARDIANS (PARANORMAL)
Heavenly Lover (Book 1)

Underworld Lover (Book 2)

Underworld Queen (Book 3)

AUDIOBOOKS
Sharon Hamilton's books are available as audiobooks narrated by J.D. Hart.

ABOUT THE BOOK

Despite his thirty-nine years, Tucker Hudson is in peak physical condition and is considering rejoining the SEAL Teams after a ten-year hiatus. What he hadn't counted on is a steady relationship with Brandy. Is this thing between them something he can count on or is it just a distraction? Now he's torn between his heart and career. Can he balance them both?

A plus-size girl, Brandy never fails to be there for her friends' and their happiness. But for her, relationships are little more than one-night stands, and she's made her peace with who she is. At least until Tucker shows up at a SEAL wedding on New Year's Eve. The intensity between them makes her wonder if marriage is a wise choice or just another misstep.

The evil forces surrounding them will test their relationship. Will their love be strong enough to last a lifetime, or will it become just a pleasant memory of what could have been?

A continuation of New Years SEAL Dream novella, Book #1 of the Bone Frog Brotherhood

AUTHOR'S NOTE

I always dedicate my SEAL Brotherhood books to the brave men and women who defend our shores and keep us safe. Without their sacrifice, and that of their families—because a warrior's fight always includes his or her family—I wouldn't have the freedom and opportunity to make a living writing these stories. They sometimes pay the ultimate price so we can debate, argue, go have coffee with friends, raise our children and see them have children of their own.

One of my favorite tributes to warriors resides on many memorials, including one I saw honoring the fallen of WWII on an island in the Pacific:

"When you go home
Tell them of us, and say
For your tomorrow,
We gave our today."

These are my stories created out of my own imagination. Anything that is inaccurately portrayed is either my mistake, or done intentionally to disguise something I might have overheard over a beer or in the corner of one of the hangouts along the Coronado Strand.

I support two main charities. Navy SEAL/UDT Museum operates in Ft. Pierce, Florida. Please learn about this wonderful museum, all run by active and former SEALs and their friends and families, and who rely on public support, not that of the U.S. Government.
www.navysealmuseum.org

I also support Wounded Warriors, who tirelessly bring together the warrior as well as the family members who are just learning to deal with their soldier's condition and have nowhere to turn. It is a long path to becoming well, but I've seen first-hand what this organization does for its warriors and the families who love them. Please give what your heart tells you is right. If you cannot give, volunteer at one of the many service centers all over the United States. Get involved. Do something meaningful for someone who gave so much of themselves, to families who have paid the price for your freedom. You'll find a family there unlike any other on the planet.
www.woundedwarriorproject.org

CHAPTER 1

TUCKER THOUGHT ABOUT his hot tub lovemaking session with Brandy the night before. It sprang from the long kiss he'd given her after he told her to just lean back, put her arms out to the sides, and fly away with him to who knew where? He'd told her to just trust him, that he'd be right there behind her, just as they'd been the day before skydiving. He'd professed his love for her and promised to take care of her.

But he'd stopped short of asking her to marry him. That was what was giving him problems today as they drove to the winery picnic the whole group of SEALs and their wives and girlfriends were attending in Wine Country. Last night under the stars he'd taken her body as they'd floated in the hot tub, thrusting as if he rammed her hard enough, he'd stick there forever. He wanted to dig deep and never leave, and she accepted all of him, begging for more as he pleasured her every way he could think of. He kissed away all her tears as she released so beautifully in soft moans, shuddering and spurring him on, stroking her insides until his full release.

He'd even carried her wet nude body back through the patio and back into the barn where their cubicle was carved out with sheets hanging over stringer wires. He laid her back on the bed and worshiped her, nuzzling all the softness of her curvy hips and wonderful breasts. Her white flesh and droplets of water shone in the moonlight as his arms covered hers and clutched her fingers in his. Even as his kisses lowered to her belly he knew she was fast asleep, and he'd put her there in the land of Nod.

Was she dreaming of him?

He hadn't slept, even after trying to sync with her breathing, but it was no use. He was not going to be able to sleep until whatever was needling him worked its way out, like an old splinter.

Morning came softly and he watched her sleepy body awaken to the sounds of birds outside. Her eyes were full of wonder as she lay next to him and stared at the wooden ceiling, like he had done all during the night.

They'd spoken very little this morning. The two of them showered together and she teased him but didn't demand anything. Their fondling and tickling and kissing was always a pleasant start of the daily routine, most the time leading to another sexual encounter. But today, it was enough that they couldn't keep their hands off each other, as if the words spoken so sparsely last night under the night sky was enough to last them a month.

Maybe that was it.

"You're so quiet this morning, Tucker. What has you so preoccupied?"

He smiled to cover up his surprise that he'd failed to mask his pensive mood. He glanced to his right and she wasn't having any of it. He could lie, of course. But he wasn't going to. He just wanted to remain silent until he figured out what was bothering him.

"I'm just happy, Brandy. Really happy." It was the truth. But would it work?

She reached into his lap and felt his semi-hardness, and stroked him, coaxing him to lose himself between her fingers. He wanted to unbutton his pants but was hoping she'd do it. He did need release.

She continued to stroke up and down as he spread his knees further and he presented to her warm palm he could feel even through the fabric of his pants.

"This what you're thinking about?" She asked. "We could always take a detour…"

He had a flash of clarity. He saw her in a wedding dress, and then he saw her belly grow large with a child. He was definitely having dangerous thoughts.

Sex had always been just that: sex. With Brandy, he'd wanted to fill her, make her have his baby.

This scared the pants off him. While that would solve one problem, it left another one glaring: the more they made love the more he wanted her. This had never happened before. Even Shayla, his first wife, when they were young and fresh and fucking like rabbits all the time, even then he didn't feel like this. He was burying himself to make roots, not to get himself off.

His hands were sweaty. His forehead too. His deep breathing was mistaken for arousal, causing Brandy to deftly slip her fingers inside his waistband and unfasten him. She seared him with a sultry smile just before she went down on him. He nearly went off the road, quickly checking his rear view mirror.

Her tongue curled around him. With one hand on the steering wheel, he placed his other palm at the back of her head buried in his lap, and pressed her onto him. She moaned as she sucked and kissed him to oblivion.

The sunshine was extremely bright outside as they continued down the winding two-lane country highway. It got brighter the more she worked on him—the closer he got to climax. And, bless her soul, just as he began to spill, she placed him between her enormous breasts and squeezed.

Brandy's tee shirts were always too small for her,

and the look of the cotton shoved up under her chin, her double large chest all ripe and firm, was a sight he'd never tire of looking at. A few seconds later and that tee shirt was desperately needed.

He laced his fingers through her hair. "God, Brandy, I've died and gone straight to Heaven."

She rose to her knees, leaned over him, removed the wet shirt, and grabbed another one from her bag in the second seat. Pulling it tight over her breasts, her nipples puckered under the new pink fabric, bulging and knotted.

"You're going to distract everyone at the picnic, sweetheart. No bra?"

She leaned back on the seat and tickled her nipples outside the cotton shirt. "No bra," she said, with her eyes the size of a small child's. "Will that make you jealous?"

"No, honey. I'm a man of action. I don't dwell in those places of self-doubt and pity. I'll beg you to ride my cock hard until you behave."

She grinned, and then stared out the windshield. "I'm happy too, Tucker. Really happy. I wish I hadn't been so afraid of this."

He nodded, understanding he'd been her nearly first sexual partner, though he would have been easily fooled to think otherwise. She was preening, reapplying her lipstick that had been smeared all over his organ, which he now stowed back into his pants with one hand.

That word again came up: *this.* Just what *was* this? Should he tell her about the fantasies he'd been having? Or, should he not distract from her delicious mood, exploring the newfound feeling of love and lust all wrapped up in one velvet package? He'd experienced the cravings, but not these cravings that only lead to that stronger desire to have her again after every encounter.

Tucker knew he'd been intense as a SEAL, and perhaps that's why Shayla left him for the other Team Guy. He'd been so focused on his career, on the brotherhood of men he was absolutely digging serving with, the danger and excitement of being a man's man doing things most people couldn't even comprehend. Now that he was out, perhaps that's why he and Brandy had made the instant hook-up. He willingly let her be needy with him because he needed to give it all back. With Shayla, their carefree spirit gave way to routine and eventually boredom, where they were just going through the motions. They were pretending to be a couple long after she'd mentally and even physically moved on.

It was fucked up, and after the breakup it caused him to force a change of scenery, but he never felt he lost something he needed.

He *needed* Brandy.

That's what made all this talk between them last night and internal thought this afternoon so dangerous. Brandy was *very* dangerous. She was lethal. And still he allowed his wrists to be bound by those golden ropes, his chest bleeding from the pain in his heart. He needed her so much he might die over it.

He saw the three Hummers and trucks pull up to the large steep-roof buildings of the winery created from a hop-drying kiln. Kyle and Cooper directed traffic and that's when it hit him. He needed them too. He missed the contact he used to have with the Team Guys all weekend between deployments. Even when he knew Shayla was staying out late, making naked calls to the Team Guy who was on deployment, he still needed his buddies. It's where he wanted to be most of all.

He barely had time to think about it as he was directed to park. But, would the same thing happen to them if he got accepted back on a SEAL Team? Would Brandy, now erupting with womanly wiles and enough pheromones to sink a battleship, find someone else to satisfy her when he was no longer around? Four and six month deployments were common these days, Kyle had warned. Would she wait for him? *Could* she wait for him?

Or, was that too much to ask?

Because he was still deep in thought, Brandy made

it out of the truck before he did, and sauntered over to Christy and Dorie. He hoped she didn't notice his lack of attention. Her voluptuous body swayed down the driveway in front of him, her long mahogany hair fluffed up by her fingers as she called out to her best friend. He could watch her all day, and had many nights.

But still, he felt like a heel. That talk show doctor would be wagging her finger at him. He was taking the cookies out of the cookie jar without paying for them. But had that doctor ever found two things she couldn't do without like he had? Was it really fair to judge him so harshly?

At the precipice of an epic change in his life, Tucker wasn't sure which pursuit he should concentrate on first. If he pursued joining a SEAL team, would marriage interfere with his training? And if he made the team, would he be able to be as devoted a husband as she required? Was it fair to Brandy to put her through all this?

He decided to wait on either event until he could see himself having both. Then he'd give the choice to Brandy and pray like hell somehow it all worked out.

Although he knew that was never the way to run a mission, it was going to have to just stay that way for a bit until he could figure things out. Because when he moved, he wanted to be balls to the wall. No excuses.

No holding back. Going for it with every ounce of his being. He'd throw his heart out there in the ring too. Mix it up, and hope she'd agree to take him, wounded, unsure of himself than he ever wanted to admit.

She could love out all the kinks and inconsistencies lodged like pieces of glass inside him, while he was planting roots inside her.

There was a chance this could work. But just a chance.

In either event, it would be worth it.

CHAPTER 2

BRANDY COOK HAD never been to Northern California Wine Country before and was stunned with the beauty surrounding her. Every direction she beheld world-class views of green hills dotted with acres of vineyard cornrows. Yellow mustard flowers and gnarled old growth vines lay before her on the famous Dry Creek Valley floor. She was so overwhelmed, she could hardly speak.

She drifted into a dreamy fantasy of growing vegetables and raising brightly colored flowers, as Amy had been doing at the Frog Haven Winery, where they were staying.

Dad would love this place!

An avid gardener himself, Steven Cook owned an organic fruit stand and general market, catering to health-conscious San Diego tourists out for an afternoon drive near the ocean. She and Tucker lived in a cottage behind Cook's farmhouse, some five miles down the road. Tucker had been helping Mr. Cook prepare the land behind for planting just before they'd left for vacation up north.

Her best friend, Dorie Hanks, slipped quietly next to her as they both approached the tasting room.

"You're upsetting the animals in the zoo, Brandy. I should have warned you." With her pert smile, the new bride showed perfectly aligned white teeth—the kind one needed shades to fully appreciate.

"Excuse me?"

"That tee shirt shows every curve and each little—" She was eyeing Brandy's chest, pointing and trying not to be too obvious.

Brandy noted that her replaced tee was even smaller than the one she'd shown up in. She blushed.

"I didn't even think," she whispered. "I *hate* wearing bras—those contraptions that feel more like some sort of Victorian torture device. I'd much rather have rounded hills than taillight rockets or peaks resembling the Himalayas."

"That's a visual. You're great with words, Brandy." Then she nodded in the direction of a bevy of young men not in their SEAL delegation, all of whom quickly turned away at exactly the same time.

Brandy sighed. "Point taken. Dammit."

"Where is your other shirt?"

"I got it dirty on the ride over." Brandy didn't want

to look into Dorie's eyes. "I'll see if they have some sort of wrap I can buy inside the winery store."

"Come with me." Dorie grabbed her hand and led her to Brawley's Hummer. She brought out a multicolored oversized silk scarf. "You have to wear layers up here. This comes in handy." She wrapped it around Brandy's shoulders, tying the front in a knot. "There."

Brandy stared down at the ridiculous colors that didn't match anything she was wearing, including her personality, but she was thankful, just the same.

"Appreciate you looking out for me, Dorie. What would I do without you?"

"Get into trouble," her friend answered, scrunching her nose up. "Probably have more fun than I'm having."

Brandy was surprised at this. "Already? The newlywed glow has come off?"

Her best friend cocked her head from side to side and rolled her eyes. "You know these guys. The chase is better than the catch. They are relentless until they get you nailed." She winked and whispered in Brandy's ear. "I mean that in every sense of the word." She stood back, adjusted the scarf at the hem so it covered Brandy's upper arms evenly. "And then they're off chasing other things."

"No way. Not Brawley!"

Dorie was examining her fingers laced together

waist high. When she looked up, Brandy could see the pain in her eyes. The sober realization between the two best friends was left unspoken, as if that would help stamp it out.

Brandy wanted to give Brawley a piece of her mind. She could put pepper in his coffee, laxatives in his morning milkshake. Maybe put itching powder in his jeans and underwear. Place some really stinky cheese in his favorite running shoes. There was so much she could do. He'd been like a brother ever since he'd met Dorie, always so respectful and fun. She'd harbored an enormous crush on him for the past eighteen months while they were dating, and then got engaged. She'd never picked up that he would be a wanderer. *That louse!*

This changed everything. This meant war.

Before she could say anything, Dorie speared her with her baby blue eyes. "Not. A. Word."

Brandy tried to look offended, frowning, but was having difficulty making eye contact.

"I mean it, Brandy. You don't do or say anything. And you never heard any of this from me, either. I'll completely deny it and call you a crazy. Don't say anything to Tucker, either."

"Is Tucker?—"

"Not a word. And no, Tucker's fine."

She was picking up the habit of fisting and unfisting her hands, along with the deep breathing exercises she'd learned from Tucker. It helped keep her calm until she could resign herself to the inevitable. She was going to have to act normal, and play with Brawley, like she didn't know. It was going to be a long day in close proximity with him. And she was dying to have the question and answer session with Tucker that she dared not have. So much to stuff down. It was totally unfair.

The two of them walked side-by-side and, as they often did, they bumped hips. It was the lazy familiarity she'd grown accustomed to being plucky relief to the gorgeous Dorie Hanks. They headed to the entrance to the tasting room, crisply crushing the pink granite rocks underfoot.

Dorie giggled.

"What?" Brandy asked.

"I can't believe how loose you've gotten. Tucker has that affect on women, I'd say."

Brandy considered her statement. Was Tucker a player? If he was Brawley's best friend, then perhaps they got into trouble together. She tried to recall if the two SEALs had been out in the evening alone since their return from Dorie's honeymoon, and she discovered that yes, they had. She didn't like not trusting Tucker, but she couldn't stop the doubt from creeping in. Her wine country bliss was fading.

"Come on, Brandy. Get over it. If I can, you can." Dorie nudged her, almost setting her off balance.

"Sorry." Brandy knew the only thing that would cheer her up would be to do something devious, hurt Brawley in some way. But not get caught—by anyone!

"It will all work out." Her friend sighed. "My father was the same way and I got a lot of practice watching my mother deal with it. After they finally split up, the first time she brought someone over to the family home, he was nearly twenty years younger and cute as a button." Dorie was giggling again. "I never laughed so hard in my life. My dad never quite got over it. Served him right for how he treated my mom all those years."

It wasn't the kind of family dynamic Brandy had any familiarity with. But then, her mother was gone and her father had been totally devoted to her and probably always would be. This type of behavior wasn't going to be what she wanted to get used to. And if that was a red line and ended things, so be it.

So she focused on getting revenge instead. An evil smile crept across her face. "I admire your mother for getting even. That was the only way to take care of it, in my opinion," she said to her beautiful blonde friend.

They slowly made their way into the cool tasting room smelling of fermented grapes. Gentle music echoed throughout the space, hushing the crowd who whispered their wine selections over the hammered copper bar to the two servers behind. The civilized explanation of all the features and characteristics of the wine was hard to hear, due to the echoes and the size of the late morning crowd. People listened. They nodded. They wrote notes on small chits of paper with little red pencils, consulted the luscious brochure laid before them, sipped their wine sample and savored the taste like it was a tiny orgasm.

As she studied the crowd, she found Tucker staring at her. He raised an eyebrow and tapped his collarbone with his fingers. She let him wait, considering what to do, and then allowed her sex-infused fantasy weekend to take charge again. Her right hand slipped under the silk and she pulled it aside, revealing her nipple pattern beneath the cotton shirt.

The effect on Tucker was immediate. He raised both eyebrows, tilted his head back, licked his lips, and then gave her a wink.

She covered her breast with the scarf again and turned to watch the tourists imbibe. Dorie pulled her toward the bar.

"Let's get something to taste. Like a mob scene in here today. Everyone's so polite, we'll never get a chance to drink anything."

Brandy chose to taste the Dry Creek Cabernet instead of starting with white wines the server recommended.

"I hate white wine," she said when the server asked Brandy about it. Dorie followed her lead. The wine was smooth and full-flavored, the aftertaste coating her tongue dangerously. She craved sharp cheese and crusty French bread, or a good steak.

"I like this," said Dorie.

"I do too," she answered. "But darned if it doesn't make me want to chow down a big steak. They say wine enhances your appetite, and for me, it certainly does."

"Makes me horny," added Dorie.

The server was holding another red selection, his eyes wide and his cheeks suddenly pink. Dorie flashed him a smile and the server nearly dropped the bottle.

"Some Pinot?" he asked with difficulty.

"Oh why not?" Dorie held her glass out and accepted the deep burgundy-colored elixir. Brandy followed suit.

Tucker followed behind Brawley as they sliced through the crowd to join the ladies.

"Find something you like?" he asked his bride.

"The Cabernet." She spoke to the server. "Can I have another taste?"

"Of course." The winery employee picked up another glass and poured Dorie a generous amount, then held out two more. "Gentlemen?"

While Brawley reached across the counter to accept his sample, Brandy turned to address Tucker, swilling the beautiful blend to coat the sides of her glass. A few drops spilled over the top and landed at the small of Brawley's back. He arched up quickly, felt the back of his shirt, and then examined his palm.

"You got me there, Brandy. A little less wrist action or we'll all be soaked." And then Brawley inhaled the contents of his glass in one gulp dismissively.

"Why Brawley Hanks. I didn't know you were afraid of a little action."

Dorie stared daggers at her while Tucker frowned. Brandy wished she'd gone with the itching powder or the stinky cheese. But for now, she was satisfied.

She'd have to reassure her best friend that the secret they shared would remain that way.

CHAPTER 3

TUCKER STOPPED TASTING at the third winery they came to, unwilling to sacrifice his clean driving record. But it humored him to see Brandy get smashed. She was going to need some food soon. The picnic had been postponed and finally, at two o'clock, they were ready to stop to eat.

The air was chilly so they decided to eat at the old Healdsburg General Store, an old Pony Express station and roadhouse that were a hundred and fifty years old. Horses in the front were replaced with Mercedes and Bentleys, and today, a herd of Hummers and four-door trucks.

The ladies lined up to use the restroom and Tucker ordered for the two of them and took his place at the long table that could easily seat twenty. The old wooden floors had a slight bounce to them. The noise of dragging chairs over the oak planks reminded him of one of his grammar schools in Oregon growing up.

His mood had lightened, but he still remained focused. Like several others, being the sober driver, he took his job seriously so as to protect the women who were mostly laughing and hanging off their men. He saw Coop grinning at him. The tall Nebraska farm boy didn't drink but that didn't diminish his enjoyment of the day. Libby, his wife, sat beside him, in a pink alcohol flush, fanning herself with a menu.

Kyle Lansdowne appeared on a chair to his left.

"So, I gotta ask you, are you in for the next BUD/S class?"

"I just haven't finished the paperwork. Collins said I can have a shot and he'd do what he could."

"You know you'll spend a few months at Great Lakes first. Same program all over again," the Team 3 LPO said.

"I'm prepared. This time I get to do it in the summer. Last time I froze my ass off," answered Tucker.

As the ladies started filtering back into the store, Kyle shot the important question Tucker knew was coming. "You told Brandy yet?"

"Not exactly."

"What does that mean?"

"I want to do that before I turn in my forms."

"So what you're telling me is that if she objects, you may not continue?"

He looked into the eyes of a Team leader he greatly

respected, knowing he had Tucker's welfare at heart. It didn't make the answer any easier.

"No, Kyle. It means that if I turn it in without telling her first, I'll have my butt on the street." He took a gulp of ice water. "I already screwed up one marriage because I didn't handle that right. If she's the one, I got to do this careful."

"If she's the one, she'll stand by something you want to do," said Kyle.

"Roger that for sure." Something tickled his insides. "You know, old married Kyle, you're what, five years younger than I am? And here you're giving me advice?"

"No advice, man. Just asking."

"So let me ask you a question. Do you ever really know what a woman is thinking until you ask her? Even if you ask her, are you really one hundred percent sure you're getting the truth? Be honest with me, Kyle."

Kyle chuckled and nodded. "Got me there, Tucker. Nope, I love my wife with all my heart and I'd lay down mine anytime for her. But, damned if I know what she's thinking every day. I just hope and pray I live up to what she wants. It ain't up to me. The woman chooses. You know that, right? We just gotta hope that they have all the facts to make a good informed decision."

Tucker laughed. "That's what I keep telling myself

every night in bed. Helping her make an informed decision."

They both chuckled again. "That's one way of putting it. But time's running out. I think you'd make a helluva Team Guy, and I want you with us when we next go over."

"Thanks, Kyle."

"And one other thing. If you're going to Great Lakes, you can't come with us to Mexico. That BUD/S class reports in two weeks, but I suppose you already know that."

"Indeed I do," Tucker said, finishing off his water. "Collins told me they've got one of my trainees going with you guys in my place. But I don't get a refund on the fishing trip I already paid for. That sucks. But I hear you, and I'm getting to it." He grabbed Brandy's water and crunched down some of her ice as he gazed at Brandy's lovely body headed right for him.

"Good." Kyle patted him on the back and slid down a couple of chairs to make way for some of the women, including Christy, to join the group.

IT WAS CHILLY back at Frog Haven. Tucker gave Brandy one of his heavier jackets, took her hand and asked her to come for a walk with him between the rows of vines just beginning to bud. At first her expression was one of surprise. But her nervous banter told him she was afraid of something. She was taking deep breaths, doing rhythmic breathing and even shivering slightly.

"You cold, Sweetheart?"

"A little, I guess. I'm hoping we can turn in early. Think I had a little too much today."

"Ah, but it was a thing of beauty to watch you and all the other ladies." He'd enjoyed saving her from falling or holding her close so she could walk steady. He also kept her separated from Dorie, because the newlyweds were having an argument, and a fairly serious one at that. He decided to let her bring up what was concerning her so he didn't appear to pry. And then he'd let her know about his plans.

In a few short minutes, she approached the subject of Dorie and Brawley. "I think they are arguing about his wandering eye. Do you know anything about that?"

Tucker was aware Brawley had strayed off the path during their engagement, and it was the one thing he was most disappointed with.

"I didn't know about the argument, or specifically what was the problem, but, well, Brawley has had lots of experience being single for many years. I didn't think he would ever get married, so I kind of suspected Dorie was pregnant, but he says no. Some men are just that way, Sweetheart."

He could tell that statement sent a jolt through her body.

"What about you?" She stopped walking and waited for him to turn around and face her.

"I've never cheated on anyone in my life. I never intend to. But, you remember that conversation we had over my magazines—the ones I *used* to have anyway. Men like to look. Women are beautiful creatures—all sizes and shapes and ages or coloring. Hard not to stare at God's handiwork.

She gave him back a weak smile that he could barely see by moonlight. The shadows made her look a bit sad.

"You and Brawley—"

"I'm not Brawley. I don't do what Brawley does. I would never do that to you. Is that your question?" He stooped down so they could make eye contact.

She melted into him, throwing her arms around his shoulders and neck. His huge hands scooped her rear up and held her against him while her knees wrapped around his hips.

"Thank you," she said before they kissed. "I want to trust you."

Tucker let her down slowly, feeling her mound travel over his member. "You *want* to trust me? Or, you *do* trust me?"

"Same thing."

"Oh no, Sweetheart. Vastly different. I need to know if you trust me."

"You've never done anything—"

"And that's not trusting. That's being okay for now. I'm talking about trust, especially when it's not convenient to do so."

"Yes, I think I do. I think some of this is new to me. Give me a chance, Tucker. I'm running as fast as I can to catch up."

He drew her back to him and held her head, raising her chin and planting a deep kiss on her hungry lips. "I like the way you run. I like the way you try to catch up. Sweetheart, I love the way you do everything."

They kissed again. He could taste the remnants of the wine from today, felt her body need him again, and his desire flamed. But before it grew to a bonfire, he needed to tell her.

There was a stack of wooden pallets left between the rows they were traversing. He moved three of them, making a seat for her. Then he sat next to her.

"I've made the decision to go back to the Teams. But I wanted your opinions about it first before I turn in the paperwork."

There. He'd said it.

She took a gulp of air. The hand he was holding clutched his and he felt her pulse quicken.

"I—I want you to do what's best for you. When would this be happening?"

"Soon."

"How soon?"

"I'd have to report in two weeks."

She dropped his hand. "And how long would you be gone?"

"About four months, maybe less. You could come visit."

"Where?"

"Michigan."

"Okay. And then when do you go overseas, or wherever you go?"

"The training will take over a year all totaled. But most of it takes place in San Diego. We do jungle training, desert training and some in the snow country—Alaska, Norway, all over. I have to qualify just like I did the first time. They won't make it easy on me, which is why this next question is important to me."

He could see water had formed in her eyes. She was experiencing already saying good-bye and it hurt him to see the pain written on her face.

"Go ahead." Her voice was timid, weak.

"When I get done with training, and before my first deployment, I'd like to marry you, if you'll have me. But only if you're sure."

She stared down, studying her fingers entwined with his, resting on her lap.

"So, no honeymoon in an exotic place like Dorie and Brawley. It's *I do* and then *Good-bye.*"

"We don't do anything like Dorie and Brawley. We are Tucker and Brandy and our lives are in our hands. Like this." He drew her fingers up to his lips and kissed them. "We're a team, you and I. But, only if you support what I'm doing."

He had to wait for her answer and wasn't surprised her reaction didn't match the movies when the girl jumps for joy and hugs the guy to death. He hadn't even bought a ring to give her. But this didn't diminish the commitment he was making this evening under the stars—a commitment he hoped she'd share.

"Yes. But on one condition," she whispered.

He braced himself for something he worried he'd not want to hear.

"I get you body and soul for the next two weeks."

Her follow-up smile warmed his heart. "I'll be your slave."

Brandy cocked her head, still smiling. "You might want to think about that a little bit before you promise. I have appetites and demands and—"

He grabbed her close, interrupting her message with a deep penetrating kiss he hoped sent her spinning. "Nothing would make me happier," he said when they came up for air. "I can't wait for my instructions, because, honey, everything you want, I *need* to give you. Everything. But I'm going to go back to the Teams to help me be the strong man you'll be able to count on." He kissed her forehead. "You understand that, don't you?"

"I do." She nodded, meeting his eyes, unflinching.

He knew they had a real good shot at this. He was going to do everything in his power to make it happen. With her help, he could have both things he wanted more than anything else. He could be the man he knew he was created to be, and he could love the woman he was created to love.

He'd spend the rest of his life blowing her mind. All she had to do was trust him.

CHAPTER 4

THEIR RETURN FROM the Wine Country began with as much excitement as the trip itself. Brandy was overjoyed Tucker didn't hesitate to discuss their future plans, although their wedding wasn't going to take place for at least another year. Tucker told her he wanted to complete his Corps School and requalify as a SEAL. That meant taking BUD/S all over again at the ripe old age of forty. He showed her his enlistment paperwork, ready to submit, naming her as next of kin and beneficiary of his insurance, should something happen while in the Navy.

Little things like this reassured her when the cobwebs of doubt crept into her frame of mind. Life was looking like it could have a real happily ever after—just like some of her friends. Lady Luck was finally smiling down on her. She realized her mother had been right.

"When the right man comes along, he's going to love you just the way you are. You'll be perfect together."

Thanks, mom.

On the fourth day back, she went with him to the Induction Center where he turned in more paperwork and submitted his lab work and physical evaluation. On the way home, he suggested they stop and go shopping for an engagement ring. She'd told herself she wasn't going to push him on it, since they had so little time together. But she was overjoyed he'd made the suggestion. She had never brought it up.

She picked out a very small diamond, insisting they could upgrade later on. Tucker argued with her a little, but in the end gave in and allowed her to get the modest token of his undying love. Brandy didn't care how their future finances went, this simple ring meant so much to her, it would forever be her most prized possession.

She'd lost count how many times she'd been in friends' weddings, but now she'd have one of her own. Every time she thought about it, her heart raced.

I'm actually getting married! Me!

The ring could have been made out of aluminum, for all she cared. It was that he wanted her to be marked as belonging to him. He even insisted on putting it on her finger and kissing her tenderly on the palm. This big behemoth of a man had a tender heart, with a great love growing stronger every day. She could see it, feel it. Brandy experienced that complete hero's devotion she had considered might never find her.

Her father was thrilled, and allowed her to take time off work, since his health had greatly improved. The new hires Brandy made were working out well for the little business. There would be time for throwing herself back into the stand once Tucker left for Great Lakes.

Until then, she didn't want to think about it—pretending they had years and years before she'd have to be separated from him. The little internal lie worked, too. His body gave her strength the more he kissed and massaged his way into her flesh. She relaxed further with her inhibitions, the more intense their lovemaking became. His need to completely wring her out and satisfy her in bed nearly left her in tears on a daily basis. She even asked him to take her to a local X-rated strip club some of the SEALs had frequented. He insisted it wasn't necessary, that he was no longer a single man, but Brandy needed to present to him the gift of her trust. No matter the environment, she loved him and everything he wanted to do, and needed to show it.

They spent little time with Dorie and Brawley. There was a rumor circulating in the community that the two of them were still fighting. One day she got a call from Dorie, which confirmed everything Brandy feared. With only five days left before Tucker was to leave, Brandy was called to the Hanks home with urgency.

"You have any idea what's going on?" he asked.

"No. Just said for me to come. Alone."

"Jeez. I don't like it. I should take you over there."

"I'll be fine. I'll text you if I see his Hummer, or he walks in. I promise."

He reluctantly agreed. They cancelled Tucker's plans to go to dinner at Kyle's house, though she had insisted he go alone.

"Oh sure. You expect me to sit there all evening and get pummeled with questions about where you are? No thanks. Just easier to reschedule it, saying something came up, or you're not feeling well. Something."

"Fine."

"And you let me know. No secrets, okay? Perhaps Kyle needs to be informed," he said.

"She made me promise not to tell you. I've broken that promise, obviously, but I won't break the other one."

"But they deploy a few days after I leave. Someone's got to keep an eye out for him. I wish I were still going as their civilian. I'd feel better if I could watch over him."

"Tucker, you can't save the world. Brawley's gotten

himself into something dark, and he'll have to get himself out of it. I want you to focus on the training. Give yourself that chance and forget about the rest of the world." She angled her head and teased. "Seriously, Tucker. If you are distracted, you'll regret it."

"On one condition, then."

"Fair enough."

"Something happens—either tonight when you go see her, or after I'm gone, you let me know. I can't leave a friend in need. That's not how it works."

Brandy could see why having relationships in this very intense environment of the Special Forces could be tricky. They couldn't have a bad day. She'd learned that the SEAL Motto: *Only Easy Day Was Yesterday*, was created to remind them that they could never let up and coast. They were always on call and it would always be tough, regardless of what else was going on at home.

"I promise," she said to him, giving him a swift kiss and then breaking their embrace to exit the cottage. "I'll text you when I'm on the way home."

She was getting used to driving Tucker's big truck. The San Diego dusk was very mysterious tonight, showing off hues of turquoise and salmon, the palm trees and profile of the coastline was dark the blacker the night sky became.

Brawley was one of the SEALs who had bought his

first house with the re-enlistment bonus he obtained tax-free when he'd been on deployment a year ago. Since that time, she'd been told the house had nearly doubled in value.

But as she approached the front door, the woman who greeted her, her best friend of nearly ten years, looked disheveled and red-faced from crying. Her normally beautiful hair had been unwashed and she was dressed in her sweats and bare feet.

She reached out and Dorie fell into her arms. To the side and back of her head, she whispered, "Come on, just tell me about it. It's going to be all right, Dorie. Don't worry. This won't last for long."

Dorie released herself, pushing to arm's length and studied Brandy's face carefully. "You can't tell anyone."

"Tucker knows I'm here, but I didn't tell him anything." It was true, since Dorie didn't go into much detail, just indicated that she needed her shoulder to cry on. "So explain please what's happened."

Brandy took up a spot on the living room couch and prepared herself for bad news. Dorie sat next to her and they held hands. "He's been talking to old girlfriends again, or, rather, one old girlfriend. But I know there are others. He slept with someone before we got married."

"Again? You said again."

"Yes. Happened before we went up to Wine Country. He promised he'd hang up that life, but something snagged him." She pulled a tissue from the box on the coffee table and blew her nose. "Or should I say some*one* snagged him. And it might be more than one former girlfriend."

"Ah, Dorie. I'm so sorry. Are you sure?"

"He has this bimbo calling him all the time. Her profile picture was of her in her lace underwear—that is, until he erased it after I caught him.

"Could it just be innocent friendship?"

Dorie looked at her cross-eyed. "Brawley doesn't do innocent. You know that. He'll cut it right to the bone. He says he loves me, but I don't know what's going on. He can't stop chasing other women. It's getting to be that I don't even want to go out with him any longer, he's so preoccupied with women who cross our paths. He gives off the vibe or something and they come flocking to him."

It was part of her own curiosity that made her ask the next question.

"Does he take any of the Team Guys with him, by chance?"

"Well, since your guy is pretty tied up with you, he hangs at the Scupper too long with some of the newbies. All his other regular guy friends seem not to want to have anything to do with him. I'm expecting a call from Kyle or Christy one of these days."

Brandy was sorry for her friend.

"Honestly, some of those new recruits look and act so young. Like teenagers—who've been trained to act with deadly force. But they're like a bunch of teenagers with guns. I worry sometimes they don't have the maturity to—and, well, now look at Brawley. You'd think he'd have sense to just quit being in high school. And he's so angry all the time. Little things set him off. That's new. It scares me."

Brandy touched her cheek. "It's a handicap, Dorie. It's a flaw, like someone who can't stop spending. He has to want to get better and work on it. If he loves you, Dorie, he will. But you'll probably have to call him on it, and demand it. You ready for all that?"

The beautiful blonde sighed. Brandy could not understand how Brawley could ever want anyone else. She was perfect in every way—the most flawless beauty she'd ever known. And she had a wonderful heart. Looks mattered little to her. She read people the right way. It was a shame.

"Dorie? You ready to take this on?"

Brandy's stomach dropped to the floor when Dorie didn't make eye contact. "You have to put a stop to it." She squeezed her hand. "You have to be honest with yourself. You're the one who gets hurt as a result if you just let it slide."

Her friend jumped to her feet, pacing back and

forth. "Ahhh!" she shouted to the ceiling. "I wish I could just understand what's happened to him all of a sudden. I never remember his fuse being so short. It's like something is wrong, and he doesn't want to tell me."

"You need counseling, Dorie. Get some help, or get with some of the other wives—call me!"

"Don't be silly. Tucker is leaving very soon, right?"

"Um hum."

"I can't take up your precious time."

"But Dorie, consider this. What if you're in danger? Physical danger?"

"Oh, it's not that bad. He's just very prone to agitation. You know Brawley. He was never like that."

Brandy admitted she'd always seen him as fairly easy to be around. "Do you feel comfortable just asking him what's going on? Or, should you try this in front of a counselor?"

"I don't want to go pouring my heart out right before he's supposed to deploy. They get all keyed up and tight before they go. It's like Brawley on steroids. Finding the right counselor will be hard for us."

"Then *you* go. You get some assistance. Bounce everything off them and give yourself a break. I think you're blaming yourself too much."

Dorie nodded.

"And come stay with me, if you want. I'll be all

alone. I could use the company."

That brought a smile to her friend's face. "You also have a lot to learn, my dear. When they're gone, especially if you fight right beforehand, it hurts so bad. I feel so guilty. He's putting his life out on the line, and I'm complaining about him not paying attention to me any longer when he's home. The last deployment they lost a guy. I know that haunts him."

CHAPTER 5

Tucker watched the little bedroom brighten, light filtering through Brandy's sheer curtains. They did nothing to stop the oncoming morning. This was the day he'd be leaving. The day he was filled with both regret and excitement. He'd told himself he'd be prepared for this big event, but now discovered he was not. So he lay immobilized, allowing the early morning sun to work its magic.

Her window was open a crack allowing a soft breeze to wash over their bed. He was on his back, his right arm holding her sweaty body deliciously close while she slept. He'd miss seeing her wake up each morning. He'd be in a dorm room with five or six other men—most of them ten years or more his junior. And it would be just his luck to get a world-class snorer assigned to his group. He had all kinds of ways to get even with one of those.

He hadn't doubted his decision to serve again in

the Navy. He didn't doubt he could pass the rigorous qualification course at BUD/S. He didn't mind that two of his recent trainees were now going to be in the same class as their former instructor. He didn't mind that another new recruit had taken his place as the lone civilian component to the next SEAL mission in Baja—an honor he was supposed to claim before they learned of his intention to re-join.

What he was concerned about was his thirty-nine year old body stressed and under pressure. The first time through, he was just a dumb kid who made it because he just wouldn't quit. It didn't mean anything to him back then. Now, it was different.

He knew guys in their late forties who still served. But most Team Guys served six or eight years on average, and less if you got injured. So, he wouldn't be the *oldest* SEAL on Team 3, or wherever they put him, but he'd be the oldest in his class, and that bothered him.

Brandy was mumbling in her sleep. It always gentled his whole demeanor when he got to trace down her spine with his palm, sliding it over her derriere and giving her a soft squeeze. This would be the last morning he could feel the ecstasy of making love to her under the soft glow of first dawn.

He inched down the sheets, opening her crossed arms and nuzzling between her breasts as she began to awaken. He watched her eyes open with lazy enjoyment as his fingers slipped over her belly to the magic juncture between her thighs. His forefinger encircled her bud until one of the little presses made her jump.

His mouth was on her opening, his tongue taking over the work from his finger. He gently bit her labia and let the delicate flesh feel just the tip of his canines. She moaned, bent her knees and arched her back, making her breasts heave and then fall as she exhaled, widened her knees and accepted two of his fingers inside her. Her hands flailed on top of his, pushing him deeper and massaging every knuckle and joint. Her arms forced her beautiful orbs with the knotted dark pink nipples to overflow. They called to him. He was hungry for her in so many ways, he vowed to try every one of them on her, until she could hardly move. It was that important that he leave her exhausted and begging him to stay. He needed to hear and feel that need in her.

Because it matched his own.

AT ELEVEN O'CLOCK sharp he kissed her good-bye just outside the gate that housed the busses to the airport. He smoothed the backs of his fingers over her wet cheek.

"No need to cry, Brandy. Nothing on this earth would keep me from coming back to you. Be good to your father and be a good friend to Dorie. I think she's going to need it."

She wouldn't take her eyes off his. "I will." Then came her sweet smile. "But I'm going to miss you so much, Tucker. Can we talk every day?"

"Not sure if the rules have changed, but if I'm off on a training, which will happen after I finish the Corps School, then no. There will be days, maybe even a week or two I'll not be in phone contact."

"When can I come visit?"

"Working on it. Good news is, Great Lakes will be pretty then. Early summer. Perfect time to come out. So, let me do a little research and I'll let you know. Have to scope it all out first."

"Roger that," she whispered.

"Hudson! Get your ass over here and quit fondling the wifey," one of the instructors barked.

Tucker winked at her. "Hear that?"

She sent him off with another quick kiss, and then watched him board the bus. He felt her eyes on his back, and then saw her face between the bars at the gate, her little ring glistening in the sunlight as she gripped the metal barrier.

Her form got smaller and smaller as the caravan of two busses traveled down the frontage road, then turned the corner around SEAL Team 3's building and hit the back road to the airport. Just like that, she was gone.

On the bus, he knew he was the object of discussion. He caught the sideways glances and the faint whispers. He was going to graduate as a forty-year-old man, trying out for a young man's job. But Tucker had never been injured and had hardly ever missed a workout. The messy divorce with Shayla had truncated any dreams of finding love, so he'd thrown everything into his Teammates, by taking a job supporting the community—helping the would-be recruits get in the kind of physical and mental shape he knew they'd need to be able to qualify. It was the closest he could get to actually being on a team these past years.

The morning's activities were a blur. Everything moved at light speed. Their soft lovemaking, the quick double check on his packing list, something he'd gotten drilled into him from his past. In a full-on retro deja-vu, he harkened back to his childhood in Oregon, when he and Brawley sat side by side and compared lunches while they bounced down the country roads in the big yellow bus. The day was judged based on what kind of dessert his mother had packed. Watching the murky water and the Coronado Bridge come up, then the city of San Diego proper, he felt just as when he was in grammar school. He was waiting for the rest of his life to happen.

He had placed a call to his mother earlier as he

drove Brandy to the base. He wanted the two most important women in his life to talk together for the first time.

"Mom, this lady is going to marry me. Can you believe that?" he'd told her.

His mom laughed. "Well, I guess there are miracles in this world after all. First Brawley and now your turn. She's probably very special if she is in love with you, not that I blame her one bit."

"She's right here, Mom." Tucker handed the phone to Brandy, who nearly dropped it before she took up a light-hearted conversation with the elder Mrs. Hudson. She promised a road trip North after Tucker's graduation from Corps School, and before he started his first phase of SEAL training back in Coronado.

A young, lanky black kid he'd been training who took the seat next to him interrupted his memories of the morning.

"Jamal. If this isn't old home week. Now I've seen four of you on this trip. Is there some kind of conspiracy?" he asked, following it up with a grin.

"Don't know that, but feel free to kick my butt if I forget anything you've taught me. Can't make you look bad now can we?" he said in his slow, Southern drawl.

"May I offer a piece of advice?"

Jamal enthusiastically nodded his head, yes.

"Not sure where we'll be housed, but if I don't get a

chance to tell you, go ahead and volunteer to take *any* tests they give you. But if they tell you you're going to dental school, sub school or some other specialized career path, tell them to pound salt. You've been promised a berth in the next BUD/S class, and if they give you any guff, give Collins a call."

"I certainly do appreciate it, Tuck."

The kid sat back in the seat and then had an afterthought, "I hear they do a timed run as soon as we hit the tarmac in Chicago. It's going to be a pleasure to see you overtake the drill instructors—*all* of them!"

Tucker reveled in always being the fastest runner in any group of men. He could also bench press more than nearly anyone else as well. He was most worried about the swimming portion of the course, and for that, he would be looking out for an expert swim buddy.

Jamal chuckled right along side Tucker. He was glad that, even though his hair was prematurely gray, his run times had never been better. He was starting to believe he was the machine Brandy always told him he was.

HE WOKE UP with a jolt when the wheels touched down on the runway. They'd been put on a commercial flight. One of the overhead bins popped open and began spilling things over his shoulder, into the aisle.

At the training facility, they were set up into quads, in sets of two rooms with a quasi-living room between them. Nice thing about it was that they had a small kitchen, equipped with a full-sized refrigerator and microwave.

Several of the men in their pod were from the east coast. One was from Montana. Tucker and two others hailed from California. One of those men, Conner Newsome, was also a SEAL candidate, and looked extremely fit, so Tucker made a point to arrange project workups and P.T. with him. He knew that sometimes it didn't take much to get a guy to quit, especially if he felt he was doing it all alone. Having a swim buddy, or someone to watch your back or help with some aspect of the course he didn't understand was a smart move. The bonding would give them both an edge they could draw on when they needed to.

As the days went by, he began to settle in to a routine, studied hard and tried to curry favor with his instructors. He knew this was a safe bet now, since when he began the first phase, he would seek anonymity. He didn't want to stand out or he would get picked on. But because he was re-qualifying as a medic, the math and science courses were more challenging. He'd been out of school longer than anyone else.

In the third week, several of the men had dropped out or been reassigned back to the fleet, leaving a vacancy in their pod of eight. It remained that way for nearly a month before they found a replacement.

The Navy allowed one recruit for roughly every ten thousand men, to try out for the Teams, and guarantees were not always given at enlistment any longer. Because Tucker was returning, he'd have his shot, unless he just blew his courses. That didn't mean they'd make it easy on him. They did want his experience, he'd been told. Having served for ten years, he walked into the field with skills and knowledge of the way the Teams operated that no amount of training could ever duplicate.

He talked with Brandy by phone nearly every day, and enjoyed hearing about life back in San Diego. It took his mind off dwelling on BUD/S, only a few weeks away now. Her dad was nearly up to his old speed and the police had some leads they were following, trying to locate the former employee who had stolen from them and nearly killed her father.

"And wait until you see Dad's garden. I've never seen him so happy," she told him.

It had been his gift to her father, rototilling the nearly half acre space. It had been part of elder Mr. Cook's dream to raise his own vegetables and then sell them through his store.

"Can't wait to be back in the San Diego climate. It's getting nicer up here, but damn, it's still cold, especially at night. And it doesn't just rain here. It monsoons, and the wind blows right in your face, coming off the lakes. Sometimes, even at this late date, the rain is laced with snow. It chills you to the bone."

"I've got some ideas how you can warm yourself up on those cold nights, Tucker. Just say the word, and I'll be up there tomorrow."

He was getting horny talking to her and couldn't wait to see her. "I think we get a weekend soon. We'll stay in Chicago. You'll love it."

"So—Kyle's group left yesterday. Not sure if you knew that."

"Figured it was coming up. How's Dorie doing?"

"Not so good. She's really struggling."

"Keep close, Brandy. It will be the best thing for Brawley, for everyone, when he comes back and she's got her head on straight. Maybe he'll squeeze those demons out of his system. He *could* come back a changed man."

"Hope so. You have any clue what's gotten into him though? I mean, was he like that at all when you two were growing up in Oregon?"

"Don't think so, but I honestly don't remember. I mean, I've known him so long, he's like a brother. What's he doing?"

"Well, remember I told you about the calls he was getting from some girl?"

"I do. That still going on?"

"Not sure. But he smashed up the Hummer. Pretty good scrape all along the passenger side, denting the rear door. The truck had to be towed since the frame was bent."

"Just a single car accident, then?" Tucker wanted to know.

"He said he was avoiding a deer. I believe him."

Tucker had noticed the increased drinking at Brawley's before he'd left. And Brawley had stopped coming by to visit him, using the excuse he didn't want to get in the way of his still new relationship with Brandy. It was one of his regrets, not being able to spend a little more time with Brawley before he left. It was unsettling. "When he gets back from deployment, I'll be just finishing up Phase I. I'll make sure to reach out, see if I can get together with him. I hope you won't mind."

"Not if you behave yourself. Because when you come home, your ass is mine, Tucker. I don't much like the idea you'd be his sidekick if he's looking for girls."

"I should be so lucky." He chuckled at Brandy's brazen attitude.

"I mean it, Tucker."

"Duly noted. I promise, sweetheart."

As the weeks progressed, Tucker still hadn't heard from anyone on the Team. He didn't expect a report on a classified mission, but he always stayed loosely connected even after disengaging from the Teams. He was hoping the new guy was being useful.

But Brandy told him Dorie had also been virtually left alone. The longer this went on, the more he worried about his friend.

As the two friends got older, Brawley attended a different high school, so most of the time their sports teams were competitors. Both athletic and gifted in multiple sports, the matchups between the two of them became the whole story of the game, and drew lots of fan interest.

But unlike Tucker, Brawley didn't have a sweetheart in high school. Instead, he played the field. Tucker wasn't aware of a reputation for being a womanizer. He'd often wondered if perhaps Brawley hadn't been the smarter one between them. There was just so much unfinished. So many holes creeping up on them, it felt like this childhood friendship might be in peril.

One day, he got the call he was dreading. Brandy was coming for her first visit in two days. Brawley's long, rambling message made no sense at all. He wished he could talk his friend down.

"Must be nice and warm in Baja now," Tucker said to Brawley.

"Fuckin sweatin' bullets. They got cockroaches the size of dogs. You should see them."

"Well, at least the local cat population is under control then." Tucker thought Brawley would find it as funny as he did, but silence hissed on the other end of the line.

The awkward gap between them made Tucker's hair stand on end. The back of his neck was hot. It felt like there was a hole in his rebreather, or tent. "Hey dude. What's up? You don't sound like your frisky asshole self." He wanted to break the frostiness between them.

"I've been seeing things. Scary shit."

"Not following you, Brawley."

"Well, we're deep into May, past Cinque de Mayo and everything. These people have those skull masks? You know the ones I'm talking about?"

"I believe they call them sugar skulls."

"Yea. They paint their faces to look like one of those bright skulls. Starting to depress me a bit. You know how that guy Randy what's-his-face said if you start to get scared, well you need to get out."

Randy had been their pre-enlistment fitness trainer, with over twenty years on the Teams.

"You're one of the bravest men I know, Brawley. You're careful. Don't go do dumb stuff. There's a little tension because of the immigrant population and border issues with the government. But we're cool. Just be glad you're not Trace. I heard Kyle and him owe their asses to some General down there who wants his daughter to marry a SEAL. I'm glad I didn't make that promise."

Brawley didn't answer.

"You there, asshole?"

"There. I just saw another one?"

"Another one what?" Tucker asked. Now Brawley was starting to scare him.

"One of those little senoritas of death. She wants a playmate."

"Horse shit. Don't go there, Brawley."

"Ask them to stop it, Mr. Tuck and Roll. That's all I see when I close my eyes."

Tucker knew a corner had been turned. It wasn't a good sign.

"Make sure you get lots of rest, Brawley. Get some meds and get a long, long rest."

Just before Brawley hung up, he whispered, "I'm being followed, Tuck."

CHAPTER 6

STEVEN COOK, BRANDY'S father, had discovered items missing from his store. It started out small, but progressed until several days in a row he'd lost a whole case of fruit. But what bothered him was that the person stealing from him hadn't tried to cover their tracks. He immediately thought about his earlier assault.

Detective Clark Riverton was on semi-retirement duty from the San Diego P.D. He was skilled in homicide cases, and missed his former job, but investigating stolen fruit from a mom & pop grocery store was where his career was headed these days. He took it like everything he did: swore and complained to anyone who would listen, but did nothing about it. He'd been reminded it was an option to just quit. Being the kind of stubborn man he was, that wasn't anything he considered for more than a second.

Riverton's presence, waddling between the aisles,

picking up oranges, apples and melons, sniffing them and then setting them back down, made Mr. Cook wonder if it was such a good idea to call him.

"You can't tell anything by smelling the fruit. At least, not those," he said as he nodded to Riverton's hands. Cook extended his hand. "Steven Cook."

"Clark Riverton." He retrieved a dog-eared card from the shirt pocket under his blazer.

"Thanks." Cook slipped the paper inside the front catchall pocket on his green grocer's apron.

"So what can I do yous for?" Riverton looked out of place. "You've got a fruit burglar I hear."

Cook winced at the obvious slight. "That's right. But it's more than that," he continued. "It's like I'm being left a message."

Despite his manners, Cook heard Riverton swear under his breath, and then clear his throat, standing tall. "And what makes you think that? The fruit talking to you these days, Mr. Cook?"

"Not the fruit—" Then he realized he'd been played. "The guy who assaulted me had been an employee of mine, Jorge Mendoza. Your colleagues are trying to find him as we speak."

Riverton's expression didn't change. "Okay, so we got a serial fruit burglar, then. Anything else you wanna tell me about? Like, when did this happen, and how often?"

"After hours, of course. He's getting in somehow. I don't keep the money here anymore."

"Smart. That's been stolen too, or did he just prefer fruit?"

Cook examined the lines on the Detective's face. He couldn't see any laughter beginning to break out but was fairly sure it was there, just under the surface. Riverton was a pro at masking his feelings, but Cook detected he was about to split a gut.

"No money missing. Not yet, anyway."

"This—" Riverton consulted his small spiral-bound notebook—"Mendoza fellow, you or any of your staff spot him hanging around?"

"Nope. No one has. The police told me he was a known gang member. Which reminds me, while I have your ear, why can't an employer like myself consult a database of known gang members before we make that hire? It sure would save us all a lot of hassle."

"It doesn't work that way. It's not like we can consult their corporate records. He doesn't carry a membership card."

Cook was annoyed with the teasing.

"Well, don't ask me how, but I know it's him and his friends."

Riverton asked other questions, making notes in his little book. He stuffed it in his shirt pocket again, and suggested he talk to every employee at the store, which Cook agreed with and gave permission to.

"My daughter comes this afternoon, should be here anytime now. Other than Kip, and Brandy, the others are part-time, going full time in the summer when their school is out."

"Seasonal. I got it."

Cook hesitated, and then asked the question he'd been dying to know the answer to. "Detective Riverton, do you believe me about all this, or do you think I've been getting high?"

Riverton took a deep breath and pulled his pants up by the belt, readjusting it. "Sometimes it takes awhile for me to get a feel of a crime. But trust me, if it's there, it will come to me. Right now, I'm not seeing why someone who is already in trouble for the first offense, try to mess with you a second time. I mean, a case of oranges? What's the point in that? What? Ten or twenty bucks of oranges?"

Cook was at the end of his rope. Riverton's attitude stunk. When Riverton didn't give him a straight answer, Cook added, "That's what I thought."

CHAPTER 7

BRANDY HEADED TO Dorie's to return the scarf she'd borrowed on the trip up north. That beautiful weekend seemed so long ago, but it was just three months. She was packed for the trip to Chicago, leaving early in the morning. She had a few hours to do at the store, then she was going to get to bed early.

Dorie's face was gaunt and appeared almost gray, not the beautiful tan and pink skin she normally had. From the appearance of the bluish circles under her eyes, it was obvious her friend had not been sleeping.

They embraced and Dorie allowed her in.

"First of all, thank you for letting me borrow this. I had it dry cleaned." She handed over the scarf, folded in tissue.

"Thank *you*. I'd totally forgotten about it."

Brandy examined her friend's body posture, her shoulders slightly slumping. She was wearing distressed blue jeans, partially unbuttoned, and a big white fleece sweatshirt and silver flip-flops. Her hair was wrapped up in a clip atop her head.

"Are you working today?"

Dorie smirked and examined her clothes. "No. I asked for a few days."

The two had met at an upscale advertising agency, until Brandy had been fired. "I have to be honest. I'm worried about you, Dorie."

The new bride attempted a smile. "I'm pregnant, Brandy. I just don't know if the father of my baby wants to be my husband anymore."

She began to melt into sobs when Brandy held her, directing her to an overstuffed living room chair, where the two collapsed. Brandy was reassuring her it would all work out. She hoped she was telling the truth.

"Does Brawley know?"

"Nope. Haven't heard from him in a month. This early in the pregnancy, anything could happen, so I don't want to distract him."

"We can always ask Kyle to let him know, if you want."

"Not on your life. It's my story. Probably my fault too, or at least that's what Brawley will say."

"You don't think he'll be happy with the baby? Perhaps it's the perfect something that would cheer him up." Brandy wasn't sure if this would help.

"He's been a ghost. I'm not sure where he's at." She

began another bout of tears and leaned against her for comfort.

Brandy was heart broken. She'd never considered Dorie's marriage with Brawley could be so loveless. And now with a baby coming, there was added pressure she didn't need.

"Whatever happens, Dorie, understand that the baby was not a mistake. One of God's little angels coming into your life at just the right time. Brawley might be acting like a jerk, but the baby is truly a gift, an angel, and messenger from up above. Just remember that."

"I'm scared. Never felt this way before, Brandy."

"Well, girlfriend, I'm certainly no expert, but I'd say you're developing some pretty powerful hormones. Mood swings are supposed to be one of the side effects early on."

"That could be part of it, but I also got another one of those calls from that girl, asking for Brawley again. I told her I was his wife, and she said she knew and hung up." She shook her head. "What a douchebag. What's he done now? Maybe I don't want to know."

"I agree. It's like he's become a completely different person. You think he's hurting about something? Something he doesn't want you to know about?"

"I have no clue. None whatsoever."

"Well, the main thing is the two of us should stick

together. You lean on me until he gets home and you guys can go see a counselor. I'm sure, in time, you two will sort it all out."

Dorie separated from her and stood. "You want some wine or something?"

"I'd love a glass of ice water."

"Done! As a matter of fact, that's what I'll have as well."

She was in the kitchen in a flash. Brandy joined her. All her life she'd envied the beautiful girls, like Dorie. The ones who just walked into a room and all the guys would come to their knees. Brandy had begun to feel invisible. She told herself everything her mother had drummed into her about character and real love. But it was a fact that she felt unattractive, until she met Tucker.

Dorie had more men around her constantly, vying for her attention, cozying up to her, even though they knew she was married. It was just inconceivable that all this be happening to her. She watched her friend play with her blonde curls, sorting and sifting her long fingers through them. She allowed silent tears to flow.

Brandy wanted to be a good friend, but she always felt Dorie was out of her league. Tonight, her perspective had shifted.

Dorie gave her a weak smile, as if she'd read her thoughts. "You must think I'm a bit crazy."

"Not at all. It's just that you don't have enough information. The waiting must be hell on you."

Her best friend appeared to be thinking about that. Then she asked, "Have you eaten? You wanna go out somewhere to have a light lunch? Or, I can fix us something."

"I ate, but I'm also due at the store." Brandy answered. "I fly out to Chicago tomorrow morning, so I was going to go to bed early after that."

Dorie grabbed her. "Here I am, raining on your parade. I'm so sorry, Brandy." The tears began to form. She covered her face with her palm. "Oh, what am I going to do?"

"Why don't you call his LPO's wife, Christy? Perhaps she can give you some suggestions, and take my place for a week while I'm in Chicago. I hear she's a great confident."

"Except for the fact that I know something is going on with Brawley. That information will go straight to Kyle, then. Brawley wouldn't want me to jeopardize his career."

"But by shoving it under the rug, you could actually make it much worse. Whatever it is, you're far better nipping it in the bud. It *could* save his life."

The two said good-bye. As Brandy was walking out the door, she heard the phone ring.

"Hang on." Dorie coaxed her to stay long enough

so she could answer the phone. She took the clip out of her hair, loosening it vigorously and grabbed her telephone.

Her expression changed after she heard the first few words coming from the other end of the line. Her forehead puckered. Her eyes squinted and she began to tremble. Brandy rushed back to her side.

"What is it?" she whispered.

"Yes. I'll be here," said Dorie, her voice trailing to oblivion. Thank you for calling."

Whatever she was going to say next, Brandy knew she wasn't going to like hearing.

"He's gone missing. Brawley has just disappeared. In Mexico. The Navy is sending someone over to discuss a possible hostage negotiation."

Her friend's normally sparkling bright blue eyes were filled with pain.

"I'm going to stay with you, Dorie."

"No. You go. You're leaving for Great Lakes and I don't want to interfere with that—"

"But I can't leave you alone. At least call Christy Lansdowne, okay?"

Dorie nodded her agreement. "I'm sure she's got some advice. I'll do that. Now go, and I'll update you when I have news."

As she drove to her father's store, Brandy knew her best friend's nightmare could soon consume them all.

CHAPTER 8

TUCKER WAS SWEATING profusely as he drove to the airport to pick up Brandy. His fingers dug into the leather steering wheel, leaving ridges.

Her plane was delayed, but force of habit still made him show up early to the original arrival time. He'd rented the bridal suite downtown at a small boutique hotel with a beautiful view of the sparkling towers of the city center that seemed to stretch for miles. It had nearly emptied his bank account, since he had to pay for the weekend in full before he could reserve it. And his check hadn't been deposited yet.

He was worrying about a lot of things these days. And money was one of them. Would Brandy be satisfied with how little he would make? Even as a SEAL, the pay was ridiculously low. And, he had to admit, he'd never been good at managing his money, so at almost forty years of age, he was still living from paycheck to paycheck. His truck was the only thing of value he owned, and it was mortgaged to the hilt. He knew a lot of Team Guys who kept re-enlisting so the bonuses they received could pay off all their debts. Lots of guys never got ahead.

He should know better. That's one thing he was going to have to fix. With Brandy's help, he knew he could.

He'd placed a call to Kyle as soon as Brawley had hung up on him two nights ago. And now, nearly forty-eight hours later, he didn't get a call back from him either.

It was strange feeling part of the team without really being on it. He wasn't allowed to know everything they were doing, but, God willing, he would be joining them in another year. So, here he was, sitting in classrooms, marching to cadences, having room inspections and having to listen to pre-pubescent conversations all around him with kids that barely shaved. He'd killed people with his bare hands. He'd married, loved with abandon, got totally dumped on while he was deployed, and probably made love to another forty women after his divorce. These guys didn't have a clue what was about to fuck with them. The medics in the class were still embarrassed to watch a woman give birth in the hospital.

He hoped Brandy had some answers for him, because he'd thought about everything so many times his brain was fried.

The world bloomed when he saw her running toward him in the airport lobby. Without caring, she'd dropped her carryon and slammed that big, beautiful body against him, he nearly fucked her right then and there. Just holding her vibrating form, smelling the sweet perfume of her womanhood and her desire for him made him drunk with all the right things. Blood flowed to body parts that had gone dormant. It could have been the dead of winter, but it was spring in his body. There were lights, music, birds chirping and all the other fuckin' things that guys feel when they're in love. It was so funny, he nearly cried from the irony. He'd signed up to kill people for his country and have to leave this woman alone while he did it. What kind of a decision was that?

"Tucker, I ache all over I'm so excited to see you."

"Baby, I haven't slept in a week. I've not thought of anything else." He *wanted* to feel that way. He just had to lie about the worries, because that wasn't how he was going to talk to her. That was going to have to be between him and his maker.

They were ushered to their room. He gave the bellman twenty dollars because her suitcase was the heaviest he'd ever seen. The guy studied Tucker, all buff and huge, easily a hundred pounds heavier than the skinny guy too small for the uniform. But he made great effort to place the enormous bag on the bed, as Brandy had requested. He loved that about her. She was oblivious to those little details, like the princess she certainly was.

So, the kid backed out the door, wiped his forehead and beamed when Tucker gave him the twenty and a wink.

"Thank you, sir."

"You earned it. Get some ice on that lower back, okay?"

Brandy had started unpacking.

"We're only here for three days."

"I don't care, I want to get all my things hung up and refolded so they don't wrinkle."

She didn't even look at him, as she picked up each article of clothing and shook it out and either added it to the closet or the drawers.

"So, you going to give me a fashion show, where you take your clothes off and put them back on every hour? That what we're doing?" He leaned against the wall, more relaxed than he'd felt in two months. And it had nothing to do with alcohol or the extremely good vape one of the boys in his dorm had brought from home. He just loved watching her do her thing. That's what he'd missed.

But his pantsbunny reminded him that he'd missed the sex, too. She'd worn a white stretchy blouse over a pair of black slacks. Lucky for him the dresser was directly across from him, and, after she'd filled up the top two drawers she had to bend over to get to the third one near the floor. Suddenly there was that vision before him that drove him to action.

He ran across the room and grabbed her so quickly she screamed. "What are you doing?"

"You can do this later. Right now, I'm here for the sole purpose of satisfying that ache you talked about in the airport. Can we talk about that now, please? I've been very patient." He said all this while he was pushing her suitcase off the bed. It crashed on the floor and spilled contents, some jars of something rolling down the carpet trying to escape through the front door.

But she didn't notice because she was laughing so hard. He hoisted her on the bed and dropped her and she continued to laugh.

"Now that, that's a heavy suitcase!" he said.

She propped herself up on her elbows, looking up at him. "Hey!"

"Oh shut up and help me get you naked please. I don't want to ruin anything, but honestly, honey, I really don't care."

He pulled her shirt over her head and viewed a spectacular pushup bra with flower stitching and pearls. The thing gave her easily an eight-inch cleavage.

"Perfect!" he said. "You're gonna leave that on."

"It opens in the front."

"Like I said, perfect. When I release, you can release that too, okay?"

She laughed again, unzipped her pants and shimmied them down her hips and thighs. "You'll want to take note of these," she said as she splayed her hands to the sides to show him the matching panties. "And just watch!" She scrambled to her knees and bent over. Just below the beautiful butt crack that was revealed, and above that perfect ass, was a little bow stitched in place.

"Hold that pose," Tucker said as he kicked off his shoes and removed his slacks, nearly losing his balance and falling on the floor. At last, fully naked, he demonstrated his treat for her eyes. "Ta-Da!" His hands splayed to the sides, revealing his enormous boner. It was nearly bright purple it was so throbbing and hard.

"Oh my."

"Indeed. Now, honey, you be careful now, because this might hurt."

"Oh dear. Really?" She whispered in return, still on her knees, looking at him with those sultry red lips and her mahogany hair mussed up all over her shoulders. "And here I can't even pleasure myself." She rolled her head back as she pressed her palms down the satin and cotton of the bra, lower to smooth over her belly and then down over her hips. She leaned onto her shoulders, placed her palms at her rear, spread her cheeks and slipped the panty elastic to the side to insert a finger in her core. "I'm so ready for you Tucker."

He shook his head. "Nope. Not going to fit, But I do admire you for trying. My dick is so hard your panties are going to chop it off. That might ruin our evening."

She nearly fell to the bed, laughing.

He crawled to spoon over her, his hands fondling her from behind.

She groaned and leaned into his touch, wherever he chose to place his hands.

"I like that. Very compliant. You want a little bit of me, baby?"

"I want it all."

"Even if it hurts?" He pulled the panties down over one hip and leg, and then removed the other side.

"You can kiss it and make it better."

"I can kiss it right now and make you come. I know I can. Shall I try?"

She didn't answer him, but nodded, viewing his face through her hair.

He slid beneath her on his back and drank from her sex looming above him. She undulated to the rhythm of his tongue, moaning and clutching her chest. He added his thumb and she started to vibrate.

"Told you so," he whispered.

"Don't stop now."

He climbed to his knees behind her, massaging her slit from her bud to her anal flower. "I've missed you. How you taste. How smooth your skin is, and how beautiful you look when you're pink and aroused, and when you come on my mouth."

He lifted her gently so he could position her over his rod, and then slowly pulled her down and back on top of him. She hissed and made little mewling sounds as he filled her with each tiny thrust up inside her. And when he could go no further, he pressed her hips down to go beyond.

Their breathing was in tandem, as he held her there on the bed. He kissed the back of her neck, slowly smoothed over her thighs and her round ass, returning to her bud where he gently pinched her, which brought another hiss.

"Love this, Tucker. No rush. I want this all night long."

"Absolutely, sweetheart. Anything you want. I'm here. Not going anywhere."

CHAPTER 9

BRANDY WOKE UP against Tucker's back. He had one arm twisted behind him, resting on her thigh. The scent of his neck was sweet, almost feminine. She inhaled deeply and let all that delicious, moist air refresh her lungs.

There wasn't any part of him she did not love. She hoped it would always be like this—each of them totally consumed in their passions, attentive, hard at work to create joy and get as close to each other's souls as possible. In bed with him was the only place on earth where she felt the true meaning of life. Where there were no barriers, only truth in gentle movements. They gave, and took. They rested and gave more. It was a cycle she doubted she could ever tire from. She felt cherished in his enormous arms. He'd do anything to protect her, and she felt the same for him.

He turned, kissed her tenderly and rubbed his thumbs over her cheekbones. Her face felt small, like a little child's in his hands. She'd forgotten that.

"I'm a big liar," she whispered.

"Oh really? What little lies are you telling me, then?" He followed this up with a kiss.

"I've been telling you over the phone I've been doing fine. I haven't. And now that I'm here, I don't want to go back to San Diego."

He started to say something and she placed her fingers over his mouth.

"I know, I have to." She kissed him.

"No, I was going to say stay. You could easily get a job out here. It's just that it's so expensive. I could try to get you a room—"

"And know that you're in a dorm with a bunch of Navy brats? Stay with a family I don't know?"

"We could find someone really nice. And then I could see you more often. Cheaper than getting a hotel on a short term. Than airfare."

"But there's my dad. I can't leave him without any notice."

"It will only be another month, Brandy. Then I get a few days off until Indoc. And they'll give me another few days before we start Phase I. But all that, Indoc, Hell Week and everything, will be done in San Diego."

A month seemed like an eternity, though she'd managed to wait three already. She pouted.

"Do that again," he whispered.

"What?"

"That thing you did when you sighed. That thing with your lips."

She sighed again, and pushed her lips out and immediately his mouth was on hers, his tongue making its way to play with hers. She pulled back and grinned. "You're so funny."

His eyes danced in the reflection of the night-lights outside. He pulled her into him again, his enormous paw on her left breast, squeezing and kneading it into submission. He kissed and sucked her nipple, getting more serious by the minute.

There was a vein in his forehead that pulsed when he was in deep concentration and right now her breasts were making him very, very focused.

He turned his head and examined her from different angles. He explored with his fingers and tongue, and then let his hand wander down her midline, stopping before touching her nub.

Tucker's were the only fingers that had ever touched her there. And every time he did it, he made her feel like it was the first time all over again.

"So sweet. So wonderful." His forefinger found her.

"All yours, Tucker."

"Yes."

He got to his knees, bringing a pillow underneath her hips, which was the perfect angle for him to go in deep. He pressed past her swollen lips and soothed her with his gentle back and forth movements, bringing his kisses between thrusts. His powerful hips ground into her, lifting her pelvis and slowly increasing speed.

She let him do everything this time. Let him open her, set her on fire so she could watch the process as well as be the lead actor in it. She waited for that little phase when she lost complete control. Ravenous for him, she bit his neck and clutched his back. Still, she could not get enough. Sweat rolled down her chest and from her forehead into her hairline. With her hunger building, she found it difficult to get air, so inhaled deeply at last and finally felt the delicious rush of her orgasm when she exhaled. Her long sensual journey lasted minutes as he continued to help her fly, kept her afloat, and gently set her back down, thoroughly exhausted.

He collapsed on top of her just as the sky was turning pink. She fought sleep, but the warmth of his body and the sweat of their lovemaking pulled her into a dream state where she fell on a cloud.

CHAPTER 10

THEY WERE AWAKENED by Tucker's cell phone ringing. He'd tried to ignore it, but a few minutes later the ringing started again.

"I'll turn it off."

He got up, wandering naked, checked the screen and swore.

"What is it?"

"It's Kyle. I gotta call him. There's something wrong with Brawley."

"Tucker! Yes, there is. Oh my gosh! I should have told you."

"Told me what?"

"He's disappeared. Yesterday—" She hit her forehead. "Yesterday Dorie got a call and he was listed as missing in Mexico."

"What? When was this?"

"Yesterday, about noon? I think? No, earlier. Eleven. That's when I went over, just before I had to go to work. She said she'd call me when she had updates. I think she was going to call Christy."

"Who called her?"

"Someone from the Navy. Oh gosh, Tucker. Why didn't I contact you right away?"

"I got a call from Brawley night before last. Very strange. He's been talking to me off and on, but this was out of the blue. Said he was being followed. I rang Kyle immediately, but couldn't get through."

He redialed the number and Kyle picked it up on the first ring.

"Hey Tuck, sorry I didn't call you sooner. So you've heard about Brawley, then?"

"Yea. Brandy's here with me in Chicago for the weekend. Dorie got a call from the Navy yesterday about Brawley missing. Is that true?"

"I'm afraid it is. Our op here got real fucked up. And we were watching Brawley like a hawk. Something wasn't right."

"What do you figure happened, if you can talk about it?"

"Well, this is a need to know. Right now, time is of the essence. We don't exactly have good support here. Not quite sure if we should just focus on finding Brawley and forget the cover we've created. But I got the go-ahead to call you, at least."

"Glad you did."

"You start with your observations. Any clue, Tucker?"

"Well, he's pretty fixated on this Day of the Dead stuff. At least that's what the call was about. Seeing faces. Skulls and stuff."

"You think he's using something?"

"I don't think he takes anything. At least nothing I know of," answered Tucker.

"I checked and there's nothing on his record of any kind of mental illness. Did you notice anything growing up?"

"Not a thing, Kyle. He did mention that kid you guys lost last year on that quickie in Africa. He took it pretty hard. Felt responsible. He told me about it right after you guys came back, and then everything got all fucked planning the wedding. I barely saw him after that until after their honeymoon. If there was a sign something was wrong, I totally missed it."

"Okay, well I'll look into that."

"So is this missing of his own accord? Or, was he taken?"

"We don't know. That's the ugly truth. But he's been drinking. That we noticed big time."

"He told me he was scared."

"Yea. He mentioned it to Coop too. Coop thought it was a delayed PTSD."

"Sorry, can't help you there. I know nothing about

that. What about the kid last deployment?"

"Brawley knew the family. Used to date his sister, of all things. This was a few years back. The kid idolized Brawley. But hell, wasn't his fault. The two of them made a wrong turn and wound up facing some bad guys. Carlos was in front and got hit. Brawley got three of the four of them, but it was too late to save Carlos."

"That's a shame. I never knew the story. Wish I had. Maybe something I could have done."

"So, if anyone contacts you, let me know immediately. We were working pretty deep, and I left my cell behind for a couple of days. Won't happen again."

"Okay. I'll keep my ears open."

Brandy touched his arm, and then took the cell from Tucker. She put the phone on speaker. "Kyle, this is Brandy. Have you called Dorie? She's been going out of her mind."

"Nope. I knew Collins and the boys back home were doing that. Was going to call her tomorrow. She should have called Christy."

"She was hesitant to say anything to either of you. She was concerned about him, and she's told me he's not tried to contact her once since you've been over there. That's not like him."

"No, it isn't. Okay, well we've got a couple of places we have to check out tonight. If either of you think of anything, call me."

"Definitely," answered Brandy.

"You guys have fun. Guess I don't have to say that, do I?"

Both he and Brandy answered in unison, "Nope."

Kyle managed to squeeze out a tiny chuckle. "Glad someone's getting laid. Sorry Brandy, just how my brain works."

"No offense taken."

"Take care of my brothers," Tucker added.

"Always. Hey, when do you start Indoc?"

"About four weeks."

"Well, hurry it up and get your butt back down here. We need you back on this team. Your boy did real good. Strong kid. You trained him well."

"Thanks, Kyle. I'll be sure to tell him next time I see him."

"Okay. Better call Christy. You guys don't be too good."

"Not a chance," Tucker said, and hung up.

Brandy was sitting on the edge of the bed, still naked. He could tell she was nearly in shock.

"Poor Dorie," she whispered.

"You need to go back home?" He sat next to her and took her hand in his. He felt her begin to thaw. Then she returned his squeeze.

"No, what I need is some breakfast, and then I

think I need a nap. And that, Tucker," she said as she punched his arm, "Is entirely your fault."

He grinned at the sight of the sun beginning to pierce the skyline and whiten the tall grey shadows of buildings.

"Yes, indeed, I am totally to blame. And I'd do it all over again in a heartbeat."

He decided he'd talk to her about all the things that could go wrong, but do it tomorrow. In the meantime, he noted she didn't panic. And she didn't run home to daddy.

Yup. I think this is going to work.

CHAPTER 11

THE WEEKEND WAS over way too soon. Tucker wasn't very familiar with Chicago, and neither was she, so after several times getting lost or waiting for a Taxi or Uber, they decided to just stay inside their room, ordering room service. Time was so precious, she didn't want to waste a minute of it.

Their parting and the long flight home were tearful. The heaviness in her heart reminded her that the love she felt for Tucker was real. This trip had cemented it. He'd even had that long discussion about all the terrible things that could happen, how dangerous it was being a SEAL.

He used the situation with Dorie and Brawley to demonstrate how she needed to stay plugged into the community. Alone and on their own, the wives never did well. The guys had it drummed into them, he said. But the ladies had to embrace that so everyone could be protected. He explained how people would be helping Dorie with meals. Someone would come and do housework or shopping for her. She didn't have to, and shouldn't have to feel alone.

So Brandy returned to San Diego with a new determination. She wanted to learn everything she could about being a wife of a SEAL. She called Christy Lansdowne and over the next week, got invited to a couple home parties and get-togethers. She found the women, as a whole, to be very resilient. They were used to juggling households without any help from their husbands, who were always gone. And when the men were home, they were allowed time to unplug and get back into the rhythm of life in California. Babies were born. Kids had lessons and recitals. Grandparents passed away. And yes, sometimes Team Guys didn't come home.

"When I was considering marrying Tyler, one of the wives told me I'd never feel as loved as I would married to him. She was completely right."

Others gave her pieces of advice. Everyone admired her for going into the job of marrying an elite warrior with her eyes wide open, and for doing her research up front. To be prepared. It still wasn't a guarantee, just like every brave or strong man didn't pass all the challenges of the BUD/S or SEAL Qualification Training. But it didn't take anything away from their bravery or honor.

Brandy's dad, Steven Cook, was back to full speed. He was already selling the squash, lettuce and peas he was raising in his new garden. He was growing cabbage and broccoli, as well as carrots and beets. His patrons delighted in occasionally being able to go out back and pick their own produce, and they paid well for the opportunity.

She took Dorie to her first doctor's visit and they both got to hear the baby's heartbeat. With Brandy's encouragement, Dorie went back to work and found it helped her get her mind off the possibility of having to raise a child without a father. Both of them hoped Brawley would be found eventually, since he had been seen on the outskirts of the village.

The girls talked about being able to accept whatever the eventual outcome was. Brandy also got offered her old job back, which she promptly turned down and felt great about it.

It had now been ten days since Brawley went missing. There still was no ransom demand so the search team Kyle left in place in Mexico was convinced he'd just abandoned his post, voluntarily because he'd been seen. He explained to Dorie that the team wanted to find him quickly, before the slow wheels of the Navy started in motion, stripping Brawley of his Trident and sending him home with a dishonorable discharge. Kyle explained that it still might happen that way. But he was confident Brawley was alive. His wallet had been found, emptied of cash. A convenience store clerk had seen him come in from the beach and ask for water on several occasions. He was also given food. The clerk said he looked homeless.

"I guess there are a lot of homeless vets out there," Dorie said. "I had no idea."

"Well, that gives us hope, then, if he was seen," remarked Brandy.

"At this point, I just want him safe. We'll sort everything else out later, if we can."

Brandy was proud of her best friend. She wasn't sure she could endure the same.

And then one day, the team found Brawley sleeping under a cardboard box at the shore. His skin was covered in insect bites, he had a distinctive red beard and his hair was full of twigs and debris. His bare feet were cut and beginning to show signs of serious infection. He'd also lost a lot of weight, using a rope to hold his pants up. The guys who found him said he didn't recognize them at first, but as he ingested some decent food, things began to come back to him.

Brawley was escorted home, along with the rest of the team. What his life was going to look like was still uncertain.

But Brawley was alive!

Tucker was pleased when Brandy gave him the

news.

"So what happened to him?" he asked.

"No one knows yet. Dorie and I've been doing some reading. There are a lot of homeless vets who just disappear—walk away from families and houses. All sorts of mental issues made worse by some of the conditions—well, you know quite a bit about that."

"Indeed I do. We're all so young when we start out. It's hard on a guy, and he probably had some things he was covering up, too. He didn't want to get tossed from the Teams."

"And have to answer to his former SEAL father."

"Yup. Something like that. Wow. So glad he's safe, for now. Going to be a long road getting him all the way back."

"Dorie's looking for a place for him. Just started therapy at the VA hospital," she answered. "She sees him tomorrow for the first time."

"He's lucky. Life on the streets, even the beach, is very dangerous."

"Well, he's even luckier than that, Tucker. Dorie's pregnant."

Tucker chuckled. "Well, if anything can make a man jump to attention, that'll do it. Good for them. I'm pulling for them."

"Me too.

They made plans for another weekend when he finished his Corps School. But the Indoc, which sometimes was postponed by as much as a month or more, depending on the SEAL Team cycles, was all set to start the following week. If Tucker wanted to wait for the next class, he could do so, but it would postpone his eventual graduation. He explained that guys who got injured during training sometimes sat out a rotation and joined up with the next class. Tucker wasn't injured, and didn't want to wait.

Brandy's father continued to have cartons of goods raided, but began viewing it as an involuntary contribution to the local population, and not the former employee.

"The way I see it, if someone's that hungry, I say give it to them. No one should starve here. I've got plenty," he said.

"But you'll report it, right?" Brandy asked him.

"Oh yes. Riverton and I are now old friends. He logs everything in quite dutifully. He said if I was willing to spend the time to call him, he could do me the favor by keeping track."

She went home each night after work, walked around the cottage, touching things that Tucker loved, even slept on his side of the bed just to be a little closer to his familiar scent. She opened his drawers and smelled his tee shirts, even organized his socks. He'd be annoyed with that, she thought, but she didn't care. His absence left a huge hole in her world that daily phone calls could not patch up.

In just two more weeks he'd be home. He'd be here, preparing to do one of the hardest things he'd ever done in his life. Brandy was determined to help him do it.

CHAPTER 12

TUCKER WAS PREPARED for the P.T. the instructors at Indoc dished out, but he wasn't prepared mentally for all the insults he had to endure. Kyle and others had said he was a welcome commodity, being a former SEAL. That the Navy encouraged re-enlistment with his skillset.

Those lying sons of bitches.

It wouldn't have made any difference because he still would have gone through being the adult Boy Scout in Great Lakes. He was kind of looking forward to seeing some of the pimply-faced crowd getting a dose of reality, where every little infraction was noted, and the instructors didn't let anyone get away with not getting humiliated on a regular basis.

He knew what they were doing. They were trying to wash out the weak ones. Especially the officers who would not be able to lead a command on a SEAL Team. They could leave the program during this phase and not have a mark against them. But if they quit during one of the three phases, that was a whole different thing. They wouldn't likely have a very distinguished career.

Tucker's class was made up of about one-third officers. The instructors called them the "Gentlemen's Club." A lot was made of the enlisted men vs. officers, with choice comments. Tucker laughed at some of these, but didn't dare show it.

"You think you can carry that boat because you have a college education, boys? That you don't want to get your hands dirty, that it? Why, that just gives you an excuse to take it easy. In *this* class, we don't get over the finish line until we *all* get over the finish line. That means you officers are at a disadvantage. Life's about to get hard. Real fuckin' hard. I don't mean hard-*on*."

This usually caused one or two of the enlisted men to chuckle. That would send them scraping the bottom of boats with their own toothbrush, or running extra laps.

Every hometown was denigrated as breeding the lowest of the low, that they should consider themselves lucky to even be in their presence.

Tucker was called Grandpa and Pops more than he was called his name. One of the worst badmouths on the instructor team was a recruit he'd actually prepared. He was doing a rotation as an instructor while his leg injury healed.

"I remember you. You were that old guy who thought he was all buff and tried to scare the shit out of all us. Oh man. Payback's a bitch. Your ass is mine now!"

Tucker had to do extra pull-ups because he'd made so much fun of him during his own training.

"Show them how you fuckin' show off. We used to dream at night we'd find you in a dark alley."

These shouts and insults did get under his skin. But it made him wish he'd been tougher on the guys than he had been. If, God forbid, he should take a turn at being an instructor and one of them decided to go back in, he knew he'd dish it out even more. Because it was good for him. It was good for all of them. And it was meant to stress out the ones who were going to wash out anyway later on. Just like carrying boats over rocks in twelve-man crews, rubbing all the hair off their scalps, over and over again, there wasn't any way around this but to find the ones who could somehow get up and over those rocks without breaking their ankles.

After Hell Week, there were only about twenty per cent of the men left. The ones who dropped out had to chase the truck with the bell in the back of it. You couldn't just walk into the office and say you quit. You had to do a good quit, not a sissy quit. You had to be humiliated and catcalled so that you were clear this was not for you.

He called Brandy at the end of that week. He needed some TLC and he was going to take it.

She met him at the training facility parking lot, and had secured a nearby motel room, and not one of the expensive ones. Money was tight for them. He fell asleep in the car on the way over. He awoke to her trying to yank his enormous frame from the passenger seat. At first, he thought he was still at the beach inhaling saltwater, but as he regained his wits, he tried to help her lead him to the second floor room.

"Should have gotten a first floor."

"I can see that now."

"I told you to get the first floor," he whined, but he didn't care.

"Shut up and save it for the third time you qualify. I'll remember then, okay?"

"Oh man, you got a mouth on you. I'll bet you do nasty things with that mouth."

"Sure I do, not that you'll ever find out, because you can't stop snoring. I'll bet you fall asleep in the middle of sex, too."

Brandy indeed had one of the most wicked mouths ever invented. He was trying to tell her so when she got him inside the door, and pushed him onto the bed.

"Ouch! I'm hurting all over."

"Really? That's what happens when you garden too much. You've just been lying on the beach, sunning yourself."

He tried to see that mouth that was making him mad, and horny at the same time.

"Come here."

"I don't do orders like that."

"Please."

"Okay, please."

"Please like *please pass the salsa* or please like *please stop talking and take off all your clothes?*" He was losing the battle and sleep was beginning to overtake him.

"Hey, lover-boy. You can talk a good talk, but I'll bet you don't even have the strength to get your clothes off."

She was smiling down on him, hands on those lovely hips. And she was wearing a nice scoop top with what had to be the strongest pushup bra invented because he could rest a basketball on her shelf with no problem. He was going to show her he could do anything he wanted. He could run five miles and still get it up with her. He could—

Tucker woke up the next morning with a smile, until he noticed he was still wearing the same clothes she'd picked him up in. She'd thrown a blanket over him, leaving him just the way he'd fallen. Even left his boots on. But, as his eyes focused and he beheld the warm fleshy glow of her body lying beautifully naked next to him, the urgency to join her was overwhelming. He suddenly had the power of a team of mules.

He sat up. He remembered why he'd been so happy. He'd made it through Hell Week. Brandy was here to help him celebrate, and heal. Yes, there was pain under his arms, and in his groin area. His feet hurt too, and soon he found out why. Every single toenail was bright green. The green algae extended to mid calf, where the socks and lace-up boots stopped. His shoes were so ripe, he tossed them against the room door. This woke her up, with a start.

"You didn't even take off my clothes!"

"What's that smell?" She held her nose and then followed his line of sight until she discovered his frog feet. "Oh dear. Your inner Shrek is sprouting. You didn't happen to cross paths with a witch somewhere in Coronado, did you?"

"That. Was. Unkind."

She rolled over on her back, giggling, one arm shading her forehead and gave him a very welcoming grin. The covers revealed just enough breast to make him hard instantly.

"Wouldn't have made any difference. You weren't going to do anything anyway. I just let you sleep." She followed it up with a sweet smile, but then she licked her lips and he forgot about his green feet, and climbed on top of her.

"Pew. You need a shower, sailor."

"Yes, I do. But you're coming with me." He kissed her, traveling down under her ear and then sucked that overzealous nipple that dared to pert up on her. He licked that thing to submission and it wasn't long before she was writhing, doing things with her hands he was supposed to do.

"Don't you get started without me, Brandy. I want to feel and taste all of it right there with you, honey."

She brought one of her hands up and saluted him. Her fingers were wet. It was so unfair!

He pulled her arm and got her to standing position, her long shiny hair covering her shoulders and those gorgeous mounds.

"Now you have to work," he said.

"What do you mean? You think it was easy getting you through that door and up the stairs? Ha!"

She crossed her arms, defiant. Oh, she was dangerous.

"Okay, so you worked a little bit. Now your job is to undress me."

Those lovely fingers slipped in and around his buttons, zippers, undoing his belt as she pulled the stiff saltwater-washed uniform off his body. When he was completely naked, she screamed and jumped back a foot.

He looked down to determine what she'd seen. Little rivulets of blood oozed from his underarms. A matching pair were in his groin area, caused by the friction of his wet suit which he had to wear or freeze to death during the midnight wet-n-sandys. But standing loud and proud, his dick was perfect. Smooth, and bright purple-red, veins bulging and ready to burst. He imagined she might think it was the cherry on top. He couldn't help it. She made everything perform like a rock star.

When his gaze returned to hers, he saw she was licking her lips again, and she began to kneel.

He wanted a shower, but, by God, if she'd just take him into her mouth, he'd take care of all the rest. He knew making love to her was going to get him healed and right with the world ten times faster than it normally would have done.

CHAPTER 13

IT HAD BEEN nearly twenty-four hours since she'd eaten and Brandy was starved. Tucker was snoring on his belly. The shower hadn't entirely gotten rid of the green.

"Lover boy," she whispered in his ear. One enormous paw grabbed her forearm.

"You're not getting away yet."

"I don't *want* to get away, but I'm hungry. Haven't I performed enough to deserve at least a cheese omelet?"

"How about room service?"

"Tucker, not sure if you remember, but this wasn't exactly the suite at the Hotel Del. The Lamplighter doesn't have a restaurant. They don't even have a coffee maker in the room. And I'm starving."

He let go of her arm, and then pulled himself up. "Oh, I suppose we could take a short break."

"*And* you did ask me to set up something so you

could see Brawley, remember?"

His eyes were roaming all over her chest again. "I think that was your idea, not mine."

She hit him with a pillow. "You liar."

He laughed and feigned being hurt with the soft fluffy material. "Down, woman! Down! Remember, I have injuries."

"Not to the parts that count."

"I'm glad you noticed." His boyish grin made her melt. It would have been easy to just say the heck with it and just play in bed all day. She loved the play, but she was truly hungry. And arranging the visit with Brawley was tricky. In his delicate condition, she didn't think it was wise to keep him waiting.

"Tucker, we have to be at the clinic at ten. That gives us about an hour for breakfast. I. Need. Food."

"Yes, ma'am."

She handed him a change of clothes he'd asked for, and they set out in search of an omelet.

AT TEN, THEY were waiting for an audience with Brawley's doctor before seeing him.

Dr. Raj was from India. His handsome face beamed when he saw Tucker. "I heard all about you, Tucker. Going through all the qualifications again. Quite impressive!"

"Thanks, doc."

"What's it like doing it again? Harder or easier?"

"I really can't say. I mean, some parts are harder, some easier."

The doctor nodded.

"Actually, sir, I'm waiting for the easy part, come to think of it. I've got some pretty big chafing holes in my skin under my arms and right here." He demonstrated the spots at the top of his thighs on the inside.

Dr. Raj made a face. "I'll bet those wounds are huge, then. I can get you some good antibiotic cream. Best thing is to not move much, and keep it dry, clean and don't irritate it with clothing. But of course, you can't walk around naked."

Brandy could see the Indian doctor blushed.

"Oh we're doing fine on the last part. But not so much on the movement."

"I understand. Well, I'll see to it that you get some of that cream before you leave. Now, about Brawley."

"Yes, we'd like to see him," Tucker said.

"And I think that would be good. We're trying to introduce things back into his life that perhaps he forgot. For instance, he doesn't remember his wife at all."

"Oh dear," sobbed Brandy.

"I think he started to disengage before he actually left the team. It is a form of Post Traumatic Stress. Gradually, his brain will let him absorb other people, and then the memories will return. But, he could have a serious gap that won't return, I'm afraid. We won't know for some time. Every case is different."

"Does he know Tucker is going to see him today."

"He's been told, yes. Just don't react if he says or does things you don't understand. We want to include him in our lives. He can't do it the other way around."

As they walked down the softly lit hallway, Tucker whispered a question to Brandy.

"Is this the VA? Not at all the facility I remember."

She realized she'd forgotten to tell him about the clinic. "Libby Brownlee's dad arranged this for Brawley. And he's bankrolling it, too. He's getting the very best brain injury care in the country, part of Scripps. I'm afraid the VA has a ways to go before we see this kind of service for our Vets."

"Good for him. I met Dr. Brownlee a many times before. He's our unofficial Team doctor, you know."

She took his hand, lowering her voice again, "Yes, I know. In fact, I know a whole lot more than I did just a couple of weeks ago. I haven't been sleep deprived and doing boat drills like you have. But I've been studying too."

Tucker squeezed her hand, then drew it to his lips and kissed her. "Thank you, sweetheart."

They were shown the doorway to a pleasant room decorated with pictures and live plants. Tucker saw that Brawley's family photos were displayed all over the wall, including his wedding pictures. On the space next to the window was a much younger Tucker photo. He was standing next to a younger version of his best friend, in front of some white mountains, their arms locked around one another, smiles as wide as Brandy had ever seen.

"From our first deployment in Afghanistan," Tucker whispered.

Behind a curtain, they heard the familiar voice. "Tucker, is that you?"

Doctor Raj gave them a thumb's up, and held ten fingers in the air. Tucker acknowledged with a nod. Brandy slipped into the corner and took a seat as her big hunk pulled back the curtain. Brawley's eyebrows rose.

"Fuckin' about time. They said you were on vacation or some shit. Get your ass over here, and break me outa this place, will you?"

Tucker embraced his buddy, tears streaming down his cheeks. Brawley also began to cry. "You're back, buddy. You came back."

"No shit, Sherlock. But hey, I didn't do the heavy lifting. They could have left me on the beach with all those senoritas, but no, they had to spoil the fun and drag my ass here." He wiped his face with the back of his hands, and then stopped as he noticed Brandy.

"Well, hello there little lady. When did they sneak you in here?"

"She's with me, you goofball," said Tucker, his lips still rubbery with emotion. "This is Brandy, and she's going to be my wife, so hands off."

"Sure. Just like you, Tucker. Tell me the prettiest girl is yours. You selfish bastard."

She approached the bed. "Hey Brawley, nice to see you again. So glad you made it back." She shook his hand and he grabbed her toward him and gave her a proper hug.

"I'll be damned. She said *again*, Tucker. So she's met me before too. Like the other pretty one." He glanced around as if looking for permission. "Can you believe it? She claims to be my wife!"

Brandy saw Dr. Raj cover his mouth just outside Brawley's line of sight.

"I know." Tucker drew his arm around Brandy's waist and claimed her back. "You could have done much worse. I'd just sit back and enjoy it. She could have been a horse-faced woman with a beard. It will be like falling in love all over again, my man. You lucky bastard."

"I intend to do lots of research."

"Yes, best to take your time and savor every moment."

Brawley blinked and appeared to lose continuity

because his expression changed. "Hey, not sure how long you're staying, but could you ask that little Indian fellow if he could get us some pizza. I'm fuckin' starved."

Dr. Raj appeared on cue. "Brawley, I'll see to it right away. Unfortunately these two have to cut their time short today." He handed his patient a photograph from his own wedding. "But they brought this for you. See? This is them at your wedding just a few months ago. See? There's Tucker, and there's Brandy."

He stared down at the picture and then took it gently from Dr. Raj's fingers. "I remember that dance. That was you!" He pointed directly at Brandy.

"It was. We were showing off, remember?" Brandy said enthusiastically. She was delighted the old Brawley, or some form of him, had reappeared.

Dr. Raj winced and shook his head slightly at the word choice, but he left it to Brawley to react.

"You were sexy as hell. And you got sick. Now, I bet you don't remember that, do you?"

His grin was a joy to watch. And he was partially right. She'd been so drunk that New Year's Eve, lots of the reception was a blur.

"That's where we met, so I owe it all to you," whispered Tucker.

"How about that?"

Dr. Raj carefully extricated them after the goodbyes were exchanged. In the hallway, all three of them breathed a sigh of relief.

"That was about as perfect as I'd hoped," he said.

"You gotta let the Team come in here. I think he can handle it."

"You might be right."

"And they'll needle the shit out of him, too. Just wait. He's gonna feel just like I do going through BUD/S. It's what he's used to. Been like that his whole life, even as a kid."

"Thank you." Now it was Dr. Raj's turn to develop tears. He was going to say something else, but Brawley's hoarse voice pierced the sound barrier.

"Hey, where's my pizza!"

CHAPTER 14

TUCKER FOUND THE next two phases of BUD/S easier. The instructors didn't yell at him so loud, which kind of pissed him off. He didn't want to be known as a weakling, or anything approaching being fragile. He wanted to be the one to show them how it was done. It was dangerous to have that attitude, so he worked to make sure it didn't show up in his team dynamics.

Because of his previous experience on the Teams, the instructors gave him hints about what might be sprung on the class the next day. "Don't bother to shower, you'll be wet all day," or, "Go light on the breakfast. A little choppy out there on the bay today." One suggestion he really appreciated was, "Pick the big guys today. The Smurfs are going to get wasted." Tucker had been nursing a cold and thoroughly enjoyed sitting on the sunny beach watching as every other boat crew had to go in and out all afternoon.

Because they'd come in first, they earned the right to rest and restore. It wasn't much, but it was as good as doing wet-n-sandy in a heated bathtub.

But the instructors discovered he was an inspiration to those men who were struggling to push themselves to finish. Tucker's swim buddy, who could have been on one of the Olympic teams, dropped one day and didn't even say good-bye. He knew some day he'd run across the man and give him the chance to explain. But the loss of his strong swim partner made the "water features" as the instructors called it, more challenging. Another good swimmer who had also lost his partner started shadowing him, and they worked the channel like he had done with his former buddy.

He also knew word had spread what Brawley had been through. He was encouraged to share some of his private thoughts about P.T.S.D. and how it could creep up on even the strongest warrior.

In the last week before graduation a subtle shift had occurred. Tucker transitioned from student to teacher. He suspected this was the role he would play in the months and days coming up.

The graduation ceremony was held in the operations building, newly renovated since Tucker's first time out. Even the chairs were nicer and they had a screen for the hot sun that baked Coronado all twelve months of the year.

Brandy was wearing dark Navy blue, and not black, because she thought it would be bad luck. Her suit nearly matched Tucker's dark dress uniform of the enlisted rank. He noted all the ladies were taken with the dress whites the officers chose to wear.

It was a surprise when Kyle Lansdowne walked into the gathering and began his address to the new class five-two-six. They were a small group, only twelve of the original group, plus several who would go on to do further training from previous classes, having recovered from their injuries. Several had developed mono, which sometimes forced them to wait six months or a year to graduate.

Tucker was seated on the left. Brandy and his parents were seated on the right, along with other friends and family of the other men. He'd given an invitation to Dorie, but she respectfully declined, since she was due to deliver any day. She'd been touched by the gesture. They'd talked earlier.

"It's like Brawley's going through BUD/S all over again, Tucker. Just without the uniform and the speeches," she told him. "He already earned his Trident. Now he's proving to everyone why."

He'd been so overcome, he didn't have words to give her in return.

So he was waiting for his time to walk up front and get his pin to add to the other one he'd kept in a box in his underwear drawer. He chuckled, recalling when Brandy asked him if he got to wear both Tridents at the same time.

Kyle began his speech. Tucker had heard many of them before, but this one was special because he felt it had been written just for him. Unless that was his ego talking, and that was always a possibility.

He shook it off, clearing his head, ready to listen to the man he hoped to serve with and under, and risk his life with, *again.*

Kyle gave the welcome to the dignitaries, and told the families that he'd remembered this day, over twenty-two years ago now. He told them he never hesitated when asked to address a new class. He'd met some of his best friends here. And some of those he lost overseas.

"We aren't supposed to say we're the best, because any man who wears a uniform is a hero. There is no rank to the word hero. You don't get a medal every time you become one, or, in some cases, claw your way back to one." He nodded at Tucker. Tucker returned the short nod.

"We are trained not to brag, but let me tell you, and then I'll shut up about it, we are the best of the best. And so are the other Spec Ops guys, and the guys who deliver and pick them up. The ones who give support on the ground or arrange to get them home. The ladies who give birth to these fine men and then have to give them up to a country that doesn't always recognize her Vets as they should all the time. But we don't do it for that. In the old days no one knew what a SEAL was. A lot of us wish it was that way again."

He paused to take a drink of water.

"We are lucky enough to find something we so love doing, that we do it even though we may have to pay the ultimate sacrifice. We were created because it was determined our country needed a group of special guys who can gut it out and just get the job done, no matter what was asked, no matter what the risk. I guess history will eventually tell us if we were smart or just plain stupid."

The audience rumbled in amusement. Kyle gripped the podium and continued, scanning the whole crowd, both right and left. And then he motioned to someone at the back.

Tucker turned in his seat, winked at Brandy, who had been staring at him that way she did. His mother had her arm around her shoulders. He continued to scan the back of the room and saw a column of familiars walk up front in their dress uniforms, which was not required. There was Cooper, and Fredo, T.J., Lucas, Armando and Danny, and each one gave their wink or nod as they passed his chair.

"These are just a sampling of some of the guys we

get to work with every day. Several of these men have saved my life. More than once. I've had a hand in rescuing some of them. We like to say that we never leave a man behind. That's true of all the branches of service. But we're a brotherhood and that never ends."

He winked again at Tucker. It was making it harder and harder to keep from releasing the tears that hurt his eyes. Hearing the sniffles from the family and friends who had gathered didn't help, either.

"Some of us come home in various stages of whatever has been our plight. We're ready to bring it on. Bring it *all* on. We may not like it, but we can take it."

He sighed and gripped the podium again. "I don't know when I'll retire. I can't imagine doing anything else with my life, and I say that with the full knowledge and love of my wife and kids, my extended family. There are some men who are made here. There are some men who leave here to go on and do other great things. And then there are some men who just belong here. I'm one of them. And I'm also proud that today, I'm witnessing the graduation of another of our ilk."

There was a smattering of clapping. As should be, Tucker wasn't named. Only the few that knew the story had that benefit and the rest had to take it on faith. But when the time came, and the men lined up to receive their Tridents, Kyle was the one to pin it on Tucker himself. His words, whispered in confidence, were ones

Tucker would never forget.

"You inspire me, Tucker. You help show them the way. Keep it up, bud. We need men like you."

All he could say was, "Thank you."

CHAPTER 15

One Year Later

THE SIGN OUTSIDE Frog Haven Winery indicated the winery was closed for a private function. Dozens of pink and deep red balloons marked the roadway in both directions. The gravel drive had been watered down the night before. Even the vines were celebrating, their shades of magenta and mahogany, golden yellows and faded greens standing fresh and proud in the fall sun. It was wine country and this time of year was always the most colorful. Harvest was just around the corner. Tourists were planning their new release tours and barrel tastings. Every weekend there was a festival honoring tomatoes, artichokes, artists and jazz. It was a feast for the eyes as well as the soul.

Brandy stood in the dress she'd picked out years ago and never told anyone. She'd gone with her mother to look at a party dress for a function she was attending, and they stopped by a bridal store. Brandy was still in grammar school. But when she saw the low-cut off-white satin gown, covered in beaded flowers and hand stitching, she was mesmerized.

"Very pretty, Brandy. You'd make the most beautiful bride of them all wearing that dress," her mother had whispered in her ear.

Brandy still remembered her mother's scent and it lingered around her today. This dress was just like that one she'd seen nearly fifteen years ago. The cut was perfect for her ample chest, showcasing it, as Tucker would soon appreciate. Even as a child, she must have had a sixth sense of what her adult size would be. She turned to see herself in profile and liked what she saw. Rose and burgundy roses were wired to the comb at the back of her head, blending with the mahogany shades of her own natural hair color. Facing the mirror straight on, she said those same words herself, but she heard her mother's voice.

"Very pretty, Brandy. You make the most beautiful bride of them all." She felt like her mother was holding her hand, fixing her hair and tending to the fullness of the big slip underneath. Brandy closed her eyes and saw it, felt it. He mother had come to be part of the celebration.

A gentle tap on the door announced Dorie's entry into the changing room, which was a converted case storage building, smelling of musty fermented and very patient wines.

"You need anything, Brandy?" Dorie's burgundy gown matched the accent flowers in her bouquet, deep pink and rose red.

"I'm good. Just enjoying the moment. All the planning, and everything, and it's all over so quickly."

"That's what weddings are. You're just walking through the doorway into your new life. It's what happens after you get there in those rooms that count. That's where you live. This is just where you mark the spot it begins."

"That's lovely." She hugged her best friend. "How's Jessica doing?"

The baby was trying to walk and was at a squirmy stage, needing constant supervision. She had Dorie's beautiful smile and blonde coloring, but she had Brawley's fearless personality.

"She's climbing all over her dad. She's already discovered his boutonniere and has thrown it to the ground."

"Serves him right. I guess he's getting a dose of what his mother probably went through."

The other bridesmaids entered, and they stood in a circle, locking arms behind them. The sound of rustling taffeta and giggles put a hush to the room.

"Thank you all. For years I never thought this day would come. And then, just like magic, Tucker appeared as my New Year's wish. It just goes to show that anything is possible, if your heart's all in."

"That's what love does. It makes the impossible possible, Brandy," Dorie began. "Or, I guess I could say, it makes possible what we told ourselves we could never have."

Dorie's mother brought them a glass of champagne and led the toast like the cheerleader she was. She and her daughter stood arm in arm while she raised her glass. "To a perfect marriage, complete with all the flaws in life that make it so perfect in the first place!"

The girls laughed, but everyone followed up by sipping the pink champagne until it was all consumed.

"Thank you all," Brandy said to her wedding party. You've made my day special and complete. And my father has enjoyed being father and mother to the bride, especially with all your help."

Everyone laughed again and began chatting nervously. Brandy glanced out the small tinted window in the corner, and caught a glimpse of Tucker in his tux, laughing and hugging well wishers. He looked stunning. But, he'd complained about it for days and the week before the wedding almost threatened to boycott the ceremony if forced to wear it. They found a tailor who fixed the fit, making the cut and style what he was comfortable with. His biggest fear was that he'd remind everyone of The Beast from the fairy tale. Or, worse yet, Shrek, which was how she'd described him that first night they met.

His SEAL buddies were lining up, so it was no surprise that just after they disappeared the wedding planner descended on them and asked them if they were ready. Brandy found herself nervous beyond what she'd experienced before. The dress had been made with a lace-up bodice that could be adjusted. She hoped she wasn't going to pass out. She grabbed the planner.

"Can you let it out a little more? I can't breathe."

"Sure, hon."

In a minute Brandy was much more comfortable, and thanked her. Maybe some day she'd decide to wear something that made her look like a skinny pencil, but for now, who she was fit her perfectly. And it was what Tucker liked.

The girls went ahead of her. Cooper's daughter and little Samantha, Kyle's daughter, were holding hands with Gretchen's youngest daughters. As flower girls they began walking down the carpeted aisle between the rows of vines. At a right angle, they turned and disappeared into the clearing where the ceremony was to begin. They threw their rose petals with abandon, and were done before they hit the tenth row. They took their place at the side with Christy Lansdowne herding them together.

They'd chosen a selection of Baroque music played by a local quartet as, one by one, the bridesmaids floated down in single file through the colorful leaves, to join the men in front.

Brandy's dad was close to having the meltdown she was worried she'd have. "What's wrong, Dad?"

His quivering lower lip gave the sentimental man away. "Your mother. She'd—"

"She's here. Honest. She came to me. She's all around us today, Dad. Everywhere. Can't you feel her?"

He nervously searched the area.

"Close your eyes. She'll come to you."

He obeyed her suggestion and soon had a smile on his face. "I think you're right," he said with his eyes still closed.

The wedding planner gently touched her dad's shoulder and encouraged him to start down the aisle. The beautiful lute music was Brandy's favorite tune. He guided her through the narrow aisle, the planner walking behind and unsnagging the dress as she made her way to the clearing. Standing erect and not looking anything like Shrek or The Beast, Tucker's chest pumped up as he inhaled big and looked startled. Her father gave her a kiss, and then retreated to the side.

Tucker's hands were shaking. He whispered something to her and she asked him to repeat it.

"I'm scared."

Though he'd tried to say it softly, everyone in the wedding party and the front two rows heard his declaration very easily.

"Dammit," he whispered.

"You're doing fine, Tucker. Just hang on. I'm right behind you. I'll never let you fall, and I'll never stop loving you."

His own words, spoken on the day they skydived together two years ago, echoed between them and he squeezed her hand.

The rest of the day whirled away like the magical ball in Cinderella's castle. The reception was held in the tasting room nearby. The mix of children chasing each other and the handsome SEAL Team members and their wives and girlfriends, plus extended family felt private and intimate, though the numbers were not small.

Tucker lured her out into the vineyard again. She had hooked her skirt up, but the long gown was catching along the way, making the trek more difficult. Tucker took care of the fabric, and stooped, carefully untangled where she was caught and did so with patience. The sight of his huge body attending her made her giggle inside.

He took her hands in his, and guided her to sit on a pile of wooden boxes.

"We were here before, weren't we?"

"Yes, sweetheart. This is where I asked you to marry me."

"That was a wonderful night."

"And it never has to end." He cleared his throat and began saying something she knew he'd rehearsed. "I was a real mess when I met you. I don't know what you saw in me. I still shudder when I think of bringing you that day to my apartment. I mean," he slapped his forehead, getting animated, "what was I thinking?"

"I had fun. I'd never met anyone like you."

"Well, that's probably true. There's only one big green monster on the planet, after all."

"No, you're wrong. What I meant was I'd never met anyone who was so much like *me*. I never had to adjust or be careful around you, because I could just be myself, without pretense. You make my life sane and you give me joy. You make me laugh."

"I never deserved this. But I promise, Brandy, nothing's going to change that. If I hadn't met you, I'd have never had the courage to try out for the Teams again. I'm always going to be here for you because you've always been there for me. No matter what."

"No matter what. That's a promise Tucker."

Want more? If you haven't read New Years' SEAL Dream, the novella that launched this beautiful love story, I've got a special bonus for you. Because you've preordered this or been one of the first purchasers, I'm delivering this to you for a short period of time, right here! My gift to you.

Or, are you ready to just jump right in and start from the beginning of the whole SEAL Brotherhood series? Consider one of these fantastic collections:

Ultimate SEAL Collection, No. 1
(Books 1-4 with two novellas)

Ultimate SEAL Collection, volume 2 (Books 5-7)

Want more Bone Frog Brotherhood?

Sharon's latest book, **SEALed Forever**, book #3 of the **Bone Frog Brotherhood**, is out now!

SEAL's Rescue, book #4 of the **Bone Frog Brotherhood**, will be released June 11, but you can reserve it now!

And by the way, did you know you can follow Sharon on BookBub? Sign up for her Newsletter? Here's how:

BookBub

bookbub.com/authors/sharon-hamilton

Newsletter Signup

sharonhamiltonauthor.com/contact/#mailing list

Amazon Follow Me

amazon.com/Sharon-Hamilton/e/B004FQQMAC

NEW YEARS SEAL DREAM

Bone Frog Brotherhood Book 1

SHARON HAMILTON

CHAPTER 1

"NO THANKS NEEDED, Tucker. I didn't ask you to be part of the wedding party because I didn't think you'd fit into a 5X tux on top with your XL waist. You're an action figure, Tuck. Besides, you drool."

Tucker growled as he turned his back on the groom, Brawley Hanks. The dressing room full of handsome penguins grunted and politely guffawed, since they were all dressed up and on good behavior.

"And there's no room for even a Barbie on his arm. Damn those church aisles," barked Riley Branson.

Another former Teammate, T.J. Talbot, grabbed Tucker's arm and drew him out of the Room of Doom, as the single SEALs called it. "Pay no attention to them. They're assholes. Also, who wants to walk down the aisle with a Barbie Doll?" He winked at Tucker.

He felt at ease immediately. Tucker's huge hands and fingers knotted themselves to oblivion, having no place to hide and looking like a bushel of antlers he was carrying. "Thanks, T.J. I hate these things," he said, pulling on his lapel. "But I've been out of commission so long, thought it would be nice to see some of the guys."

"And now you've seen that nothing has changed." T.J. was nearly as tall as Tucker, perhaps an inch shorter. He bumped foreheads. "But the girls will be younger because of Dorie, and that's probably a good thing," T.J. whispered.

"You having regrets, you old married fart?" Tucker murmured back.

Brawley's dad appeared in the church hallway before T.J. could answer and slapped both the former Teammates on the back simultaneously. "Glorious day, isn't it?"

Tucker knew old man Hanks was relieved his son had finally settled down and picked somebody. Brawley had more breakups than a pre-teen homeroom class.

"Yessir. Just took the right woman." T.J.'s face was shriveled up, like his last comment had soured his tongue. Tucker knew he was lying through his teeth. Privately, he thought, it took more alcohol than could fill a battleship to convince Brawley it was time to man-up.

"Dorie's a real nice gal," Tucker offered up. "You're gonna be a lucky father-in-law. She should fit in well with the rest of the family," he added, trying to keep a straight face. He knew it would be painful for T.J.

Both gentlemen looked back at him, T.J. not showing an ounce of expression. Mrs. Hanks was raised in the local Mennonite community. She was as plain as a saltine cracker, without any makeup or hair curling or adornments. Her two daughters were younger, even paler copies of her. Whereas Dorie looked like she could handle a Las Vegas pole and entertain a whole room of men. Those were going to be some interesting family dinners during the holidays, Tucker figured.

When he had the courage to look back into Mr. Hanks' eyes, he realized old man Hanks married her probably because little Brawley was on his way, and for no other reason. He felt the man's pain.

"You believe in miracles, son?" Hanks said, his eyes folded into thin slits.

"Yes, sir, I do. I surely do. That and redemption, too."

T.J. cleared his throat. "Well, congrats, sir. Must be a load off to have Brawley settled. I think those two will be happy together."

The far away look Mr. Hanks gave them back was difficult to read. Tucker had been feeling a little lonesome and sorry for himself until he encountered Hanks Sr. today. Now he was damned pleased he'd never hooked up with anyone.

Sure, they're pretty, but they're dangerous. Unpredictable. Who needs them? Certainly not me!

At last, Hanks pushed through the two younger men, heading for greener pastures, having exhausted any thought process he was following. He turned his head back to them and whispered, "Happiness' got nothing to do with it. All a state of mind, gentlemen." His fingers pointed to his temple, oddly positioned to look like a gun. "All a state of mind." He sauntered off, straightening his jacket and making room for his crotch as he walked, swinging his feet at the ankles to shake off wrinkles.

"Close your mouth, Tucker. You're gawking," T.J. reminded him.

"That's a complicated man right there," murmured Tucker. "I can see how he gutted out twenty years on the Teams. Thank God Brawley made it. Would hate to be a son of his and not make a Team."

"You know the family better, but I'm guessing being on the Teams was summer camp compared to growing up in the Hanks household."

Tucker knew T.J. was right. They'd grown up together in Oregon, and the two boys got acquainted by competing for spots in high school sports teams. They joined their BUD/S class together, but Tucker disengaged after ten years. Brawley re-upped for a short tour and was going to leave as well. Then he met Dorie, so he extended and used the bonus to buy a house. Dorie had a lot to do with that decision.

The rest of the wedding party began to spill out onto the walkway leading to the sanctuary. Blossoming orange trees gave off a gentle and pleasant aroma. Tucker punched Brawley hard in the bicep, nearly knocking him over before he gave the groom and his groomsmen a fat-fingered wave. He was going to find a seat toward the front, but not too close, give himself enough room to spread out in case he fell asleep during the wedding. His goal was to keep his big mouth shut and his eyes glazed over so he could just swim a little with his former Teammates without getting into trouble. That meant he'd keep his hands to himself and wouldn't ask anyone to dance. He'd also pretend not to look for cleavage or evidence of a proud bony mound or ample ass beneath layers of swirling chiffon and taffeta.

Piece of cake, he thought as he entered the sanctuary. Organ music played, accompanied by a violin and flute combination.

Hospital music.

The two Hanks sisters were dressed in identical maroon dresses with white lace collars, revealing their beanpole stature. Both girls had their long brown hair parted in the middle, tied in a bun at the back of their neck. No curls, ribbons, or sparkles to adorn them.

Each had a deep pink lily wrist corsage on their right hands, folded identically next to each other.

The moms were ushered in next. Mrs. Hanks wore a darker shade of maroon, but her brownish grey hair was pulled back similar to her daughters'. Mr. Hanks looked around the room, catching eyes of friends and landing briefly on Tucker's face. He sat down hard, making the pew squeak.

Dorie's mom was lead in by Riley Branson. The lady was the same kind of bombshell for the older crowd, and Brawley had told Tucker stories of her younger years growing up in San Diego. Though she was close to sixty, her hair was as blonde as her daughter's gorgeous locks. She wore a tailored light pink suit with a flared waist jacket covered in glistening crystals that flashed all over the interior of the narthex and the aisle going down. The skirt below her tiny waist didn't leave much to the imagination. She wasn't as tall as her daughter, so the high heels were giving her some trouble on the cushy rug.

Dorie's mother sat next to her already seated boyfriend, an obvious sign that he might not be a permanent fixture in the family, but he gave her a peck on the cheek anyway.

The organ music crescendo rose, and a majestic non-wedding style march was on, signaling that the audience should rise for the bride and her father.

Everyone came to their feet, Tucker one of the last to stand. He turned to the narthex and saw beautiful Dorie all decked out in bright white. Ahead of her were several bridesmaids, all Barbies, except for one, who was a big girl with about the largest chest Tucker had ever seen. He found himself praying for a clothing malfunction as she paraded down the aisle with Riley. Her tight bustier looked like it was going to explode any second, which might even knock Riley off his feet. He found himself chuckling under his breath at the image in his head until someone in the row ahead of him turned around with a frown.

But Tucker's daydream was shattered by the presence of Dorie, looking every bit the virginal angel. She was probably the prettiest bride he'd ever seen. Her veil was loaded with little crystals, like her mother's suit. By candlelight at the evening service, it created the effect of a thousand little faeries dancing down the aisle all around her. Mr. Carlson looked tanned and about as proud as a father could be, since his daughter was marrying a war hero.

Brawley was gaping and looked pale as the creamy skin on his bride's beautiful face. His best man whispered something to him, which caused a quick glance to his crotch, followed by an annoyed sigh as he realized his best man was messing with him. He presented his elbow to Dorie as her father kissed her good-bye. Dorie grabbed Brawley's hand instead.

Tucker prepped himself so that he wouldn't fall asleep, but found he needed very little help. The girls were ten point fives, even the heavy one. He told himself to stop it several times, but he was used to ranking women in front of him. Dorie would be number one, of course. Then there was that red-head, but the dark-haired heavy one kept catching his eye. He matched them all up to her, and, to his surprise, his dick preferred her.

The Hanks sisters began a duet that was about as bloodless as the middle-aged female lab tech at the VA who actually sported a five o'clock shadow. It was about as pleasant, too. The slightly off-key rendition of a country song he couldn't remember had people in the audience coughing to clear the pain in their ears. Tucker was going to burst out laughing if he wasn't careful. He opened a package of gum, made too much noise, and found people frowning at him.

Who cares? He chomped his gum silently and appeared not to notice.

With that out of the way, he tried to concentrate on the words of the reverend's message to the audience, and that's when he fell asleep. He startled from a very pleasant dream to find several in the crowd reminding him they still didn't approve. An older bony fist leaned over his shoulder to hand him a tissue because he had drooled on himself.

Can I help it? Sermons put me to sleep.

Then he noticed the dark-haired plus sized girl staring right at him with daggers. Okay, so he messed that one up. But he wasn't there to take home a date anyhow, so he shrugged, stopped looking at the girls, and started staring back at the people in the audience who had caught the snoring or grunting or drooling—maybe all three.

I need some spiked punch.

He knew that someone was going to do it. Mrs. Hanks had forbidden alcohol, but she was about to learn a lesson. It was no SEAL wedding if there wasn't a heavy dose of alcohol.

Come on. Come on. Let's get the party going.

The rings were exchanged. The kiss was pornographic, as a good SEAL should behave, and included a gentle squeeze of the bride's ass, which made her giggle when they both got tangled up in her veil. Tucker noticed the big girl didn't like that, either.

Mercifully, the wedding was over. Brawley and his young nymph floated down the aisle, followed by the bevy of lovelies, Tucker was suddenly jealous that T.J. had accompanied the brunette. The shit-eating grin he gave Tucker in exchange meant he knew full well what he was doing as his elbow leaned a little deeper into the lady's chest, which extended her left boob and created about eight inches of mouth-watering cleavage.

I got assholes for friends.

But since T.J. was happily married to the lovely Shannon, Tucker didn't have to worry about anything.

Except to keep from drooling, get drunk with dignity, and pretend this was a good idea.

Because it wasn't. He knew he'd made one of the biggest mistakes of his life.

CHAPTER 2

BRANDY WAS GLAD the party was beginning. Her plan was to get considerably sauced, dousing and putting out the fires of a disastrous year. She'd been let go earlier in the year for speaking a little too plainly to a customer of the advertising firm. A competing agency hired her the next week—until she found out they were moving their operation to Silicon Valley from San Diego. Her father still owned and operated the local organic grocery store, and so Brandy came back to work for him until something else came on the horizon.

When Dorie asked her to be part of the wedding party, her decision to stay in Southern California was set in stone.

Thinking it would be helpful to meet her diet goals for the wedding she took up a part-time job as a weight loss counselor. The free meal plans and extra income were at first a double bonus. She had some early success, but then her diet stalled and crashed. The food started tasting like cardboard, and she was secretly supplementing with things from her dad's store. Her lack of progress and her MIA at weigh-ins caused another termination.

But that was last year. This was New Years Eve, and she was going to have a great year. She'd land that dream job after all, get down to a size eight or ten—one she'd never achieved before—and who knows what else could happen? Perhaps Prince Charming would notice her new svelte physique. She'd start lifting weights and perhaps learn to run so she could enter a 5k with Dorie.

She watched the bride and groom glide over the dance floor. The weather was spectacular and clear, surprisingly warm. By candlelight, they swayed and swooned, and there wasn't a woman in the crowd who didn't want to trade places with Dorie and her handsome new husband. The hush that fell over the group made her begin to cry. The glittery twinkle lights and silky drapes at the sides of the tent blew in the gentle breeze coming right off the bay.

She approached the group of her fellow bridesmaids and noticed their chatter stopped the instant she was upon them. Several brittle smiles greeted her.

"Having a good time, Brandy?" asked one of them.

"Isn't it the most gorgeous wedding you've ever

seen?" she answered, aware she was gushing like a schoolgirl.

"I'm looking at all the eye candy," one of the other girls remarked, nodding to the group of nearly twenty young men, all fit and handsome, dressed in black tuxes and suits.

"Your Randy is deployed, Sheila. You can look, but better not touch."

"I hear that the guys on SEAL Team 5 don't have much to do with these boys. They're all Team 3."

Brandy was disgusted with her attitude, but the rest of the crowd tittered, and closed ranks. Soon she was left alone as they wafted off to grab some punch. On the way, two girls were asked to join the dance floor, as other couples from the partygoers began to pour into the revelry. In a matter of minutes, the bride and groom were hidden by other dancers. When the tune turned lively, the dance floor got even more crowded.

Earlier, she'd watched one of the SEALs on Brawley's team add some rum to the punch, along with something else, so she was fairly sure it would be strong. But just in case, she had a flask of brandy, her namesake and always a good companion in case the evening turned lonely.

She checked her watch as she headed to the punch and saw it was forty-five to midnight, the beginning of the New Year. Soon all those bad dreams of this year would be wiped away forever.

As she reached for a glass, another hand crossed hers. In the collision, several drinks fell to the floor, and several more fell over on themselves on the pretty lace tablecloth, making a light pink stain. The hand she'd collided with could easily palm a basketball or clean off a windshield with one swipe. Enormous beefy fingers, dripping in the sweet mixture, shook, sending droplets of punch all over her face and upper chest. The surprising spritzer caught her off guard.

A deep voice made an apology to the plain woman behind the punchbowl who looked like she'd faint from fear. Then the voice came her way.

"So sorry. I didn't mean to make a mess."

It was the beast from the sanctuary, the one who reminded her of Shrek. And now he even sounded like Shrek. She stared up at massive shoulders and a puffed out chest so large he could have trouble getting through a doorway without going sideways. He wasn't young, like the other men, with a healthy dose of salt and pepper in his hair and a solid white full beard. It was a lot to take in, but she finally found his eyes, and that settled her nerves just a bit.

"Are you okay?" he whispered. His warm eyes twinkled and were kind.

"Y-Y-Yes." Then she felt the coolness of the punch covering her. "Napkin."

It was quickly delivered to her flailing hand.

"Another one. I need another one," she said since the small napkin began to fall apart as she dabbed her face.

He handed her a fistful nearly an inch thick.

"Oh! That's too many," she mumbled, but took the wad anyway.

"You got a lot on your-your-your chest there. I hope it doesn't stain." He pulled her aside to make way for one of the caterers to mop up the floor.

The slip made her angry. He gave her a fistful of napkins because of the *size* of her chest. She turned her back to him and continued to dab off the droplets dripping down between her breasts. Out of the corner of her eye she saw one of the other bridesmaids whisper to her neighbor.

She abruptly turned again so she could address the monster, but the area was vacant. She caught sight of his back and head as he ducked under the tent cover and walked out into the night.

The young catering staff member brought her a filled cup of punch. "Here you go. Don't be concerned about this. That guy looks like an accident waiting to happen. Not your fault."

"Thanks." It was all she could think of to say.

The punch was indeed strong, and Brandy discovered upon finishing it that, although she was relaxed, her breathing was still just as difficult. She tried not to think about the help she'd needed getting the big undergarment on before the bustier could go on. It took two of the bridesmaids to work alternating to get the large zipper to close. At one point, she thought her breasts would reach her chin, but she was able to position herself until she was somewhat comfortable. The bustier was easier, since it closed with a row of large hooks and eyes.

She wobbled her way to the women's restroom and reapplied lipstick, really laying it on heavy. She loved the bright red shade of her new purchase. Adding a little blush, removing two dried droplets of punch, and rinsing her dress with a little water, she felt put together and ready to take on the world. It was only twenty minutes to midnight. All this would go into the folder of old news in just a little while.

Brawley was standing at the edge of the dance floor, watching his friends taking turns dancing with his bride.

"She's lovely, Brawley. I'm surprised you share her," she said and smiled.

The handsome SEAL had always been nice to her. Her crush on him was hard to hide. He leaned over and whispered in her ear, "Well then, let's make her jealous. You game?"

When he leaned back to check her expression, she

gave him the biggest smile she could muster.

"Game on, mister."

They danced a modified swing to a lively Motown classic. She knew Brawley had benefitted from the instructions he had taken with Dorie. Brandy had taken lessons with her father after her mother passed. The two of them moved around the floor like a choreographed routine, causing a clapping circle to be formed around them. Brawley's bow tie was undone, as were the top two buttons on his shirt. Brandy wished she could remove or disconnect something, too, but in the end, she stopped just long enough to take off her shoes and throw them into the corner. Brawley swung her around with his powerful arms. She felt lighter than air.

This is a good way to usher in the new year.

Finally the music ended and the crowd cheered them. Brawley gave her a big bear hug that nearly toppled them both. She regained her balance, and, breathing heavy, she accepted his polite kiss to her cheek—a cheek she would hate to wash off.

Dorie was smiling as she re-attached herself to her beau, using his handkerchief to wipe the sweat from his forehead. All Brandy could do was watch them.

The room seemed to rumble behind her, but it was only the sound of the beast's voice.

"Tell you what. I'll go kidnap Dorie, and then you

can have him."

Even the hair at the back of her neck stood straight out. Her shoulders felt the tiny beads of moist breath against her flesh. It set up a vibration that traveled briefly down her spine. It was a curious reaction, especially for someone so beast-like.

Upon turning, she faced his warm brown eyes again. They were still twinkling little laugh lines evident at the sides. Somewhere the bevy of bridesmaids and their friends were laughing, and she didn't care.

"That would never work. Brawley would be too heartbroken. He'd probably throw himself off the Coronado Bridge." Her tongue nearly stuck to the roof of her mouth. "I need something to drink."

"I think we should try this punch thing again, don't you?" His voice was gentle, almost melodic, but very, very deep. She felt the words vibrate in her chest.

"Yes, let's try to do it better this time. I think they're out of napkins," she answered.

Was that a growl she heard? She wasn't sure. But it was a wicked growl that could fend off anything.

They walked together side by side.

"I'm Tucker," he said flatly.

"And I'm Brandy."

At the table, he chose the larger clear plastic cups, handing her one and taking the other for himself.

"To a new year. No accidents," he said.

She met his cup with a dull click. "No accidents. To a perfect year."

The cool drink was refreshing, and she finished the whole glass faster than he did. His face was full of surprise.

"All that dancing," she said between deep breaths, "I needed that. Probably should have had water—"

All of a sudden, she felt light-headed. The air constriction had finally caught up with the alcohol floating around her stomach and brain. As she began to see black spots in front of her eyes, she felt his arm underneath her back, holding her, keeping her from falling. Just before she blacked out, she heard the words,

"I've got you. No worries."

CHAPTER 3

TUCKER CARRIED HER to a row of chairs setting just outside the tent. He hurried to get her out before they attracted much attention. Instinctively, he knew she'd be embarrassed if she caused another incident.

She was beginning to moan as he did a light jog towards the chairs. He laid her down, then removed his coat and placed it over her, pulling it up all the way to under her chin.

"Brandy, stay right here and stay warm. I'm going to get some water and a clean washcloth for your forehead. But stay here, okay?"

He saw her nod. Her face was pale, and she'd attempted to open her eyes, but closed them again with another moan. He suspected she'd be sick next.

He ran to the curtains where the catering equipment and staff were housed and got a clean dishcloth and a bottle of sparkling water. When he returned to Brandy, she had already rolled over on her side and was starting to vomit.

"It's okay. You eat anything today?"

She shook her head and then retched nothing but a pink liquid. All she had on her stomach was alcohol.

"You need to eat something. That will soak up some of the alcohol."

She ignored him and retched again. He held her hair back from her face before wiping her forehead, cheeks, and then finally cleaned her lips. He helped her roll back.

"Not too far back. Stay on your side. It might help."

She sighed and snuggled under his jacket. "I hope I didn't get your tux."

"Nope. All's safe. You were actually quite dainty about it. You should see it when I get sick. Not a pretty sight."

"I can only imagine," she mumbled. Then her hand searched and grabbed his as she opened her eyes. "Sorry. Sorry. I'm so sorry. I didn't mean that."

"Yes, you did." He held her hand, and then his thumb began to rub over her knuckles. He stopped himself. "You didn't eat anything before you drank. It happens to the best of us. I'm going to get you something."

"No. I'm on a diet."

"Hogwash," he said as he got up and headed for the food tables. Glancing back, he saw that her gaze followed him. He loosened his tie and unbuttoned his collar. Brawley was on him with concern written all over his face.

"Is she okay?"

"She's gonna be fine. Liquor on an empty stomach. She just needed some fresh air, and I'm getting her something to eat." He searched the small finger sandwiches and bypassed the frittata and vegetables.

"You let me know, promise?" Brawley answered. "We're cutting the cake at midnight. Just a couple of minutes now."

"I'm on medic duty, but I can only imagine what that kiss is gonna look like. You gonna mess up her face with it?"

"Nah. I wanna get laid tonight, Tucker. It's my wedding night."

"Smart move. Don't worry about Brandy."

"She's in good hands." Brawley winked and left to join the crowd gathered around the cake.

Tucker piled the dish with the sandwiches and returned to Brandy. She was attempting to sit up. He knelt in front of her. "I've got some bread here, which should be good for your stomach. Some kind of mystery meat in the middle, so go easy."

She had pulled his jacket around her shoulders. She smiled. Her beautiful chest and cleavage was hard not to stare at, so he focused on the plate offered to her.

She popped the little sandwich into her mouth and closed her eyes.

"Hits the spot."

"Good." He took one. "They're not bad. You should have another."

Brandy did as she was instructed.

"Feeling any better?"

She nodded. Her hair was hanging down over her shoulders as she put her elbows and forearms on her thighs. The gap in her bustier was enormous.

"I wish I could take this damned thing off and go topless."

"A dangerous thought," he said, slightly embarrassed she'd caught him looking.

She smiled. "So tell me something, Tucker. Did someone put you up to this? Be nice to the fat girl?"

The thought had never occurred to him. He was surprised.

"No. No one put me up to anything. Why, you think there's something unattractive about you? Are you an axe murderer or serial killer or something I should be afraid of?"

She shrugged and gave a small laugh. "You know the expression. Age old tale. '*Always a bridesmaid, never a bride.*' That sort of thing."

"Whoa!" Tucker handed her the plate and stood up. "Who said anything about being a bride. If you're thinking—"

"Happy New Year," came the shout from the tent.

He looked down at her. She'd set the sandwiches to the side, took a deep breath, and said, "Shut up and kiss me, you idiot."

With the room erupting in horn and popper noises, Tucker came back to his knees, reached for her face, and melted his lips into hers. It wasn't the wedding cake kiss Brawley would have, and tasted like a ham sandwich, but it definitely got the sparks going deep inside him. Almost painfully, his libido lumbered into full action mode. He felt like a battleship heading out to sea on its final mission. His heart pounded, almost hurting from inattention and need. The subtle scent from her perfume and the way her hair felt on his cheek nearly made him dizzy.

He pulled back and looked into her eyes.

"You okay?" he asked.

"I'd be better if you kissed me again. I needed that."

Her fingers sifted through his hair. Their deep kiss left them both breathless. As his cheek set against hers, he whispered, "What was that?"

"You okay?" she asked, twisting the conversation and letting her eyes flirt. Her forefinger traced over his lips as she focused on them. He squeezed her shoulders but kept his hands in place. He desperately wanted to explore what was being so cruelly smashed underneath all that fabric.

He'd promised himself he wouldn't be looking tonight and would keep his hands to himself. But his promise was going down in flames. He just wasn't sure what he should do. He knew what he desired, but he didn't want to take advantage of her, since he was fairly sure she was still pretty drunk.

"I don't do this," he finally said.

"I don't, either."

"I mean—what I meant was, you're drunk, and I don't think it's right to—"

"If you've changed your mind, just say so. Don't blame it on honor or some other BS, Tucker. I'm a big girl. I can smell a turn down when it's coming. I'm used to it."

His heart was breaking for whatever her experiences had been in the past. It was clear there was some damage there. But it just didn't add up. He could not see any reason she should feel that way.

She'd started to stand, began to remove his jacket.

"Wait, Brandy. You got it all wrong."

"It's okay. Don't patronize me."

"Damnit. I'm not patronizing you. Would you get that goddamned chip off your fuckin' shoulder, Brandy? What I'm telling you is I'm attracted to you. And I don't want to take advantage. I'm not that kind of guy."

He stood with her, putting the jacket back around her shoulders.

"Cake?" A silver tray with slices of wedding cake was presented to them by one of the wait staff.

Brandy eyed the tray, and Tucker could tell she wanted a piece. He took two plates. She was weaving slightly, so he guided her to sit back down. Then he got on his knees again, setting one plate aside. He cut a piece without frosting and held it in front of her. "Probably not the best thing for you to eat, but it might not be that bad."

She watched him while she opened her mouth. He placed the cake on her tongue.

"Perfect. Delicious. More. With frosting," she said.

"Brandy, you sure?" He could see some of the earlier dreaminess return to her eyes.

"What if I put some frosting here," she said as she touched the top of her cleavage with her forefinger. "Or what if it got smeared lower. Would you lick it off?"

Tucker's knees were shaking as his groin refused to behave. He inhaled her scent and the way her eyes were half-lidded while she dipped her finger in the frosting and slowly slid it down between her breasts. She leaned back on the chair, spread her knees, and dared him with her eyes.

His mouth watered as his tongue tasted her flesh

beneath the sweet fluffy frosting. He sucked, pulling the top of her right breast into his mouth just short of creating a mark. But he wanted to. He wanted to see her naked, her nipples dripping with frosting, her sex wet with her desire for him. He needed to lose himself in those breasts as he took her deep.

Her fingertips touched his temples. She kissed his forehead, holding his head to her chest. Then one hand slid down the outside of his shirt to his waistband.

"Can I take you home with me?" she breathed into his ear.

"Darlin', I'll go with you anywhere. You just name it."

"I should go get my shoes."

"I'll get them. But I don't think you'll need them."

"Why?"

"Because, sweetheart, I'm going to carry you."

"Really? Why?"

"Because it's just what's done on New Years. You stay right here, and I'll go get them. You think about having that perfect year. You think about what a perfect night would be like, and then let's go do it. Okay?"

He could feel her eyes on his back as he made his return to the party. One of the bridesmaids tried to drag him to the dance floor. She got his shirttails untucked from his waistband before he got away. In the corner were Brandy's heels. He dipped to pick them up and sauntered right through the center of the dance floor, carrying his trophy in his right hand.

He saw the looks. He saw the surprise. He saw Mr. Hanks nod and smile some secret appreciation. Dorie winked at him. Brawley gave him a thumbs up.

He was back. Tucker was back in the real world. The night had turned from the biggest mistake of his life to something else quite extraordinary.

It was going to be the best night of his life. And this was only the start of a new year.

CHAPTER 4

BRANDY SAT BACK in Tucker's bright red truck that set so high she doubted she'd be able to mount it without help. But Tucker had placed her delicately on the seat, strapping her in securely, and then pressing a warm-up kiss to her willing lips. In his own way, he was gentle, but it took effort to not break or hurt things, she noted. The engine revved, and then the truck lurched, headed to Brandy's cottage. She decided not to tell him her father lived in the house in front.

The inside of the cab smelled like him. He fiddled and adjusted the heater, asking if she was comfortable. It was only a ten-minute ride, but in that short time, she noted how he and the huge truck were one giant machine, like a Transformer. The dash and black leather seats were immaculately polished. The floor mats washed like a brand new vehicle. She noted a little decal on the driver's side of the windshield, shaped like an anchor.

When they arrived at her cottage, she was grateful all the lights were out at her father's house. Tucker insisted on carrying her to the front door and then let her slide down the front of him. There were bulging body parts she rubbed against, which would be impossible to miss.

She fumbled for her keys and then led him inside.

Tucker made her small living room feel even smaller. The cottage was a converted outbuilding. Therefore, the ceilings were a few inches lower than normal. He ducked and followed her to the single bedroom. Along the way, she asked, "You want anything to drink?"

His eyes were fixated on her. The slow shake of his head was sexy and deliberate. "No ma'am."

"I'm going to need some help getting out of this."

"Just show me what to do."

"There are these hooks at the back," she said as she turned to show him. "You have to undo them one at a time."

Tucker fumbled with the fabric and the closures. She could tell he was getting frustrated. "Holy cow, Brandy. How in the devil would you get yourself out of this thing by yourself?"

"I can pull it over my head, but it would be easier if—"

At last several of the hooks were released, and she was grateful for the extra breathing space.

"You got it."

The bustier fell to the ground. Brandy unzipped her skirt and laid it over a chair. The ugly diaphragm-squeezing undergarment was the only thing between them. She removed her stockings and panties, and once again presented her back to him.

"This is going to be hard. You have to unzip me here."

Tucker was on it, his huge fingers slipping beneath the off-white fabric, while his other hand grabbed the zipper and had it undone in just a couple of seconds.

"Piece of cake."

The rush of air to her lungs was so sudden she nearly fainted again. He braced her before she could fall over. He pulled her to his chest while his hands took hold of her ass and squeezed until it hurt.

She began to unbutton his shirt, then lifted the cotton tee shirt up, and kissed him, placing her palms over his pecs. She reached below, fingers creeping into his pants when he quickly undid his belt and stepped out of them.

She was going to step to press herself against him, but he abruptly picked her up and brought her over to the bed, where he gently placed her down.

"You have some protection?" he whispered as he kissed her neck. One callused hand squeezed her left breast and then slid down lower.

She started to sit up to grab the condoms from the bedside table, but he pressed her back, rising to his knees and staring down at her.

His hands massaged both boobs now. “You’re incredible. I think I’ve died and gone to Heaven,” he said as he nuzzled her cleavage, sucking and pinching her nipples. His scratchy beard tickled as his kissing moved lower until he was at her core. His thumbs pressed her open, rubbing her nub as she shuddered with anticipation.

She watched him pleasure her, his giant shoulders rising and falling as he dipped lower. He kept one hand massaging her breast. He was nearly delicate the way he explored with his fingers and tongue. It filled her with electricity as she heard him moan between her legs. She pulled his hair, massaged his temples, and then writhed to the feel of his fingers inside her, calling her to ride his hand and lose herself for him. She came up to her knees, reaching for his cock while she pressed herself into his giant palm.

She gripped him, moving up and down, squeezing his balls and covering his tip with precum. After some minutes of play, she raised herself up and reached for the drawer, bringing out the condom, then tearing it open with her teeth. As she looked up to him in the moonlight, their mouths closed on each other, tongues exploring, becoming more and more intense. Her fingers slid the thin condom down his shaft and massaged him while they finished their slow, sensuous kiss.

Tucker leaned back and brought her up on top of him. With her knees hugging his hips, he gripped her body, snagging her sex on his cock and then pressing her down so he was deep inside her.

He was urgent to move against her, raising and lowering her on him, drawing the rhythm faster and faster until he quickly picked her up, threw her back against the mattress, and mounted her. Plunging deep, he buried his head in her chest.

They moved together like old dance partners, reveling in the miracle that was their bodies. Beneath him, she felt delicate. She melted under his kiss, rising again into multiple orgasms as he plundered and then softened his penetration.

He was an innovative lover, consumed with desire for her, yet very attentive to her needs, begging her to come and then thanking her as she shattered beneath him over and over again. She knew that as the minutes turned into the early pre-dawn hours of the morning, she had never before felt so loved, so coveted and consumed. As the first rays of early dawn shone through the window, he held her close as he came hard and deep inside her, then folded her into his arms, and fell asleep.

She worried her beating heart would wake him as she luxuriated in the heat between them. Every cell in her body screamed for him. Her ear was pressed against his chest, and she listened as air filled his lungs and then expelled. Her skin was bathed in the sweet sweat between their bodies, the way her legs wrapped around his enormous thighs, and how his arms squeezed her so tight it rivaled the bustier just before she fell asleep.

But in the shelter of his arms, there was room to breathe, and finally to dream about a perfect evening, and the beginning of a perfect year.

CHAPTER 5

A SLIVER OF bright sunlight traveled slowly across Tucker's face like a laser. At first, he startled, since his own apartment was heavily draped in blackout shades. Even on workdays, he was able to sleep in until at least eight. This seemed just minutes from when he'd last closed his eyes.

And then he felt her moist flesh melting all over him. He carefully opened one eye to peer at the lovely brunette resting on his chest. Her lips were still puckered and red, her cheek bulging against her nose. *And she drooled!*

He tilted his head back to avoid giving a belly laugh that would surely wake her. He didn't want to be robbed of these delicious moments. How could he have met a girl who drooled in her sleep?

He scanned the walls of her bedroom. She had tacked several tissue paper sketches of what looked like produce labels and several other ones of large flowers done in chalk or pencil. There was a sketch of a light pink sandy beach cradling white surf coming from a bright turquoise ocean. He noticed a poster made from a picture of Brandy dressed in a large purple grape costume. She was holding a bottle of wine and standing next to Dorie, in an identical costume. Their legs were bright purple from the knees down as they stood in a large stainless steel vat, stomping grapes.

She had a calendar with pictures of beaches from around the world and a photo of her as a young girl sitting beside an older gentleman driving a tractor at a pumpkin farm. Her burgundy bustier and bridesmaid skirt were draped over an easy chair, mixed with his black pants, white shirt, and red white and blue cotton boxers. He was a little embarrassed at the rah rah in his underwear, but he couldn't help it. It was the way he was.

Her bookshelf burst with paperbacks, spilling over onto the floor in several stacks. It appeared every one of them had a picture of a naked man on the cover. The bedside table still gaped with the open drawer containing a box of condoms. He noticed she owned a bright pink vibrator, and that nearly ruined his composure.

But it was all good. All normal. These were the trappings of a woman he'd been trained to protect. Her precious way of life was valuable, something worth saving. This was evidence that what he'd done as an elite warrior was all worth it. He hoped to God she never had to endure some of the things he'd seen out there on the other side of the planet, where children inhaled a steady diet of uncertainty, misery, and smoke from the ashes of their crumbling civilization that knew nothing but war. His job was to make sure that war stayed there and didn't come home.

Brandy was moving against him, stroking him like she'd done so delicately last night. Her pubic bone pressed into his thigh. He raised his knee to help intensify the feeling.

At last, she placed her chin on his sternum and fed from his eyes. What did she see? He hoped she wasn't disappointed. He wasn't. He remembered every kiss, every stroke, every shudder, and every time he pinned her to the bed with her arms outstretched, as if he could will himself to climb inside her and shelter in place.

She was twirling his frosty chest hairs, biting her lip, and waiting to say something, or waiting for him to speak first. But he didn't feel under any pressure to talk so he just watched this dark angel with the red lips he was ravenous for. He wanted to see her enormous breasts bounce in the morning sun as she writhed above him. He wanted to see her face as he filled her, made her come.

She opened her mouth to say something when the door to her living room opened and a man's voice called out, "Brinny?"

Brandy scrambled to sit up, taking the sheet with her, which left Tucker completely exposed. If the man in the next room came to the doorway, he'd also notice the enormous hard-on Tucker had developed.

She smirked, whispering, "My father."

He sprung to action and quickly slipped on his patriotic boxers, but remained seated on the bed.

"Just a minute dad. I've got someone here," she shouted to the next room. Twisting the sheet around her, she stepped to the doorway. Tucker got a nice view of her shapely rear, her long mahogany hair falling everywhere about her shoulders and upper back. He'd kissed every vertebra last night, kneaded the cheeks of her ass until she squealed. She could take everything he could give out, and then some. He hated having to be careful in his sex play. Brandy played at the same intensity.

"Oh, fine. Look, I'm headed off to the store. You coming in today?"

"Maybe later this afternoon. Would that work?"

"Sure. Sorry I didn't let you know yesterday, but I'm going to be one short today. If you can, that would really help me out."

"No problem, Dad. How about one or two

o'clock?"

"Great. Hey, how was the wedding?"

She adjusted her sheet again, briefly shooting him a gaze as Tucker lay back on the pillow, his hands clasped behind his head. "Dorie was gorgeous. You should have come. They had a great band, lots of people you knew were there."

"A friend of Brawley's?" her dad whispered, but Tucker could hear it clearly.

Brandy nodded. "Dad, I've gotta go."

"No problem. See you later on this afternoon."

The door closed behind him.

Tucker watched her face recovering from the blush that also sent pink blotches to her upper chest. "That was awkward," she mumbled, fiddling with her fingers and refusing to look back at him.

He was charmed with the blush, but even more interested in getting the sheet off her. "Come here," he whispered.

Her face pinked up again, and he chuckled.

"After all the things we did last night, you expect me to believe you're really shy?"

She began twirling her hair around her forefinger, still avoiding eye contact.

"Come here, Brandy. Just for a little bit. Then I'd like to take you out to breakfast. I'm thinking pancakes."

Her large brown eyes snapped to attention. She crawled on all fours toward him. By the time she reached him, the sheet had been left behind. Her breasts overflowed in his hands as her young body undulated over his groin, pressing against the ridge of his hardness. Her fingers deftly slid his boxers down over his thighs while she guided him to her core. He held the sides of her hips, raised her up, and then plunged her back down on him.

Then he remembered. They'd forgotten the condom. Again. With his fingers digging into her flesh, he stopped her movements completely, knowing he had to ask the question and leave it up to her.

"Is it okay?"

"It's perfect," she blew back at his face, and then she kissed him.

THE SAMOAN PANCAKE House was always a Team favorite on weekends. But today was a holiday so the place was packed. He nodded to several former Teammates, a couple of whom were at the wedding last night.

She chose a corner at the back of the restaurant, and ordered.

"So you used to serve with Brawley, right?"

"About ten years ago. We grew up together in Oregon."

"You're from Oregon?"

He noticed she had a dimple to the right of her mouth, which was cuter than all heck.

"*What?*"

"You have a very sexy dimple right there." He touched the spot and loved her blush, as she held his hand.

"I love it up there. My parents had plans to retire near McMinville, but my mom passed before they could sell everything and go do it. Now Dad's stuck with the store."

"That's close to where Brawley and I grew up."

"That's what I thought. So your family was farmers, then?"

"Still are. My sister and her husband and kids live with them and they all work in the family business."

"Sounds nice. What do they grow?"

Tucker was hesitant to explain the details of his parent's venture, so he deflected the question by giving a half-answer. "They do hydroponics, greenhouse stuff. They used to grow wheat, but over the years, they've sold off parcels so now they only have a few acres left. It's all they can handle."

"You miss Oregon?" Brandy asked as their breakfast was served.

Tucker poured syrup all over his pancakes and even his eggs and the extra biscuit he ordered. "I worked up a regular appetite, Miss Brandy." He winked at her, amused by the way her jaw dropped as she watched him take his first bite. Then she blushed again.

"I don't miss Oregon at all. I like it here. More sun, less rain. More to do outside, and I don't have to prepare for monsoons to do them, either. San Diego suits me just fine."

"Yup," she agreed.

"You grew up here, then?" He knew she had, but wanted to keep the conversation going.

"Right here. I'm not sure if I stay because of Dad or he stays because of me. I work for him, help him out a bit, since I'm between jobs at the moment."

"I thought you worked with Dorie at the ad agency."

"*Used* to. I guess I pissed off a customer. I don't think the advertising business is for me."

"Brawley said your dad's store is quite upscale? Can he make it with Amazon and all those other players fighting for the retail dollar?"

"I think he makes just enough to live on. Dad's not someone who could ever work for anyone else. He owns the market outright, and the half-acre lot behind. He has some fantasy of doing a little truck farming, perhaps grow his own organic produce."

"Farming, even on a half-acre, is a lot of work."

"I think that's the point, Tucker. When he gets tired of it, then he'll sell. This gives him something to do. Keeps him from missing my mother. She was everything to him." Then she added, "I don't think our family does well with retirement. It's kind of a dirty word."

Tucker nodded and completely agreed. "Smart man. Men have to do things. They can't just sit around and watch the world go by. They have to get into action, or at least the men I hang with do."

"So now that you're off the Teams, what do you do?"

"I run some trainings for guys, mostly high school age, who are interested in joining the SEALs. I try to get them in good physical shape to help them pass BUD/S. I'm kind of the guy who tells them the truth, dispels the garbage the recruiters fill them with. I make sure they know what they're signing up for."

"They're lucky to have you."

"It's only part-time, but it gives me a chance to give a little back to the community. I also do some personal training and I work at the glider port, instructing for the skydiving school."

"Skydiving? Wow."

"You should try it sometime. You'd have a ball."

He was surprised to see she appeared resistant.

"No, thanks. I'll stick to the ground, thank you. If

God had wanted me to fly through the air, he would have given me wings."

"Or an expert tandem buddy. It will change your life, Brandy."

"Or end it."

"No. These guys are safe. They train all the SEALs down here. Some of the most experienced skydivers and stuntmen in the country. It's all completely safe." He drew her hand to his mouth and kissed it. "All about trust, Brandy. And finding out about your limits."

They finished breakfast, and Tucker reluctantly took her back to her car. She turned towards him before she got out of the truck.

"I had a great time, Tucker. I had a goal to have one perfect evening, and it was all that and more. Sorry I got sick on you."

He leaned over and cradled her jaw with his palm before kissing her. "I did, too. I don't want to tell you my goal because you dashed it all to hell. This is the part where I ask you if I can see you again. I'm hoping the answer is yes."

She held his hand between both of hers. When she looked up, he thought at first she might say no.

"I was just looking for one perfect night. I guess I could handle two."

CHAPTER 6

BRANDY CHANGED HER clothes and put on her comfortable cross trainers since she'd be standing the entire afternoon. She drove down the strand past the SEAL Qualification course and thought about what it had been like for Tucker and Brawley going through the training together. Many times, she'd watched the boat crews of new recruits working their way over the rocks or running down the beach carrying telephone poles over their heads. She mused that Tucker could actually make a telephone pole look small.

She turned off the highway and into the tree-lined streets of an older suburban neighborhood then headed away from the bay where things were a little more spread out. Small ranchettes dotted the landscape. She came upon the boutique strip mall containing a cluster of specialty stores with her father's organic grocery and deli at one end. She could see his silver pickup truck parked at the side, as well as Kip's beat-up VW. The five time college freshman had worked for her dad ever since he'd mastered the art of riding a bike. He was practically family. There were only a couple of other cars in the lot, indicating they were having a very slow day.

She loved the smell of the produce and the bright colors of the vegetables and fruit every time she arrived. It was like the smell of flowers at a florist. Her dad was famous for carrying unusual fruits from all over the world, but he specialized in California and Florida citrus and always did a huge business every Christmas sending fruit baskets to customer's relatives all over the globe.

She ducked under the portable canvas awnings shading the lovely displays, piled up in pine boxes. Two shoppers wandered down aisles inside the building itself. One was headed in the direction of the checkout, having spotted Brandy arrive.

"I'll be right back," she told the woman. "Just got to grab my apron and punch in."

Inside the store's tiny office was her father's desk, covered in catalogs, papers, and envelopes—most of them unopened. It was obvious he needed help with his bookkeeping and office organization. She intended to have a discussion with him about that very thing, and soon.

Brandy placed her purse inside the top file cabinet

drawer, noticing it had been pushed aside and was slightly crooked. With a couple of shoves she righted it to stand snug against the desk, where it belonged. Her dad's chair was pulled out, and his glasses were folded on top of the closed laptop that was so old the Apple store refused to work on it any longer.

Slipping the kelly-green apron over her head, she deposited her cell phone in the large center pocket, tied the straps behind her waist, and began to look for her father.

"Dad?"

There was no answer so she figured he might be in the large cooler room at the rear.

That's where she found him. He was sprawled on the floor, his face turned to one side. A trickle of blood had seeped into the floorboards coming from under his upper body somewhere. His face was pale, lips slightly purple. She was immediately worried he might be dead.

"Oh my God. Dad! What's happened?"

She fell to her knees and tried to revive him, but his body remained limp. Then she checked for a pulse and was relieved to have found one. And he appeared to be breathing, but when she tried to arouse him again, he didn't respond. His face was cold and clammy.

With her own pulse racing, she dialed 911 and gave instructions to the paramedics who promised they'd be there within minutes.

She called out for Kip, but again received no answer.

"Hang in there, dad."

But her father didn't register any response, which sent a spear of panic down her spine. She wasn't sure if she should roll him over on his back and decided it would be safer to just leave him on his side. Beneath his head she felt the sticky dark red blood. Finding a clean hand towel, she applied slight pressure, hoping to stop the bleeding. In mere seconds, the towel was bright red and soaked. Her hands were dripping in her father's blood. She carefully rested his head against the soaked cotton and staggered out front to see if she could find Kip. It was hard to concentrate, but she managed to calm her nerves.

The customer was waiting not-so-patiently by the checkout, but when she spied Brandy's bloody hands, she began to scream. Brandy jumped as if she'd been slapped.

"Hold on. My father has taken a spill, and the paramedics are on their way. Give me a minute to get myself gathered. Have you seen Kip?"

The woman closed her mouth and merely shook her head briskly. "Who's Kip?"

"He's the other clerk here."

"I didn't see anyone."

Brandy looked at the woman's basket, then at the

counter and discovered the cash register drawer had been pried open and was completely empty. A check was crumpled at her feet. It began to dawn on her that perhaps this had been a robbery attempt gone badly.

"Ma'am, it looks like we've been robbed, too. You sure you didn't see anyone?"

"No. No one was here. These folks," she said, pointing to a couple behind her, "arrived after me. Is your dad okay?"

"No. I'm worried. He's unconscious, but help is on the way."

Just then, she heard the familiar sound of Kip parking the company van. He entered the store, tossing and catching his keys. Upon seeing Brandy, he gave her a big grin. "Hey there."

"Kip, Dad's fallen. He's in the back. I've called the paramedics and they're on their way. This woman wants to check out, but I need to stand guard with Dad until the paramedics come. Can you get the backup working? If not, can we just close down the store?"

"Sure thing." Kip was already on his knees, extracting another register from under the counter, connecting the telephone feeds, and adjusting the paper. "I've got this. You go be with your dad."

She jogged to the back of the storeroom. Her father still hadn't moved.

She was relieved to hear the sirens getting closer

until she saw just flashing red lights. Someone must have directed them to the rear because two paramedics ran through the back door and bent over to attend to her father. Their fingers deftly poked and repositioned his head and neck, checking out his neck, arms, and legs.

"Did you see him fall?" the handsome dark-uniformed rescue worker asked her as he scanned her bloody hands. He turned his attention back to her father, focusing on the bleeding from his head.

"No. I got here like ten or fifteen minutes ago. I expected to find him in the store, so I went looking for him and found him here. Just like this. I put the towel under his head. But there was so much…blood." Her voice wavered.

The other paramedic was up on her feet, barking instructions into the com strapped to her shoulder.

"Are you a relative or co-worker?" the male paramedic asked.

"I'm his daughter."

"What's his name?"

"Steven Cook."

"He have any illnesses or things I need to know? Medications?"

"Geez." Brandy wracked her brain, trying to remember if he'd told her anything about his health, and came up blank. "I don't think he takes anything. As far as illnesses, not that he's told me."

"How old is he?"

"Sixty-two."

"No pacemakers, history of stroke or heart attack?"

"No. Not that I know of. I really don't know. He's been healthy."

"So you didn't see how this happened?"

"No."

"Anybody angry with him for some reason?"

"No, why?"

"Sorry to have to tell you, but this was no accidental fall. It appears he was hit at the back of the head, you see here?"

He showed her a dark mass of clotted blood, hair, and tissue at the back of his head, slightly underneath him.

"And then it appears he fell, because this other wound looks like it happened when his head hit the floor. So we got two head injuries to deal with."

"I see." Brandy tried to sound as calm as the paramedic was. But in spite of her efforts, her teeth began to chatter.

"You going to be okay?" he asked.

"I don't like blood," she whispered. Black dots began obscuring her vision, and she could tell she was close to passing out.

The paramedic's quick thinking had him grabbing

her upper arms with his bloody gloved hands and positioning her on a nearby chair. "Put your head between your knees if you need to. I'll get you some water in a minute. Better?"

She was starting to get confused and could feel her breathing becoming labored. So much was happening.

"Breathe. Take deep breaths," he commanded.

Her father still wasn't moving. His dark lips were getting darker by the minute. She abruptly threw off his hands. "Dad. He looks terrible! He's worse!"

"We got it. Just don't want you to die on me, okay?"

The woman paramedic returned with a gurney, which she lowered and positioned next to her father. She cut his long-sleeved shirt with scissors and then started an IV before helping her partner lift him onto the bed. They raised the legs on the cart, clicked it into position, and ran toward the back of the van. The woman stayed behind while the male worker came back to check on Brandy.

"Where can I get you some water? This *is* a store, right?" he asked.

"There's a case on the other side of this wall. Take a couple for yourselves, too."

He was back in seconds, snapping open the plastic cap and holding the bottle up to her mouth.

Brandy guzzled the cool liquid, trying to keep up,

but wound up spilling much of it down her front. She didn't care.

"That help some?"

"I'll be fine."

"You have someone you can call?"

"Kip's here. I want to go be with my dad at the hospital."

"No, not in your condition. But we're taking him to Scripps. You can meet us there. No way I want you driving by yourself."

"Gene?" his partner inserted herself in the exit. "We gotta go now."

"Okay, we're outta here. The police will be arriving soon, so you'll have to give them a statement. Then get someone to bring you down. Right now, we gotta focus on Mr. Cook. So, you take care."

"Thank you so much." She started to stand, but he pushed her shoulders down.

"Don't be stubborn. Be smart."

She didn't like the comment, but she didn't have the energy to fight him back with some quick witty thing. If he only knew.

Stubborn is my middle name.

THE POLICE INTERVIEWED them both, promising to be brief so she could get to the hospital to see her father.

Kip answered another question. "He asked me to

do the home deliveries because he knew you were coming in." He spoke directly to her.

"How long were you gone?" the officer persisted.

"Hour? Maybe an hour and a half. Normally, I'd go later, but I asked to get off early." He turned to Brandy again. "I got a date."

That's when she realized so did she. She'd promised to meet Tucker at the Rusty Scupper after work. He was working at the skydiving school all afternoon.

"You know of anyone who would want to hurt Mr. Cook?" the officer asked.

Brandy shook her head from side to side. "He doesn't have any fights or enemies of any kind. Everyone loves him."

"Well," Kip interrupted, "there is this one thing. He had a guy he let go last week. Several customers complained about him. Too friendly with the younger girls. I'm talking thirteen, fourteen-year-olds."

"When did this happen?" the officer asked.

"Thursday, I think. Jorge Mendoza. I never liked him. Steve got him from some church group recommendation. He'd been staying at a halfway house. I told your dad he was stealing beer and drinking on his breaks, but he didn't care until he started getting the complaints. Tats, even on his face. He stared at people. Cold eyes. Not a good dude at all. I was glad Steve let him go."

"I didn't know about any of that." Brandy admitted it was just like her dad to give someone a chance.

Several customers came asking questions, after hearing the sirens and seeing the police activity. Brandy told them they were closing for the day, and that her father was in the hospital. The police reminded her afterwards not to give out many details.

"Your father keep records here? Any way we could get this guy's address?"

"Um, yes. He keeps his records in the office, but I'll have to dig a bit. He's not the most organized owner out there. Some of it, he keeps in the safe," Brandy answered. One of the officers followed her, and she was able to get the employee folder from the second file drawer. She lifted a heavy canvas seed sack to access her father's safe and found it gaping open. "Holy crap."

Kip was at the doorway in a flash. "Ah shit. I was afraid of that." He put his hand over his mouth. "Sorry, Brandy."

"Did everyone who worked here know about the safe?" one officer asked.

"I wouldn't think so, but then, Dad was pretty trusting." shrugged Brandy.

Kip added, "We were really busy over the weekend with New Years coming up. Everyone was shopping for last minute things. I think he closed early last night. I'm sure he didn't make it to the bank. It's a shame, but

I'm guessing he had a lot of cash in that vault."

"Which points to Mendoza again," said one of the officers.

Brandy took another long gulp of her water, finishing it off. Her eyes filled with tears. Her day had gone from spectacular to tragic. She needed to go be at her father's side. And what if he didn't survive? What would she do? She just couldn't bear to think about it.

The officers agreed to let her go if they could question her further at the hospital. Kip was in charge of closing the store. Brandy agreed to keep the place closed until the police had finished their work, and Kip agreed to open it for them in the morning.

Alone and headed back down the freeway, she left a message for Tucker, and then she burst out in tears, flushing out all the pain and pent up worry all the way to the hospital. By the time she arrived, her eyes felt like her lids were made of cardboard.

This was not the way she'd expected this day to go. As she entered the Emergency Room doors, she began to find some of her courage. She hoped it would be enough for whatever news they'd give her. She said a little prayer before she approached the admitting desk and strained to keep her lower lip from wobbling, Taking a deep breath, she told the admitting clerk, "I'm here to see Steven Cook. Can you tell me what room he's in?"

CHAPTER 7

TUCKER HAD REMOVED his flight overalls, stowed his equipment, and repacked his chute and the tandem chute, double checking each fold twice. He felt the vibration from his cell and noticed he'd gotten a message from Brandy.

"It's me, Brandy. I'm on my way to the hospital. Scripps ER. Dad's been hurt, and they rushed him by ambulance. I'm meeting the police there. I have no idea how long I'll be, but I don't want to leave him until I know he's going to be okay. So I'm afraid I'll have to take a rain check on that burger and beer. Call me when you get a chance."

He dialed her back, sorry that he'd missed her call earlier. It had been nearly an hour. She picked up on the first ring.

"Brandy, what happened? Is he okay?"

"I don't know yet, Tucker. He was unconscious when they took him away. I'm waiting to find out if they'll let me see him. He's alive, and that's a good thing, but I don't know anything else. I wasn't able to talk to him. I don't know if he's still unconscious."

"But how did he get hurt? Why are the police involved?"

"It was a robbery at the store. They got the cash in the till, the contents of his safe, everything. The police are following up on a lead Kip gave them."

"Kip?"

"I'm sorry. He's dad's helper."

"So how did he get hurt?"

"Apparently, he was hit at the back of the head, and then fell. I found him on the floor near the cooler. He didn't look good at all, Tucker. Lots of blood. I'm worried."

"Of course you are. Listen, can I meet you there? I'm about a half-hour away."

"I'd like that," she murmured.

Tucker could tell she was trying to stay collected but was having difficulty holding herself together. Her breathing was forced and ragged.

"He's at Scripps you say?"

"Yes. I can call you if they take him somewhere else. But their ER and critical care is one of the best in the country."

"You got that right. Okay, I'll be there as fast as I can. You need me to bring anything?"

"Honestly, I'm not focusing on me at all. I think I'm still in shock. Just come. That would help."

Tucker stopped by his apartment, wanting to take a shower, but knew he didn't have time. He changed his clothes, picked up a pillow and blanket, threw a couple of waters in a bag, and headed up the freeway.

The sunset was a rosy pink, which sent a glow throughout the waiting room at the ER. His arms overflowing with the blanket and queen pillow, he scanned the seats and didn't see Brandy, so asked the desk clerk. He peered over the top of his bundle, since the woman was taller than he was.

"Are you family?" she asked, examining his armful.

"Yes," he lied.

"Well, hon, the daughter is waiting outside the treatment room. They're getting ready to take him up to ICU."

"How's he doing? Can I come in and wait with her?"

"Sorry, can't give you his status, but let me ask her if she'd like some company. I'm betting she would," she said, scanning the pillow again, squinting her eyes and smiling. "Can I have your name, please?"

"Tucker Hudson."

"I'll be right back." The heavyset nurse winked at him and then moved with the speed of a linebacker, disappearing around the corner. It wasn't every day

Tucker spoke eyeball to eyeball with a woman who towered above him. In a few seconds, the side door opened, and the clerk called out, "Mr. Hudson, this way, please."

Brandy was in the hallway, speaking to a uniformed female officer. She abandoned the conversation temporarily and ran to his arms. An instant before she collided with him, he dropped his load and pulled her to him.

"You holding up?" he whispered to the top of her head.

"Better now." She snuggled to press herself hard against his chest, wrapping her arms around him beneath his jacket.

"How's you dad?"

Brandy pulled away, biting her lower lip. "Haven't talked to the doctor yet, really. Dad's had a brain scan and some bloodwork and some other tests. They told me his vitals were strong, but I don't know anything else. Hoping someone will talk to me before they take him upstairs."

The female officer appeared behind Brandy. "If you give me just a couple more minutes, we can get my questions answered, and I'll get out of your hair. That sound okay with you?"

"I'm sorry." Brandy walked back to the row of chairs they'd been sitting at, remained standing, her arms still about Tucker's waist. Good as her word, the police officer finished her questions and then was gone within a handful of minutes. Brandy leaned against him as they sat down together. A male nurse had picked up the blanket and pillow and placed them nearby, neatly folded.

"So how did this robbery occur? They hold him up at gunpoint? In the middle of the day?" Tucker asked.

"We still don't know that. Don't even know how many of them there were."

"Your dad have cameras in the store?"

"Only for looks. They don't record."

"All this is appearing like it was someone who knows your dad. Knows his way around the store. Knows the routines."

"I think that's what the police are going on. But, honestly, I don't care about the money. I just want to be sure he's okay, without any major—"

"Ms. Cook?"

Dr. Harrelson shook her hand and motioned for her to remain seated. He extended his hand to Tucker. "I'm Dr. Harrelson. You the husband? Boyfriend?"

Tucker found himself stumbling for his words, a bit put on the spot. "Family friend," he answered grasping the doctor's paw.

"Now *that's* a handshake!" Dr. Harrelson barked, feigning injured fingers.

Tucker thought he'd been rather careful and wasn't in the mood for jokes. "Sorry, sir."

"Okay, well we have good news and bad news, Ms. Cook. We're not seeing much brain damage on the scan, and the wave patterns are normal. He's got a little swelling, especially in the back here." The doctor demonstrated on his own head, palming an area behind his right ear at the base of his skull. "There's probably some pressure, which also could be from blood pooling, but we will monitor that, and it doesn't seem to be increasing, thank God."

"That's good. So what's the bad news?" she asked.

"He's lost a considerable amount of blood, and he definitely has a minor skull fracture, probably a concussion as well. The next twelve to twenty-four hours will be the most telling, but we should know more once we see how he weathers this."

"Is he awake yet?"

"No, and right now, I'm not anxious for him to be. I think we need to watch him, let his body heal and stabilize itself. There's a chance we'll have to go in there to relieve the pressure, but the bleeding has been stopped. We're thinking the bones in his skull will heal on their own."

"That's good news." Tucker was feeling encouraged and hoped Brandy felt the same.

"I was able to contact his primary care physician.

Your dad's in remarkable shape for sixty-two. His doctor gave me his medical history. That's going to help us out a lot."

"So what's the plan?" Brandy asked.

To their side, they all watched as her father was wheeled out of the treatment room and down the hallway by two male attendants.

"His color is much better," she remarked.

"Yeah. We were a little worried when he first came in, but he's responding quickly. We hope that continues," Dr. Harrelson added. They followed Mr. Cook's gurney as it entered the elevator.

Tucker noted the strong jawline and the shape of her father's nose, indicating a strong family resemblance. His face looked relaxed. A large white bandage was wrapped around his skull down to the level of his eyebrows and ears. Tufts of graying hair stuck out the top where it had been left open, some of it still caked in dark red blood.

"So we're taking him upstairs, now," the doctor started. "He'll be in ICU, on the fourth floor, tonight. Once we get him situated, if you want to briefly come in and say goodnight, that would be fine, but no more than five minutes. He probably won't hear you, and he definitely won't respond. Just preparing you for this."

"Thanks, doctor."

"I have rooms upstairs, if you need a place to crash,

but honestly, it would probably be best if you just went home and got some rest. Nothing like sleeping in your own bed."

Brandy searched Tucker's face. "What do you think?"

"I think he's right." He knew his apartment was not more than five minutes away, but he was hesitant to suggest he take her there. He hadn't entertained a woman at his place in several months and was in the habit of trying to avoid it at all costs. He was trying to recall how bad the place was, since it would be Brandy's first impression of how he lived. Though a tiny niggling voice whispered caution, he found himself overruling it.

"I don't live too far. But if you want to stay here, I'm willing to sleep in a chair by your side. I've learned to sleep just about anywhere."

"You a Team Guy?" Dr. Harrelson asked.

"Former."

"That explains the handshake. So, you two talk about it and then let me know. Give us about ten minutes to get him all situated, okay?"

Brandy nodded as the doctor left.

"I think he's doing really great, Brandy." Tucker had never seen the man before, but in light of what he'd been through, he thought Mr. Cook was looking good. "If he's stabilized, no reason for you to get worn out trying to sleep here. Hospitals make me nervous. Just too much going on."

Tucker had an aversion to hospitals. Even when he'd broken his legs twice in combat, he demanded he be able to walk out on his own, whether in cast or crutches or both. The first time it was nearly impossible to navigate. He got good at asking people to get out of the way by swinging his crutch high above his head like a hammer throw. He even resumed his skydiving, until his LPO found out and put a stop to it.

"You sure it's no trouble?" she asked. "Do you have a roommate?"

"No roommate. It's sparsely decorated and probably not to your taste, but I guarantee the bed's great."

She smiled, slowly swinging her head from side to side. "Why am I not surprised?"

"There. That's what I've been looking for." He angled her chin up and kissed her lightly. "I wanted to see that pretty smile. Ready to go?"

"I want to see him first."

An ICU nurse accompanied Brandy to the expansive room housing several beds, most of them filled. Tucker waited against the wall, sneaking a peek through the wide open doorway. He was able to see Brandy sit in the chair provided, reach over, and take her father's hand. She spoke to him, but too softly for him to make out. A few minutes later, with a gentle pat on her shoulder, she was ushered out.

"How's he look?" he asked her.

"He actually looks comfortable, but the nurse told me they'd be on high alert all night in case something happened. It's amazing he didn't break his arm or one of his legs, the way he must have fallen."

"Someone definitely looking out for him," Tucker answered back. "Let's go."

He drove in complete silence the short ten blocks before he arrived at the gates to his complex. He was grateful he didn't have to ruminate any longer than five minutes over his choice to bring her to his place. He'd have been a nervous wreck. Putting it all out of his mind, he helped her climb down from his truck, tucked the blanket and pillow under one arm, and took her hand with the other.

The first thing that hit him when he opened his front door was that he'd never before noticed that his room smelled of man sweat. Her room smelled of lavender and other floral fragrances. Before he turned on any lights, he stumbled in the dark, picked up the clothes he'd worn skydiving today under the jumpsuit, and tossed them behind the closet doors. Before he could choose the right lighting, Brandy turned on the bright kitchen lights, exposing the sink full of dishes. It was over three day's worth, even though he ate mostly frozen dinners on a regular basis.

Why hadn't he thought about this?

He hung his head sheepishly, hoping it didn't leave too much of a negative impression. "Between housekeepers," he mumbled, rolling his neck and left shoulder.

"You already warned me, so no worries. You also mentioned you don't have a decorator." She smiled, seemingly to enjoy his squirming. "I wasn't expecting an extreme makeover," she said, batting her eyes at him.

Tucker was definitely not feeling the least bit romantic. He was scared out of his gourd. He was on uncharted territory and regretted not paying attention to that little voice that usually gave him pretty good advice.

She wandered around his living room, examining the walls and bare corners. He had one couch, and it conformed perfectly to the contours of his large frame, even if it was ugly as sin. The table in front was a wooden shipping crate. She leaned over it and studied his choice of reading material. Several nudie magazines with specialty titles like *I Love Titties* and *Booty Call* were stacked five or six issues deep. All he could do was close his eyes and wait for her reaction. It was too late to whisk them away out of sight.

She picked up one cover and showed him the enormous boobs on the unfortunate girl. "Do mine look anywhere like these?" she asked, her face showing no expression.

"Holy cow, Brandy. No. *Fuck* no! Yours are...well, they're just right. A nice, full," he began to hold out his palms, fingers splayed and pointing up, "handful, just overflowing."

She had her hands on her waist. It was one of those attitude things women frequently gave him. He knew he was in some trouble, but wasn't sure how much. With his lack of sleep last night, his radar was not working, and his blood was inconveniently pooling elsewhere. He hoped she didn't notice. He wished she'd say something.

"But completely inadequate, compared to these." She held the magazine up, covering her chest.

"God, Brandy, those are unnatural. I mean if I wanted to play with a couple of deflated basketballs, I'd go take a drive to Sports City."

She flipped the magazine over to examine it again. "They do sort of look like basketballs."

Since she wasn't smiling, he carefully waited for the whole scene to pass. He tried to reassure her he liked her just the way she was built.

"And you have lovely curves, sweetheart. She's like a human tuck and roll. I like nice, curvy hips. I mean look at me. I want a woman I don't have to worry about breaking her pelvis when I make love. I hate skinny women."

He wasn't sure it was enough, so he waited, squinting as if bracing for a blow. She tossed the magazine back onto the table, and picked up one of the big butt issues. "Big Book of Booty. Nice."

Her darting glance at him was painful, but his dick was having great fun at his expense. Luckily, Brandy didn't look there. Instead, she smiled and asked him, "Does my ass look like this?"

Tucker was stumped. Brandy's ass did indeed look like the cover model's. She was round in all the right places. He decided he'd have to live or die, but he'd be honest with her.

"Yes, your butt looks sort of like that, only better. Smooth as silk. I love the way it looks and feels, sweetheart." He was hoping she didn't catch on that this was his favorite magazine.

"So why'd you buy this other one if you don't like basketballs with nipples? Or are you lying to me?"

"Look, Brandy, we're going places we don't have to go. But the truth is, there are some nice pictures on the inside. They aren't all like this. This is shock value, to make men buy the magazine. That's all. This is like a cartoon, a comic book, something men do to pass the time, like playing a video game or something. It's all fantasy."

He carefully maneuvered himself behind her, removing the magazine from her hands and turning her around.

"I don't need those things anymore. I got the real thing right here. You were created perfect for me. I mean that, Brandy." He massaged the top of her spine. With the other hand, he slipped it around her waist and slowly pulled her to him. "Perfect, in every way," he whispered. He let his hands massage her ass, squeezing and pressing her against his hardness.

"Why can't I be your fantasy, Tucker?"

"You are. You totally are. Men look. That's what we do. You do it, I'm sure. I mean, I saw all those romance novels overflowing your bookshelf. Some of those guys were *naked*. I'm sure it's done to sell those books to women, right?"

He suddenly felt like a louse. Here her father was in ICU, and he was having this discussion about boobs and booty. His lust was driving the conversation, clouding his better judgment. It wasn't fair to her. It wasn't even fair to himself. He wasn't acting like a real man. He was acting like a wolf—and everything he didn't respect. He was disgusted with himself.

He stepped away.

"I'm sorry, Brandy. This isn't right. I brought you here so you could get a good night's sleep, to help you rest." He chanced stepping back to her until he could feel the heat of her body again. "Let's just keep things simple and do that, okay? Let's forget about all this crap. I'm beat, and I'll bet you are, too. Can we call a truce and just sleep? I'll even keep my clothes on if you like."

He could feel her soften as she bridged the gap between them, all those lovely curves fitting so nicely, making him come alive. She placed her palms on his chest.

"It was my fault, Tucker. But I think you have a good idea there. Why don't we just go to bed?"

"You're on. No objections here," he lied. He tried to keep his grin from looking too lecherous. He took her hand and gently pulled her to the bedroom. He pretended he didn't notice the posters of well-oiled ladies on motorcycles, stark naked, or how she was staring at them with interest. She approached the poster with the row of ten perfect asses. He heard her inhale and hoped she wasn't going to object. If she did, he was going to rip all of them off the wall and toss everything from his balcony to the pool level below.

But what she did next surprised him. She removed her clothes, giving him one of those looks that made him nervous. It was the thing that scared him most about women. He had no way of knowing what was really going on inside her mind. While she stood in her bra and panties, she undid the center clasp and allowed the magnificence of her breasts to shine in the moonlight, beckoning to him. He was holding his breath, mesmerized.

"I like your idea. Let's just sleep." She pulled back the sheets and slid her naked body under them, invading his man bed, defiling his private sanctuary that would forever after smell like her and bring back memories of what it was like to have her there lying next to him.

He hurried to discard his pants and shirt and then his red, white and blue boxers, turning to sit on the edge so she wouldn't see the enormous hard-on he had for her. She snuggled close, wrapping her arms around his upper torso and squeezing her lovely upper chest against him. She moved her head just enough so her lips touched his ear when she said, "And then maybe tomorrow morning you can fuck my brains out."

Tucker knew he was hopelessly flawed. But he also knew he was utterly hooked on this woman. And he'd only known her for less than twenty-four hours. This had never happened to him before. If he wasn't careful, he'd be taking her to dress fittings and window shopping jewelry shops.

It would be the end of his life as he knew it.

And he'd love every minute of it.

CHAPTER 8

AS THE DAYS and weeks flew by, Brandy's father recovered with only a slight amount of memory loss. He still had headaches that drove him to bed from time to time. He was able to identify his attacker as Jorge, his former employee. Although both the Sheriff and the San Diego PD searched, when they couldn't find him and he stopped reporting for meetings he was required to attend, it was assumed he had fled to Mexico. With his prior record, when he was apprehended, he'd be going away for a long time, since the assault caused injury that necessitated a hospital stay, and drew blood.

Brandy and Tucker spent time with Dorie and Brawley when they returned from their honeymoon in Hawaii. She also worked longer hours at the grocery, and assisted her father in hiring two more experienced clerks. She hired a professional organizer to work with her dad to get the office looking more like an office than a storage unit.

But Brandy knew she'd have to get another good job like she had with the ad agency. The rents in San Diego weren't cheap, and with Tucker staying over at her cottage so much of the time, she wanted to get someplace more private and not under her father's watchful eye. But she was in no hurry. She allowed her relationship with Tucker to take it's own path. The longer she was around him, the less of a difference their fifteen-year age spread made.

But today was going to be an important test of their relationship. Tucker had worked on her non-stop until she finally relented. She was going to allow him to take her tandem skydiving. Although she'd visited the glider port and watched him jump and land safely a dozen times, it did nothing to remove her fear.

"You just have to ignore it. Just like you did when you learned to ride your first bike," he'd told her.

"But I wasn't going to fall thirteen thousand feet if I had a mishap on the bike." She couldn't imagine she would enjoy falling through the sky, even with Tucker securely strapped to her back.

"Trust me, it doesn't feel like you're falling. It feels like there's a blast of wind coming straight from the earth, holding you up so you can fly. It really does feel that way, Brandy. You'll see."

The old converted bomber with the door removed

loaded everyone and their buddies up after some ground instruction. Brandy and Tucker were to be in the middle of the jump, since it was her first one. Several SEALs and former Teammates of Tucker's jumped solo, doing cartwheels and in-air formations. At last it was their turn. She stood at the edge of the door, barely able to see cars moving below. Houses looked no bigger than her pinkie fingernail. The air that blew back through the jump door was freezing cold.

She wasn't sure when she was supposed to jump, and worried she'd catch her foot or shoelace on the flange at the opening.

"When do we—" she began to shout, until she felt Tucker's weight behind her and effortlessly they were out of the plane and freefalling. As her heart rate began to return to normal, she realized he was right. It didn't feel like she was falling at all. It felt like the earth was slowly moving to reach out and touch her, but very, very slowly. He tapped her arms, signaling her to make a human "W" as she extended them out to the sides and spread her feet.

He kissed the top of her head and shouted, "Close your mouth. I'm getting slimed."

Her wonderment and awe had caused her to forget that little part of the training. "Sorry," she shouted back at the top of her lungs.

Tucker handed her the cord to the chute and together they pulled it, which yanked her straight up several hundred feet, or so it seemed. As the glider extended, Tucker steered them around in circles, even driving them through wispy clouds, soaring up and then doing high-banked turns in mid air. As she came closer and closer to the earth, the air began to warm.

He pointed out the border. "That's Mexico right over there." He also pointed out several other landmarks. The San Diego Bay appeared like it was a shallow bowl of silver pebbles as it glistened in the morning sun. She took his hand and kissed his palm.

"Thank you," she said to him in the quiet. It felt like the ride went on for an hour, that they would be suspended all day, but finally the ground began to loom large. She threw her legs out in front of her as they landed on Tucker's, collapsed and rolled together in the long grass, entangled in the chute.

Looking up to the sky, it appeared twice as big as before, and twice as blue. A gentle breeze rearranged her hair when her cap fell to the side. Tucker's face and beard was pressed to her cheek. "I knew you could do it," he whispered. But even that whisper had the deep raspy tones that made her whole body vibrate.

"Amazing," was all she could think to say in return, as she continued searching the blue spans above her. "It wasn't anything at all what I imagined."

"It's like a lot of things. Scarier to think about than to do. We do thousands of these jumps on the Teams. Twice as high. At midnight when you only have your night vision specs on. You see oceans of glittering lights and hope that they're harmless animals, not the eyeballs of the enemy."

"I could never do that," she answered. "But I can see you doing it. Must have been fun."

Tucker hesitated before he said anything at all, and then she couldn't make out the words. She left him to his private thoughts. She knew he missed the life, and would ask him sometime how he replaced the adrenaline he used to have coursing through his veins. She wondered if being a farmer, or a father or husband would ever be really enough.

"Come on, we gotta get up before we get overrun with the newbies." He pulled her up by the straps, unhooked her from him and from the chute and began gathering the colorful fabric, shaking out the blades of grass and small rocks. She noted how happy he looked, with the sun shining behind him, greying hair blowing in the breeze.

She touched his cheek, making him stop, his hand wrapped around her wrist.

"I mean it. Thank you, Tucker." She stood on tiptoes and kissed him until he swept her up and carried her off the field, the lightweight nylon chute tucked under his arm.

Afterwards, they went for a seafood lunch down by the marina. She scanned the million dollar vessels and the people out walking their dogs or jogging on this sunny Sunday. Every day was sunny here.

"See, you wouldn't have this in Oregon," she chided him.

"That's very true. This suits me."

"Me too."

Over their soup he asked her, "Where do you want to go for Valentine's Day?"

That sent a zinger up the back of her legs. She recovered quickly, but couldn't make a decision. "Anywhere. You just name it."

"How about we go up north? Several of the guys and some of the wives are doing a road trip to Sonoma. Can you get a couple of extra days off? It takes a day up and a day down. Gotta stay and do some wine tasting. And I understand you're proficient at grape stomping."

"In February? You know anyone who has grapes this time of year?" She wrinkled up her nose and then winked at him.

"I love that picture with you and Dorie."

"Ah, the good old days, when I thought I had a job." She allowed her voice to wander off.

"You want me to move in? I could help with the rent."

Brandy's pulse quickened as her stomach turned. "I was thinking I'd move someplace else." She drank her water and didn't look at him for a couple long seconds, not sure she understood how he'd take it. "And no, your apartment is completely out of the question."

"Why would you ever want to move? Your place is perfect."

"And it's right behind my father's house."

"So? You don't think he understands what we do all night long, Brandy? Come on. He knows his little girl is all grown up, with grown up appetites. Besides, I think he'd be relieved you had someone to watch over you when he wasn't there to protect you himself. Give him a break. Let him relax. I'll do the heavy lifting for awhile."

The "for awhile" stuck in her chest. But, she had it coming. The conversation had come to the edge of their limit on what was safe to discuss. They never talked about long-term futures. It was way too soon.

"I think dad likes having me around, but it's hard to make ends meet with what he pays me. It's like my life's on hold each week I stay there."

Tucker was quiet, and then he spoke down to the tabletop. "Why not look at it like you don't have to decide right now. If you stay there you'll probably make him happy. He gets to see more of you than most fathers get. You're not pressured to go knock yourself out trying to swim upstream with all the other people clamoring for a fat paycheck."

She knew there was more he wanted to say, but was finding the choice of words difficult. She reached out and took one of his hands. "And I'm hoping you wouldn't mind, right?"

His brown eyes saw everything about her. He saw her insides, how her heart was beating, saw all her uncertainty. Saw how grateful she was that they'd met.

"That would be an understatement." His thumb caressed her knuckles and she thought she saw traces of a blush. "Can I ask you a question?" he asked.

"Shoot." She inhaled deeply and braced for something momentous.

"If we did decide to move in together, could I keep just one of my posters?"

CHAPTER 9

TUCKER HAD SCHEDULED a fishing trip to Baja for early March, but that wasn't going to change his plans to take the road trip to Sonoma County. As they were preparing, he received an enormous rent increase, so Brandy presented him with a key to her cottage.

"You sure?" He was thrilled, but surprised.

"Nope. But I think it's time and I did ask Dad. You were right, he said he was relieved."

"Just human nature."

"So have you decided which poster will come with you?" He loved the way she teased him.

"I'm leaving them *all* behind. Why have an imitation when I've got the real thing?"

He'd been doing extra workouts with several new boys graduating in June, looking to enlist after the summer. His back and knees were bothering him somewhat, so he decided he'd take his time moving his stuff, do it gradually so he didn't send himself over the edge. For the first time in his life, he was feeling his age. He could still bulk up, and work all the machines at Gunny's even better than when he was on the Teams, but his agility and speed was lacking. He was stiff in the mornings and sometimes woke up with leg cramps.

But when Team 3 got orders to do a temporary deployment back to Baja, everything changed. The Team Guys were to work on the sex trafficking ring they had slowed, but now had flared up again. The fishing trip was still on, but Tucker was going as the real civilian, and it would be no picnic for the active duty SEALs. He'd gotten special permission after initially having his participation rejected. He was excited to be of service, even if it was logistics support, to the men he'd previously served with.

Brandy wasn't pleased.

"I think the Navy is using you as bait, Tucker. I mean, you have to pay for your part of the trip, but you don't really get to do whatever you want to. You have to hang with them. They should at least pay for your way down and back and the cost of the rental when you're there."

"I'm actually happy about spending more time with them than I would if it was a real vacation. We usually can only get two or three days, like our Sonoma trip."

But she didn't understand Tucker would have paid

anything he could afford just to be embedded deeper within the community. He knew it was a hard thing to explain, so he didn't try.

He was nearly settled with the move, just ahead of their road trip. He had so little furniture, only the closet revealed the secret of his residency. Brandy got rid of her bed. He got rid of the old couch. Everything else he left behind for a young recruit who was beginning his first workup in BUD/S—someone who also appreciated his stash of magazines and posters.

He offered to rototill the back lot for Mr. Cook as a thank you for letting him share the cottage with Brandy. He even offered to pay a little more in rent, but Cook wouldn't have any of that.

Tucker fixed the clutch wires on the "mangler", as he called the tiller, switched out the gasoline after installing a new gas tank and filter. The machine purred like a kitten. Afterwards, the sandy light brown soil looked like chocolate sugar. He imagined Cook would have a field day while they were gone, planting all his early spring seeds.

At last, they took off for Northern California, driving in one long caravan of ten vehicles. Their destination was Frog Haven Vineyards, where several of the SEALs had invested some of their re-up bonuses. Brawley told him it was run by the infamous *Pirate,* who had also been a member of Kyle's squad. Tucker had never met the man.

But he'd also been on earlier road trips when he was active and knew all about Nick Dunn's winery in Santa Rosa, which was on the way. His sister had left the property to Nick. He and Devon converted the nearly bankrupt nursery site into a world-class wedding center, lavender farm and winery. Tucker had been part of several work parties in past years, but had never seen the final result, and knew Brandy would love it.

After only two stops along the way and nearly ten hours later, they arrived in Sonoma County, not stopping until they got all the way up to Healdsburg and the famous Dry Creek Valley. Traveling the winding country two-lane freeway through the valley floor, they found it covered in blooming bright yellow mustard flowers between rows of blackened and gnarled old grapevines. Vineyard workers were cutting back last year's growth to make way for trellising new ones. The air was lightly scented by the smoldering piles of clippings and farm debris all along the way.

"I can't believe I've missed this area," Brandy remarked. "Never thought I'd find anything prettier than Coronado, but this comes pretty close."

"People come here from all over the world just to drive around, eat incredible food and taste great wines. Barrel tasting is really big in the early fall."

"Sounds like Heaven," she answered back.

"These guys have it good. Zak's nickname is the pirate. He got injured on his first deployment, shot in the eye and is real lucky to be alive."

"I'd say. But except for the eye, he was okay?"

"Yes ma'am."

"Were you close?"

"He came on board after I'd gone, so I never got to meet him. But after the injury, he wanted to come back. He worked like a dog and qualified Expert with his other eye, and went through most of the BUD/S training again. You don't find many guys who could do that."

"So he went back?"

"Well, Kyle wanted him back, I was told, but in the end, the Navy thought better of it and asked him to scratch. He met a local Realtor and they found this property and bought it, along with a whole bunch of Team Guys and their relatives. Now they're making beer, along with the wine. I hear it's real tasty."

"Zak sounds like one tough dude."

The caravan slowed down, the first car turning up a crushed granite drive, quickly disappearing from view. As Tucker began his approach up the driveway, he drove past a handful of mailboxes, and pointed out the winery sign.

"Frog Haven. That's it. Got the Bone Frog logo and

everything, not that the average tourist would know. You won't see a Trident anywhere."

They drove past more vineyard workers doing pruning and cleanup. A herd of small goats was grazing between several rows, hedged in by portable fencing.

"Am I seeing this correctly? Goats?" asked Brandy.

"They keep the grass down, leaving behind nutrients. A lot of the wineries in the valley are doing the same. Pretty smart. Rent-A-Goat." Tucker could see she was amused.

"No way. Really?" she asked.

"I don't lie. This herd is special. They make artisan cheeses the owner sells for big bucks. Your dad might even carry some in his store."

Once they approached the top of the swale, the jockeying for parking space began, with a couple of the big trucks nearly colliding. One by one everyone poured out, stretching and adjusting themselves after the long ride. In front of them was a quaint farmhouse with a large covered porch surrounding three quarters of the sides. It had been restored to perfect condition. An attractive woman in a smock apron, with two children hugging her legs stood at the entrance. Leaning against one of the porch posts next to her was a handsome man dressed in black, sporting an eye patch over one side. It had to be Zak. Tucker was looking forward to meeting him, finally.

Brandy shuffled over to Brawley and Dorie, striking up a conversation. Kyle's wife, Christy, ran to the porch and gave Zak's lady a big hug. A couple of the other wives did the same. Zak and Amy's two kids scattered into the vineyard to go play with a group of workers kids.

Tucker took Brandy's hand and they joined the small crowd that had gathered in front of the house, just as if Zak was going to make a speech to all of them.

Instead of Zak giving the speech, it was his wife.

"Welcome to Frog Haven. I'm Amy and this is my husband, Zak. I guess the kids are around here somewhere, so be careful pulling in or backing out of the driveway, *please!*"

The group chuckled.

"We're so excited to have you with us for a couple or three nights. We can sort all that out later. I don't think Zak has been able to sleep for a week, he's been so looking forward to your visit."

"Thanks you two," directed Kyle, taking charge. "Let's give them a big round of applause for making this one of the more frugal vacations we've been able to take."

The group clapped and several whistled or cheered.

Amy thanked them with a big smile. "Now, we have two unoccupied bedrooms here in the main house, but the bunkhouse sleeps twenty-four. No queen or king beds, so you'll have to put your singles together and negotiate the crack down the middle."

"Notice she said two beds together? No threesomes!" yelled Kyle.

After the laughter died down, Amy continued. "I'll let you sort all that out on your own. We eat in an hour, family style out back on the other side. I've got some heaters but there's no way I can feed you all in my little dining room, so wear your sweatshirts and jackets. If it's too cold for you, tomorrow we can arrange for supper to be served in the bunkhouse."

"Dinner attire?" T.J. Talbot asked her.

"Something you wouldn't mind getting stained with tomato sauce. We're going Italian all the way."

A cheer broke out, and as the crowd dispersed, Zak called them all back.

"Almost forgot. Short showers or only the first five of you will get one. My personal favorite is sharing, two-by-two. We have a nice hot tub you can take your time and soak in after dinner, if you like." Zak checked his cell phone. "On my mark….Go!"

The group took on the atmosphere of a church camp. The men were in sync because they were used to working together that way without anyone having to bark instructions. Tucker noticed several of the newer wives and girlfriends were completely confused, and

Christy was a big help with some timely advice, discretely placed here and there.

Tucker and Brandy selected a dark corner in the bunkhouse. Wire cables worked like stringers, attached with hooks to the walls in both directions so old sheets could slide into place, giving each couple some privacy like in a hospital room. Tucker moved their two mattresses together and then re-made the bedspread to stretch over both sides. He'd been told to bring some comforters, so he retrieved them from the truck, and added them as well.

At the opposite wall, there was an old Franklin potbellied stove and a generous pile of wood stacked halfway to the ceiling. Several rocking chairs made a semicircle around the stove for evening chats. Against one wall was a tiny kitchen with a sink, a refrigerator, a picnic table that could seat eight and a microwave toaster oven.

But the highlight of the entire bunkhouse was the bathroom, containing a two-stall unisex toilet and one shower. Tucker was looking forward to the hot tub after dinner to work out the kinks in his neck and shoulder. He doubted he could even fit in the shower, let alone share it with Brandy.

They washed up quickly and then joined the whole group outside on Zak and Amy's patio. Zak placed both their kids at the head of the table on a loveseat with pillows so they could see everyone. They were bundled for the ski slopes, wearing matching bunny hats.

At this time of year, the vines were bare, so the trellis they sat under left gaping holes where Tucker could see the stars. Some of the magic rubbed off when it turned very cold, with a slight breeze. He excused himself and grabbed their comforter from the bunkhouse and wrapped the two of them together while they devoured their steaming hot lasagna, green salad and a little too much red wine. With the slight buzz relaxing him, soon even the nippy night air stopped bothering him. He'd forgotten how different Northern California was from San Diego, where no matter what time of year, the temperature never fluctuated more than ten degrees.

Brandy was laughing at Christy's story of how she met Kyle, when she attempted to hold the wrong house open and found him naked and asleep—stretched out on the master bed.

Although the ladies were last to bond as a unit, as the wine continued to flow and the stories got louder and more daring, Tucker could tell they were already well on their way to coming together on their own team of sorts. It was important that the sisterhood of the wives and girlfriends stay strong and tight, since they would help hold each other up in case the unthinkable were to happen. Dr. Death stalked them all: men, women and children. And with the world exploding more and more every day, he was making house calls at home, in the good old US of A.

You son of a bitch.

Tucker had only had to hold one of his buddies as the young man's life passed from him. He never wanted to repeat the experience.

By candlelight, he studied the faces of those men he'd served with, and served under. He felt so lucky to have had that opportunity to be a grown up Boy Scout, doing crazy dangerous things, all the while making the world a safer place. He'd been able to push himself to his limits, the adrenaline nearly exploding from the veins in his neck, but as a force for good. Never evil. It was hard to explain to someone who hadn't experienced it for himself. It was probably the heavy wine, but right now he couldn't explain why he'd ever left. There just wasn't another job on the planet as good as being a Team Guy.

Amy put on some music and the ladies rushed to their feet to dance. It was fascinating to watch how women could just be so demonstrative, so ready to just throw their heads back, laugh and toss their cares over their shoulders.

Brawley scooted over next to him, and shared part of the blanket.

"You guys are getting along most excellently, my man. Brandy's a good influence on you."

"Nah. I still got the dirty thoughts, same as ever."

The two men chuckled. Brawley's eyes were sparkling in the candlelight as he watched his new bride dance with Brandy. Christy and several of the others became the girl group backup singers, line dancing in unison to the funky rhythm from an oldies satellite channel.

"We've missed you, Tuck."

"Missed you too," Tucker returned without looking at Brawley. "So you're staying in for another turn?"

"For now. Honestly, I don't know what I'd do if I didn't have this community or these things to do with my friends."

"I hear you." Tucker was trying not to dwell on it. He wanted Brawley to change the subject, but it was awkward sitting next to him, wrapped in the same blanket. He was sensitive about that sort of thing. As a youth, he'd probably spent more time with Brawley than he did his own parents.

"You'll have to hang around more when we get back to San Diego," Brawley said just before he finished his wine. Zak placed another opened bottle in front of the two men.

Tucker read the label out loud. "*Frog Haven Winery. A little piece of Heaven.* That's about how I'd describe it up here." He was hoping the change in focus would get the discussion off the Teams.

"First time I've seen it all built out. When they first bought it, I thought they were nuts." Brawley scanned the patio, smiling at the girls. "Now look at it. Piece of Heaven, indeed."

"Thought you invested like Kyle and Coop and everyone else," remarked Tucker.

"Nope. I bought a house with my re-enlistment bonus instead. Maybe the next time."

"So you're going career, like your dad?"

"I'm thinking PA school, or maybe med school, if I can get some tutoring."

"Geez, Brawley. You won't have any time if you do that. And you'll owe them another ten years at least."

"Well, it's a pipe dream." Brawley casually glanced at the ladies again. "They're getting smashed."

Tucker found this funny. "I think living here and doing this would be a whole lot easier. And no schooling or the cost of it."

"We'll see. First, I have to get in."

"By then, you'll have chipmunks running all over the place," Tucker reminded him. "Bills, gymnastics lessons and soccer practice. You ever spend any time with Kyle and his brood, or Coop? We can hardly get them to come out with us to the Scupper."

Tucker was convinced Brawley had forgotten his

earlier remark, until his friend cruelly drove the point home again.

"Hell, Tuck. What's stopping you? I mean Kyle says you're paying for a vacation chaperoning the Team all over Baja next month. Some vacation. Why don't you just re-up? Come back to us."

"Because I'm thirty nine, Brawley."

"So am I, nearly."

"But I've been doing other things. I'm just not sure I could get through BUD/S again."

"They'd have to give you a pass on that," Brawley barked.

"Nope. I already checked."

The two of them sat in the few seconds of quiet while the ladies searched for another station. In San Diego, there would be crickets on a night like this, even in February. Tucker had heard an owl earlier, but no crickets.

Brawley turned, speaking to the side of his face. "Well, you just confirmed what I've been thinking for the better part of five years now. Don't deny it, Tucker. You want back in."

He wasn't going to make a big objection to Brawley's remarks because that would make him look guilty as charged. But his friend had nailed him fair and square. That little confidential talk with Collins about whether or not the Navy would consider a re-entry for him was kept under wraps. But he had to go open his big mouth tonight and tell Brawley he'd checked. He wondered if he'd done it on purpose.

Wouldn't that be something if I could do it?

Brawley stood up and positioned the entire blanket around Tucker's shoulders and gave him a gentle pat on the back. "I think I'm going to go out there and rescue Dorie before someone gets hurt."

Tucker nodded. "Think I'll do the same," and stood to join him.

Brawley grinned like he'd been told a dirty joke.

"What's so funny?" he asked the newlywed.

"I think everyone's gonna get laid tonight."

CHAPTER 10

"WE SHOULD HAVE taken a week off, Tucker. I had no idea there was so much I wanted to see." Brandy was folding her clothes when Tucker made his way into their sheeted cubicle. He'd been stacking wood and making sure the fire was fully stoked so they didn't have to wake up in the morning to a cold building.

"Next time. I promise." He pulled her to him, fingering the red lace bra she'd bought for the trip. "Where on earth did you get this dangerous device?"

"You like it?"

"Turn around. Let me think about that for a couple of minutes."

She loved taking direction from him. She peered over her shoulder. "Like this?"

"Keep going."

Brandy slowly kept moving until she was facing him again. "Should I take my bra and panties off now?"

"I can't make up my mind."

His smile was bringing on a wave of hot, wet lust she could smell.

"Is it my imagination, or are these lovely lace things even more sexy looking when they're so—so—ample?" He darted a worried look her way. "Did I just make a huge mistake?" he said as he winced. He bit his lower lip and, in spite of his enormous size and white beard, looked like a little boy about to be punished.

"I used to let things like that bother me." She slowly slid her panties down her thighs. "But—"

"Don't touch that!" he whispered.

Brandy had her hand on the front clasp of her bra, ready to peel it away and stand before him naked. Instead, she splayed her fingers over the satin and eyelet lace, squeezed her flesh and took two little steps until their bodies touched.

"How is it that I'm always the one who's naked first?" she asked, her lips just barely touching his. She could hear his heart pounding in tandem to hers and took a gentle moan from him as they kissed.

"I guess it's because I always like to watch, and I forget myself," he whispered.

"I think it's healthy to forget yourself now and then, don't you?" They kissed again, but deeper. "You want me to leave it on or take it off?"

"I think you should leave it on for now. I'll get to it

in about an hour. I have other things I want you to do first. Is that okay with you, Brandy?"

She watched him remove his jeans and underwear, his erection bouncing with anticipation. She held him between her palms like she was praying.

"It's perfect."

IT WAS PAST midnight when she awoke, grateful Tucker held her tight because the room was freezing. Someone in one of the other spaces was snoring up a storm and would have rattled the windows if there were any.

Her heart was still racing from their urgent love-making. He'd played her body like an instrument, hard, and incredibly deep, expressed both in body language as well as their frantic whispers. It had been so intense, at one point she broke down in tears and Tucker thought he'd hurt her somehow.

But in a way he had. She was forever altered as if she was a willing participant in her own destruction.

It was hard not to notice a man as tall and strong as he was. But now that she knew him better, had kissed every inch of his body and answered his need with her own, she understood that everything he did he was the master of, except sometimes finding words. But he loved with abandon, never holding back, pushing her to the edge, and then just a little further, until she'd collapse in his arms. The coiled, cloud-of-butterflies-feeling in her belly were physical manifestations of what she knew to be true in her heart. She was falling in love, as she never had before. She also knew this came with risks, since there would be no getting over that kind of intense love. In fact, it was delicious and painful at the same time, even with the absence of a breakup on the horizon.

She tried not to think about where it all was going. She'd been included in the community of brothers, felt herself blend in with the ladies who were lucky enough to also be loved by one of these warriors who turned their worlds upside down. Brandy just took the waves of emotion and passion as they engulfed her and tried not to focus on what it all meant. She knew that was a rabbit hole.

It hardly seemed possible they'd known each other for such a short period of time. He'd been the missing piece she didn't even know she'd been missing. If she ever had to be without him, life would never be the same.

She thought about Amy and Zak, who was nearly killed on his first deployment. Shannon had lost her first husband, T.J.'s best friend. She'd also heard stories about the women who couldn't handle the lifestyle, the intensity of their play and their hearts. Still, it was a family, a community of brothers and the women they loved.

But one thing bothered her. Tucker had been talking with Kyle and Brawley, and she knew he missed being a SEAL. What would she do if he decided she wasn't the right one? What if he tried to re-join his team and failed? How could she ever make up for that incredible loss he would feel.

Or, what if she never could keep him happy enough to stay? Could she meet him halfway, match his energy, and carefully tend to him if he ever fell apart? She wasn't sure she was cut out for it, any of it.

Try to sleep. You have to rest. You'll drive yourself crazy with all these thoughts.

"Everything okay, Brandy?" His words startled her.

"I'm sorry, did I wake you?"

He sifted his fingers through her hair. "Yes."

"I can't sleep."

"That happens to me sometimes too when I drink too much. It's like I'm over-drunk."

She lay on her back and enjoyed the feel of his large callused hand caressing her breast. The plank beams on the ceiling were barely visible in the reflection of moonlight. Brandy waited, trying to notice some sign her eyelids were heavy and her mind was quieting, but that sign never came. She inhaled and tried to sigh very carefully so he wouldn't detect her worry. But even that was unsuccessful.

"Talk to me, Brandy."

"I don't want to do it here."

"Hot tub?"

They threw on some clothes and took their towels, discovering that they were able to be alone under the stars. The warm water helped Brandy put her thoughts into words.

She wrapped her legs around his waist and floated with her arms about his neck. The white in his hair and beard made him appear to glow in the dark.

"Is it that bad?" he teased.

"What?"

"Whatever it is you don't want to tell me."

"No, Tucker." She paused and thought carefully before she spoke. "Let me ask you a question. Does the speed of all this scare you just a little?"

"You mean does it fall somewhere between skydiving at midnight and getting my ass shot off by a sniper? That what you mean by scared?"

Now she felt ridiculous. "I got the impression you weren't the kind of guy who just jumped into relationships."

"Oh. Okay. So now we're talking *relationships*. Is that what this is?"

She would have been worried but saw the goofy grin on his face. "Watch it. Don't you make fun of me. I don't like that, as you know."

"Well, you're right about me. I don't do this. I've

never done this."

She didn't want to look at him in the eyes, thinking he might begin to get uncomfortable. The last thing she wanted to do was put him on the spot. But she wanted to know where she stood. And maybe that was the right way to put it.

"Tucker."

"Yes ma'am."

"Would you be able to give me some indication of where all this is leading? Like, do I fit into your life anywhere other than in your bed?"

He tilted his head and stared back at her without smiling, and her heart fell to the bottom of the hot tub.

"First, if you'd have asked me that about ten years ago, I'd be gone by now. Maybe even five years ago. But, believe it or not, I've mellowed. When I went to the wedding on New Years Eve, *my* goal, and remember I told you I didn't want to tell you what it was?"

"I remember."

"My goal was to keep my hands to myself and to not rank or otherwise check out the ladies at the reception."

"Okay. And how did that work out for you?"

"I didn't even come close to achieving my goal. I sat there in the church, and I watched as you walked down the aisle, and into my life."

Brandy was stunned. It wasn't what she'd expected

at all.

"I've been watching you when you were sleeping, talking to other people and didn't know I was looking. I watch you from across the room and out of the sides of my eyes when we go places. And I've come to the conclusion that I don't ever want to spend a day when you are not a part of my life."

She scrambled to her feet, separated herself from him and stood with her back pressed against the other side of the hot tub. Her heart felt like it was going to jump right out of her chest and go running down between the vines.

Tucker just waited. And then that grin overtook his face. "Oh my God. You're scared." He approached quietly, relentlessly, and without hesitation gently took her head in his hands and kissed her. "It's just like skydiving, sweetheart," he said between kisses. "You put your arms out to the sides, and fly. And I'll be strapped right there behind you. I will never let you fall. And I'll never stop loving you."

TRUE NAVY BLUE

Prequel to Zak

Book 1 of the True Blue SEALs Series

SHARON HAMILTON

CHAPTER 1

THE RED LIGHTS flashed, pulsing dangerous images across her white skin as she lay unconscious. Was she dead? He hoped not. Paramedics were pouring over her with care, asking hushed questions, obviously looking for some kind of response. And then, thank God, he heard her whisper something back and cry.

Where am I?

They were rougher with him. Zak Chambers was used to people around him making up their minds before they got to know him. Santa Rosa used to be a small town, back when his father was sowing *his* wild oats. Half the cops in town were kids of the same cops who used to arrest his dad for pranks he was legendary for doing—things like throwing pumpkins into the Redwood Motel pool at Halloween, making the headlines in the local newspaper. His father still had the article hanging on his garage wall.

And what was so wrong with pouring red Jell-O

into the fountain at Santa Rosa High School? They were *his* high school colors and they'd just creamed Santa Rosa's football team 47 to 6.

Why am I thinking about all this stuff? Where the heck am I? What's happened?

This time, however, was no prank. His father's Camaro, a twisted and partially melted hulk in front of him, looked even more ghastly because of the red flashing lights, this was no prank. This wasn't about Jell-O or pumpkins or anything that could be construed as a high school caper. This was a first-class grown up tragedy, getting worse by the minute. He didn't have a clue what he was doing here or how he got here.

"Can you sit up, Chambers?" the gruff uniformed man with a badge and white plastic gloves asked him.

Where are the pretty nurses? His dad always got lucky with the nurses.

He tried to right himself, but the blow to his head had him confused. And he'd had a glass of wine, but just one…

"Need your permission to take a breath sample, son."

Fuck me. The guy looked younger than Zak did.

"No. Not going to happen," Zak mumbled.

"Oh, it's gonna happen. Either here or down at the station, but you better cooperate or you get an automatic suspension." The guy squinted. He had pimples. He looked like one of the boys he'd hassled in school.

"Do I know you?" Zak asked. The word "suspension" was rattling around in his head like a bad idea. He tried to focus on it, but nothing came.

"Oh yea, you do. You used to buy our booze with your fake I.D. when I was a freshman."

It was beginning to come back to him now. Little flashes of color. Painful things. Things he didn't want to remember.

"Except one time, you kept the money. You freakin' robbed us, man. Ain't life a bitch, Zak? Look at us now, dancing here on the pavement with your wrecked souped up Camaro your dad probably spent his year's pension on, and me here with my badge and gun and all. Oh yea, life is a real bitch sometimes."

Zak remembered him. Had an upper crust name like Dawson, or Drew or…

"I remember you, Dirtbag." It was what Zak always called him, not because he was a real dirtbag, because he worshiped Zak for the ladies he got to hang with. But it was given him because he was unlucky enough to be named Dirk by his parents. And Zak didn't want to be anybody's idol. He wasn't *that* fake. He just didn't deserve it. In those days, Zak was still a promising football player courting a couple of full ride college scholarships. He'd walked away from it all.

But what the hell am I doing here?

The kid administered the breathalizer and Zak saw the instrument yanked from the kid's hands.

"Still scoring points with the authorities, I see." An older man with a nasty gravelly voice and a nastier-looking face peered over the top of his head and blinked down at him, upside down. It made Zak dizzy. "And you're drunk," he said looking at the device. Instead of showing it to Zak he placed it in a plastic bag and shoved it in his large jacket pocket. "Works for me."

"Sir." Dirtbag stood up. "Should I test—"

"Yeah. He's drunk," the older officer said. "He needs to be taken in until we can figure it out."

It occurred to Zak he knew the man but couldn't remember his name.

When they stood him up, that's when Zak saw the other vehicle, a vegetable truck loaded with melons. Half of them were escaping over the freeway, bouncing like a girl's oversized tits with an agenda of their own. Cars were swerving and Zak expected to hear another crash any minute.

The older deputy barked some instructions. Two Highway Patrolmen took off with their lights flashing, while someone lit flares and started to direct traffic slowly in one narrow lane taking up part of the shoulder.

Ginger had not really been his date, but she was going to be his fuckbunny for the night, sure as shit. He'd made the mistake of letting her long lip lock go a little too long, distracting him enough to miss the overloaded melon truck swerving into his lane. The impact was on her side. As he heard it, he noticed the seatbelt firmly pressing into her chest, and like a dog, he had a second or two of turn-on before he realized they'd been hit.

Seatbelts were a good thing. In this instance, it probably saved Ginger's life.

"*He* hit *me*," Zak tried to protest as he was led, handcuffed, into the back of the patrol car. His shouts were falling on deaf ears as they closed the cruiser's door after shoving him into the rear seat. He saw the ambulance leave in a blaze of red and blue flashing lights ahead of him. He felt bad about not saying goodbye to Ginger before they took her away. He hoped she'd be okay.

The dark-skinned truck driver had a child clinging to his side. Zak noticed he wasn't being handcuffed and carted away like Zak was.

No, this wasn't going to wind up being a very good day.

THE WORST THING about getting taken down to the station was that his mother had to come down and pick him up. They'd not fingerprinted him or taken pictures, just put him in a cell with about twenty others, mostly drunk drivers, which made for a very uncomfortable sleep on a metal bench with a full-on fluorescent light buzzing overhead. But he didn't have time to tell her. She looked at him like road kill.

"I wasn't drinkin' Ma." He insisted. It was *almost* the truth.

"Zak, you're just one good time after another," she said, dragging on her electric cigarette.

"Where's Dad?"

"Sleeping. Right now that's a good thing."

He'd known that was the answer before he'd asked. He'd seen his dad down at the Irish Pub, rubbing shoulders with the computer nerds and yuppies who worked for Medtronic and Agilent. His dad was still better looking than he had a right to be, and though twice their age, could occasionally chat himself into someone's bed. Zak was glad he'd made it home. Now there was a *real* alcoholic, Zak thought.

"You know anything about Ginger?" he asked her.

"That the girl you were with last night?"

Zak nodded.

"News says she'll be released today. You're the one that needed the hospitalization."

He was relieved. "So that's where we're going?" he asked.

"They should have brought *you* to the Emergency Room. Dobson didn't do you any favors. He'd have probably let you bleed out, Zak."

Dobson. Holy fuck, Amy Dobson's father, the chief. He let her take a drag on her eCig.

"Can't believe it's your first day back and already you're in trouble. Surprised they didn't arrest you."

"They still could," he answered.

Now he began to remember. It was his day back only to attend his enlistment party a few of his friends were giving him. He was to report to Indoc in three days.

Thank God they didn't arrest me. This was way too close. Time to grow up and be smart if I want to really do this. His SEAL career would be over before it started.

Then he thought about his Dad's Camaro and was grateful he'd spent the night in jail. He had no idea what the old man was going to do when he woke up. Zak had completely blown his $65,000 ride. That cherry red beauty he kind of borrowed.

"I'll pay you guys back for whatever the insurance—"

She gave him a long horse-face look like he had a purple horn protruding from his forehead.

"I promise. I will, Mom."

"In your dreams lover boy." She sighed. "I never

had to give this advice to your sister, so I might as well waste it on you. I hope you keep some rich little thing happy, Zak. If you can manage to unzip it for just one lady, you'd have a nice life making someone happy. I don't see it in you to be any kind of provider."

"I'm in the Navy now. Maybe I'll get killed and leave you the insurance policy, Ma."

She slapped him harder than he thought she was capable of.

"Word of advice. Stay away from the Amy Dobsons of the world, Zak. They'll make your life miserable, just like they always did."

Oh yes, now it was coming back to him. The fog was lifting. That summer when he was dodging classes and staying good and wet inside Amy Dobson's treasure chest. He'd fucked her so many times that year he thought perhaps his pecker would fall off. The girl was insatiable, used to multiple partners and always pushing the envelope faster than he could keep up. In the end, she tired of him and left him handcuffed naked to one of the oak trees outside the Admin building at Santa Rosa Junior College.

And then she called her dad, then Lieutenant Allister Dobson of the Santa Rosa PD, who got out his bolt cutters. He hesitated a moment, staring down at Zak's penis, swearing under his breath, halfway making Zak worry his pecker would be clipped. Dobson released him with a grunt. Zak couldn't help it if he was hung. Apparently that fact wasn't lost on her father, either.

He got off with a warning and he had to promise he'd leave town by the end of the summer. He was flunking out anyway. The scholarship was toast and his world was looking pretty small.

"Son, you either go away to college, or you go into the armed forces, or you hang out in Vegas with drag queens. Makes no difference to me. But Amy is off limits in a most permanent way."

No, Dobson, who had now made Chief, wouldn't do him any more favors. And now he didn't even get a chance to tell the Chief he was just passing through on his way to becoming one of America's finest. Probably wouldn't make any difference anyway.

They arrived at the Emergency clinic close to ten that morning. Zak's mother already had one message from his dad asking where the Camaro was.

It was going to be a very long day.

CHAPTER 2

AMY DOBSON GOT a call from her friend Margrit at the Santa Rosa Police Department informing her that Zak had been held overnight. And he wasn't alone when he crashed his father's Camaro. He was with a girl.

Amy knew full well how much Zak's father loved that vehicle. But that's not what piqued her interest. She wanted to know about the passenger. Had Zak brought someone up with him to Santa Rosa? She'd followed his journey to Santa Cruz spying on him through Facebook. But this had come to an abrupt end when he joined the military. It was like Zak just dropped off the face of the earth with no posts on social media. Perhaps he'd blocked her.

She'd told herself whatever became of Zak was of no consequence to her. But it was an indisputable fact, when she was underneath some hulk of a guy who was trying his hardest to rock her world and cause the next earthquake, Zak's was the face she saw as she tried to get off. Back when they were dating heavily, all Zak had to do was look at her and her panties would get wet. He had more sex in his index finger than most the guys she knew would ever amass during their lifetime.

"Who is she, Margrit?" Amy knew the clerk wouldn't tell her, but she needed to ask anyway. She'd helped to get Margrit the job at her father's station.

"I'd have to go check—let me—"

"No. I'm good. Was she okay?" Amy wondered if the passenger was Zak's new girlfriend.

"Took her to Memorial. No serious injuries, and he didn't go to the hospital, if you want to know."

"You said that, Margrit. Said he was held over."

"And released to his mother this morning," Margrit said helpfully.

"Thanks."

Amy played with the screen on the phone, scrolling down through pictures. She and Zak at the ocean. She and Zak with selfies in bed. She and Zak completely shit-faced kissing in that photo booth at the fair the summer she turned eighteen, the legal age. Except that hadn't mattered to either one of them, since they'd been screwing since she was sixteen.

Even back then he was the only one who rang her chimes. He was the only one who didn't fall all over himself to get in her pants. She loved that he tried to exercise restraint, and in the end, he would always cave. That's the way he was. He was hers for as long as she wanted him, despite what he told himself, and despite whatever promises he'd made to some mystery woman who was in his car last night. Curiosity snaked its way up her spine as she wondered if he still felt the same way about her.

Rich Wilson, a new addition to her Dad's force, was coming over to take her to the Police Community Day at the park. Her dad would be there, of course, and she allowed Rich to curry favor with him by bringing his daughter to the party. She didn't like local cops as dates because they were more concerned about what her Dad was thinking than what Amy wanted, but today she would put up with Rich as a means to an end.

She fluffed her hair, adding some spray and fingering through it to add volume. Staring at herself in the mirror, she added a little extra eyeshadow and lip gloss over her red lip crayon. It was her reward for putting up with Rich. It made her feel a little naughty, wicked. Maybe Rich would get lucky tonight. What she really wanted was something else, but she refused to let herself dwell on it too much.

"You look awesome, Amy," Rich said on the front stoop of her father's house. He was attractive in his clean-cut way. He wore a dark polo shirt that hugged his nice torso. He wasn't huge, just well-built and took pride in how he looked. Eyeing him as she passed, she stepped out the door and let her heels clickety-clack down the concrete pathway, wondering why she couldn't fall for the really good guys. Oh yes, it could be a fun night, rocking his world, blowing his mind with some things she'd learned, but her appetite was tempered by the smell and feel of hot fresh sex with Zak. She couldn't help it if she was addicted to him. The taste of his kiss and the feel of his hands on her was still something she carried with her every day. It was like breathing.

Young cops in his father's Department always drove muscle cars or pickups with stick shifts. In either case, they didn't hold a candle to the souped-up Ford with the bench seat Zak had in high school. His dad had helped him restore it. She loved the smell of the old leather seats and the way the crackle of the radio sounded as they parked and watched the lights, as if trying to find their story out there amongst the strings of twinkling gold and silver. There wasn't any way to describe their relationship, really. They'd stare out at the jewel display, breathing hard, aware of the other, touching on that crackled leather seat. In the end the sirens always spooked him, as if her dad was sending a warning to him just before he did what he was no doubt going to do. She liked their little routine. Zak would protest, saying they shouldn't get so physical again, and, in the end he'd lose to Amy's persistence.

"We never talk," he'd said one time.

"Seriously? You want to talk? With me?" Amy let her eyebrows drift up into her bangs. "Do you know how many guys want to take a taste of these?" She had pulled her shirt up and when Zak tried to take just a discrete peek, it was all over. His hunger burst forth like an exploded water balloon. They couldn't get naked fast enough. Several times he fucked her before she could stop giggling at his urgency.

They never talked about what it meant. It was just assumed it was only sex, not a lifelong commitment. Back then, that was all it needed to be. As Amy looked outside her window, listening to Rich describe how awesome her father was and what a good leader and example he set for all the young recruits, Amy realized for the first time that she missed those carefree days. She considered, briefly, that perhaps it had meant something deeper, but then she brushed that consideration away like a dust bunny.

She let herself out of the car before Rich could get around to her side. "Dammit, Amy. I told you to let me get it."

"Oh, I'm sorry, Rich. I keep forgetting you are a gentleman. Just not used to it is all." She smiled up at him and she could almost see his buttons melt as his chest extended. She gave him her hand as a peace offering.

They walked across the bumpy lawn area that sometimes doubled as a Rugby field to the gathering of long tables covered in red and white checkered oilcloth. She heard her dad's gruff voice carry from the barbeque pit he usually manned, followed by several deep guffaws and some back slapping. He was a well-liked Chief, Amy noted, but he also had a temper and never forgot a betrayal, no matter how small. The respect he earned was more derived from his boundaries than his easy going nature.

Out of the corner of her eye, Amy saw that he'd noticed her arrival with Rich.

"Going to pay my respects to the Chief," Rich said to her ear as he gave her a little squeeze on her upper arms.

"Fine," she smiled back at the young policeman as she stifled a burst of irritation.

Margrit joined her. She'd come alone, as usual.

"Ginger Cooper. Not from here," Margrit said, her cheeks bunched like those of a hairless chipmunk stuffed with peanuts. For a second, Amy wasn't sure what she was referring to.

"Where's she from?"

"Listed an address in San Diego."

"Oh." It wasn't what Amy wanted to hear, finding

out a girl from where Zak was stationed had come all the way up to give her competition. Amy knew she didn't have any claim on Zak, but if this stranger was something special to him, she needed to know, for her own edification.

"Jealous?" Margrit's horn-rimmed glasses and frizzy hair made her look dorky, like a librarian.

"Hardly."

Margrit sighed and looked over at the gene pool, most of them with wives and children. "You don't fool me a bit, Amy. You're as addicted to him as he is to you."

"Now you're talking nonsense," Amy said as she moved on.

CHAPTER 3

ON THE WAY home from the hospital, Zak's mother headed over to an attorney's office. Zak had kept mum all during the hospital visit, halfway expecting they'd get a call or the police would show up saying they were going to arrest him. His mom seemed to be on the same wavelength and mirrored his silence.

He'd needed this chance, and now perhaps it was all going to be taken away from him. After finally getting himself together, going through the Navy's basic training and an A school, he was finally allowed to try out for the Teams, something his recruiter had promised him. The Navy said they didn't know anything about that promise. When he tried to reach the recruiter, the guy was gone.

So he'd begged and insisted, passing up opportunities to go to Submarine School, based on his test scores which were the highest in the class. He didn't care. He wanted his shot at the SEALs. Finally his orders had come through after months of arguing and fighting with the bureaucracy. It would totally suck if today, because of one fuckin' going away party and a pissed off father of his ex-girlfriend, all of that was going to take away the one chance he had to turn his life around.

Weston Stark was a tall man, easily six-foot-five or so. He loomed over Zak and squeezed his hand like he was at an arm wrestling competition. The handshake hurt like hell.

"Congratulations, son." He motioned for the two of them to take a seat in front of his desk. Zak resisted the urge to flex and unflex his fingers to determine if any of them were broken.

"For what?" Zak shrugged as he lowered himself to the chair. "For ruining my father's car?" He could feel his cell buzzing from messages he'd not picked up.

"No. For enlisting in the Navy. Your mother is quite proud of you. I'm an old friend of hers from college years, you know." Weston gave a feral smile at Zak's mother while she stared down at her lap.

"Well, that must have been yesterday. I doubt today she's very proud of me now," Zack said, trying to get his mom's attention.

"So what line of work are you going for?" Weston was wound up tight, sitting on the edge of his desk, still looming over both Zak and his mother. His suspenders held up expensive dark blue suit trousers. He wore cufflinks, something that wasn't in Zak's wardrobe either.

"I'm starting BUD/S training next week. Qualification to become a SEAL."

"That right?" Stark let his eyebrows raise nearly to his hairline. "Wow. That's admirable. Best of luck with that. A tough course." He quickly glanced between the two of them, his mother still examining her fingers.

"Thanks."

"What made you decide to become, or at least try out for the Teams?"

Zak remembered the day he'd read the article about the kid from Petaluma who had become a Navy SEAL. Ten years ago he and Zak played on the same soccer team for a bit. The boy went on to distinguish himself, and then was killed on his last deployment. Something in Zak's DNA kicked in, and he realized it was time to go prove himself. Though living in Santa Cruz, he snuck up and attended the funeral, dodging local people who would recognize him. Their old coach was there, though. Coach Bardy gave Zak a heavy dose of reality.

"You're a fuckin' screw up, Zak. Had all the potential Joel had, and you just threw it all away." The coach was legendary for his in-your-face sidelines soccer dress-downs, when they were skinny kids just trying not to cry in front of all their teammates. It was what ultimately pushed Zak to football from soccer.

Bardy went on talking about his friend, the home-grown hero, and how Zak didn't have the balls to make it as an elite anything and would never measure up. As the man walked away, Zak was shaking in his shoes, fisting and unfisting his hands, tightening all the muscles in his upper torso. There and then, he decided, with the deepest conviction he'd ever had, that he'd live to make this man wrong.

Stark was still staring at him when Zak looked up. Even his mom was waiting for him to answer the question.

"Just something a man's got to do, I guess. My rite of passage." He carefully calmed his breathing, but his insides were boiling.

Stark crossed his arms over his flat abdomen and slowly nodded, like he expected a longer explanation. Zak had never told anyone about this decision, and wasn't about to do so today.

"Mr. Stark, thanks for your time, but am I going to need a lawyer, sir?" He held his breath for his answer.

"Good question." Stark said as he pointed his fore-finger to Zak like a gun, winking his left eye. With surprising speed, he whipped around the desk to sit in his wine-colored leather chair. Zak sensed the man had been an athlete at one time. He methodically laced his fingers between each other as if it was an art form, resting his forearms on his leather blotter perfectly centered in the middle without any other adornment except for an old snowglobe of a Christmas scene. The globe was missing nearly a third of its liquid and seemed out of place in the office. When Zak focused on it, Stark picked it up and placed it on the credenza behind him like he'd left it out by mistake.

"You live under a lucky star, son." Stark used a lot of big words and said several sentences before Zak realized the likelihood of charges being pressed were minimal. "They could still come after you, but I have it on good authority they're not looking to cite you. I think holding you was just to shake you up a bit, to be perfectly honest."

He felt every muscle in his body relax with the relief that the accident wouldn't taint his chances for the SEAL training. That took the number three concern from Zak's mind. Number two was still the well-being of Ginger. His biggest worry was the confrontation that would in all likelihood take place today with his father.

"Seems your blood alcohol came back clean."

"I told them I wasn't drinking."

"The young woman you were with was way over the legal limit, poor thing." Zak saw the feigned sadness in Stark's face, like that of an undertaker.

"I'll bet." Zak also knew that was the only reason

she'd agreed to go home with him. At first it had been so she wouldn't have to go home with one of his buddies who were all shitfaced. But after she kissed him and perhaps misinterpreted his meaning, he decided to go right along with the little charade and let the drama unfold.

"I think the fact that you were a Navy guy garnered you some points, son."

Thank God for a little break, at least.

"So like I said, your mother brought you in here to beg for me to represent you in what was looking like an ugly, ugly case." He emphasized *ugly* like the preachers he saw on television. The more time Zak spent around Stark the less he thought of him. The word "beg" stuck in his craw.

"Well, that truly is good news, then." Zak put his hand on his mother's shoulder and squeezed, silently asking her to look back at him. He was rewarded with a tired gaze followed up with a smile. The big elephant in the room was that there was still no cause for celebration.

"We even have a good Samaritan who came forward and said she witnessed everything, said the melon truck driver hit *you*. She's a security guard at the Junior College so she's a credible witness."

Stark leaned back in an arch, hands clasped behind his head, elbows out to the sides, looking as pleased as if he'd just told them they'd won the lottery and were millionaires.

Zak nodded. "Okay, then. All I have to do now is go see Dad. Might as well get this over with." Zak stood up and his mother popped up right beside him. Stark came to his feet and leaned over the desk to present a card.

"You make sure your father calls me in case he has any trouble with the insurance company. I have all the information about the woman who was the eye witness, and I'd be happy to share it with him, if he likes."

"Thank you," his mom said as she turned. Zak could tell she was trying to be polite, but when she took his arm, her fingers clutching his forearm, he could tell she wanted to get out of Dodge quick.

Zak held up Stark's card and waved goodbye. "Thanks for your time, sir," he said as he ushered his mother safely out of the office.

He helped her down the brick steps nearing the parked car. Zak finally found his voice. He was always careful with his mother's feelings. She was the only one in the family who supported and believed in him, but she was in a lonely crowd of one. "Geez, Mom, a friend from college? The guy's a shark."

"Was then too," she answered. "Don't ask."

"I just can't see—"

She stopped him before he could finish. "I said,

don't ask. He's good at what he does and let's just leave it at that." She grabbed his arm and they continued to the car.

Zak started to chuckle. "Mom, you got a little bit of the bad boys in your blood, I see."

"I said, shut up."

But Zak could see the little quirk upward on her lips. She was about to smile and really didn't want to.

They drove to the Chambers' residence in silence. Just before they pulled up, Zak dialed Ginger's cell and got her voicemail.

"Hey there, Ginger. This is Zak. Just callin' to see if you're okay and all. I'm so sorry about last night. They told me you were released today, and I just wanted to check in. Give me a call, if you could."

He ignored the several other messages left by his friends. There would be time for that later on. He'd probably need their company soon, after his visit with his dad.

Zak saw a car door open across the street and noticed Amy Dobson walking toward him. He got out quickly, hearing his mother mumble something. She exited the car and proceeded up the walkway to their house ahead of him. Amy waved to her and got a brief return gesture as his mom continued to the house without even pausing.

His ex-girlfriend was looking attractive in a short

black and white polka-dot dress with a neckline he usually liked, showing off her cleavage. He braced himself for an insult, but despite his internal alarm, his unit was reacting, just like every time he saw her. He sighed, but that didn't ease the tension in his body. He'd just dodged a bullet with the accident, and now Amy's presence threatened to drag him back into trouble. All his past poor decisions loomed. He didn't need another one.

She looked up at his bandaged forehead and briefly scanned below to the rest of his body.

"Hey Amy. Today's not a good day." He heard the front door slam shut, which distracted him until he looked back into Amy's eyes.

"I can see that, Zak. Glad to see you're not too hurt." She peered around him to examine the car. "Where's your girlfriend?"

"I don't have a girlfriend."

Amy nodded and stared at her red toes peeking out from high heeled sandals. When her head rose, their eyes connected like they always did, flaming something in his gut that wasn't healthy, like an itch he could never scratch. He gave up trying to analyze it. It was just chemistry.

He had the strength to step back. Zak knew it also wasn't fair to her. Why start something he couldn't finish? Besides, didn't she deserve more respect than that? He just needed to keep that up a little longer, and she'd be gone forever. "I'm just here for the day, headed back down to San Diego before I finish my training, Amy. I'm not back in town."

Her lip curled, and her left eye squinted. Zak looked away down the street trying to find something else to focus on.

"You have time to stop by my place later? I got a couple of things I wanted to discuss with you."

"Nothing to discuss, Amy." He was surprised his resolve was holding.

She rolled her head back, raising her eyebrows. "You never did like to talk much, Zak, but I kinda like it now."

"Well, that's a good thing then. Look, I've got to go. My folks are waiting. If I do anything tonight, it will be with Stan and Roger and the guys."

"And the little girl you brought up from San Diego?"

"I doubt that very much." He wasn't going to tell her she was Roger's little sister and had flown up to attend a family function.

"Love to see you in that uniform." She stepped closer to him but didn't touch. "Even better out of—"

He grabbed her wrists before she could lay her hands against his chest. "Amy, you got me all wrong. Those days are gone. I'm not that man anymore. I have a whole new life I'm going after, and I'm not interested in anything here. Anyone, either."

He released her wrists and watched as she stood before him with her mouth open, those red kissable lips gaping like she'd just seen a ghost. Her hands went down to her sides. He walked past her and up the steps to the front porch of his parents' house, never looking back.

CHAPTER 4

AMY RACED BACK to work, arriving a full half hour late from lunch. Her boss wasn't back yet herself, so she was a bit relieved, but she'd stay the extra thirty minutes just in case anyone else was keeping score.

She knew where they would in all likelihood go tonight. Something told her that if she didn't see him one more time before he went off to the Navy, she'd never see him again. Amy wasn't sure why that was important. But it was.

In the two years since they'd graduated high school she had been restless. She should have gone away to college like so many of her friends had done. But she stayed behind and attended the Junior College, waiting.

For what?

With her mother gone, her father had wanted her to stay in the big house just so he wasn't alone, and at first she agreed. He was lonely after the long battle with cancer her mother had gone through all during Amy's high school, and she secretly hoped he'd start dating again. But his work seemed to occupy all of his time. He seemed to lose all interest in women, and began working such long hours she didn't know when to expect him home anymore.

Being picked up and dropped off at the Chief of Police's house was creating a major damper on her love life. But she didn't want to confront him about it, especially to tell him that. The new recruits on the force were safe for her, because they dared not act out of turn for fear of their jobs. But she wondered how much of their attention was just brownnosing and how much was serious.

She had a stack of brochures from some technical schools on the peninsula in Silicon Valley and San Francisco. That was more to her liking rather than being stuck in Santa Rosa. She was in the process of applying to them when she found out about Zak.

Were they just too young to get together? Was that the problem? God, how she wished she had something like a fantastic new job or some huge opportunity. But she had nothing except a healthy sex drive and a whole lot of history working that angle. Her reputation was legendary. For the first time in her life, she regretted not taking advantage of other choices some of her friends had made. She was being left behind.

She decided perhaps what she needed was just one

more goodbye, and then she'd be done with Zak. Done with Sonoma County. She'd follow where her heart took her, move out of the house and start her new adventure. All she needed was a nice sendoff, and she knew Zak could do that. No strings. Just like the old days. Just a night of sex. And then forget about it until maybe some little high school reunion he probably wouldn't attend. He'd stand there, look at her, and she'd realize—whatever. All this stuff was foolish. She needed to get away from her father's circle of protection and out into the real world.

When she looked back at her life, there were lots of exciting days. But being with Zak made her feel like a woman. Had made her feel like a woman from the first time she'd kissed him. It was something she'd never allowed herself to admit until today.

So, this time, she'd just walk right into his arms with intention, and make the most of her last, carefree fling.

And then she'd grow up.

CHAPTER 5

ZAK'S FATHER WAS waiting at the kitchen table as his mother worked over the stove. He halfway expected his dad to come yelling out the front door, punching and fisting him, making a scene for all the neighbors. But the man he saw sitting there before him was calm, with murderous red eyes. Zak was more scared of him today than he ever had been.

He sat down and his mom handed him a beer, which he waved away. He noted his dad was drinking water.

"I'll take some ice water, Mom."

"So I got a call from my insurance agent this morning. That's when I heard you wrecked the Camaro. You wanna tell me, son, what you were fuckin' thinking borrowing a car *I* didn't even want to drive around last night?"

"I'm sorry, Pop. It was stupid. I should have asked you first. I wasn't gonna drink—"

"Drinkin's got nothing to do with it, Zak. *I* chose not to drive the car, because I was going to go out with friends. Some friends make you stupid. Especially *your* lowlife friends."

Zak bristled. His dad's assortment of friends weren't even allowed in his mother's house. Zak had known Roger and Stan for nearly ten years. But they still weren't saints.

"I'm going to pay you back, Dad. Every penny. I don't care how long it takes."

"That's not the point! The car was never yours to borrow." His father stood, his face bright red, and his ruby-colored eyes looked like they were about to burst. Veins at the sides of his neck pumped venom. Zak was concerned he'd have a heart attack. Even his mother came over and stood between him and his father.

"Jack. Stop it right now. This won't bring the car back, and you could do some serious damage to your health. Sit down. We need to talk about this."

His father piled his arms up over his head, sucked in air and screamed. "Goddammit, Zak. Why? How could you be so stupid?" When he lowered his arms, Zak could see he'd been crying.

Zak jumped up and hugged his father. The car had meant more to him than anything else he owned. How he wished he could bring back the last twenty-four hours and have a do-over. "By everything inside me,

I'll get you another car. I'll help fix it up with you again, Dad. I'll pay you back every penny for all the parts, all the work done to it."

"You don't have that kind of money, son, and you never will." His father's arms pushed him away, shoulders lowered, face resigned. Zak's heart broke for the man.

"I don't care how long it takes. I'll pay you back. That's a promise." He said from the space between them.

His mother added, "Jack, at least Zak wasn't hurt, or we'd be sitting by a hospital bed. Don't forget that. The girl is okay as well. And from what I understand, this had nothing to do with drinking, either." Her stern gaze to her husband's eyes told him she meant business. "We have to keep things in perspective. Zak goes off to the Navy. We find out what happens with the insurance. We just hope they don't come back and find him at fault or charged with anything. That would restrict him from joining his SEAL training, right?"

Jack Chambers was still red. He listened, nodded his head. "I have to get away from here, or I'll say things to both of you I'll regret." His lined face looked painfully up to Zak. "This is way more beyond insurance, or the fuckin' money. It has to do with trust. I can't trust you anymore, Zak. I don't think I ever could!" His father turned on his heel and left the house.

His mother waited until her husband started the motor to their Toyota and sped down the street.

"I'm so sorry, Mom. I wish I'd thought about all this last night. I just didn't use my head. I'm going to work very hard to make sure those days are gone forever. Forever, Mom. I want to be the kind of son you can depend on."

"You already are. You have your whole life ahead of you. Jack will learn to get over it in time. I guess helping him is my job now. You go be with your friends, say your final goodbyes, and then you get out of this town and don't look back."

STAN AND ROGER met him at the brewpub. First thing he asked Roger was how his sister was. Zak ordered mineral water.

"Ginger's fine. She didn't even want to go to the hospital. But they thought she'd had a concussion. I guess she just got the wind knocked out of her, and yeah, she was pretty scared."

"I tried to leave her a message," said Zak.

"Yeah, she got it. She's going home tomorrow. Taking it easy at my folks today before she flies home. She's not mad. My mom is, though."

"I'll bet."

"Zak, it could have happened to anyone." Stan's upbeat voice didn't cheer Zak.

Zak thought about it for a minute. "I kissed her, Roger. Took my eyes off the road for one second, and that's when the truck hit her side. I'm so sorry, man."

"Yeah. She told me. Nice to hear it from you, though." Roger wasn't smiling.

"God, I've really fucked up, guys. I've got to change my ways. This is a wake-up call."

"We feel kind of responsible for inviting you up for the party. Some send-off this is. I wouldn't be able to live with myself if you'd done something to mess up your Navy gig, Zak," said Stan. "You were talking last night about Joel, and how you wanted to go do something like he did, be a hero, make something of your life, and look what happened. It would kill me if you messed up that chance."

"I think I'm more determined than before," said Zak.

"You know Joel very well?" Roger asked.

"Not since we were teens. Helluva soccer player. I don't know, he was a born leader. It's like we'd be down, he'd stand up straight, look into the sunlight almost, he'd say something inspirational and the guys on our team would just come together. We'd win against teams we had no right to win against. Never seen anyone like that before, or since."

"He liked you, too," said Stan.

"Yeah, he did. Tried to keep up with him through

high school, though he was a year ahead of me. After he joined the Navy, I never heard from him again. Wish I had."

"He had a big influence on you. Never realized that until last night, the way you talked about him," said Roger.

"He's the reason I joined. No this, this thing I'm doing. It's exactly the right thing for me. I'm ready for this. I may not make it, but I could be a Navy guy. I just wanted to test my limits, you know, see how far I could go."

"You've got a lot more balls than I do. Gotta respect you for trying, Zak," said Roger.

"So you going back tomorrow?" Stan asked.

"Wish I could take off right now. But no, I think I gotta say goodbye to my folks one last time, maybe say goodbye to Ginger?" Zak looked up at Roger who looked like he'd chewed a sour lemon.

"Whoa! I wouldn't do that. She's fine. Besides, you can always look her up in San Diego later. She's okay. I'll give her your goodbye wishes. Just stay away from my folks."

Zak agreed. He stood. "Look, I'm going to head back home. Been a long couple of days, and I want to be rested for the drive back. Thanks, guys, for everything. Maybe the next celebration will be under better circumstances."

Zak took a last look at 4th Street, a street his father had driven up and down on Friday and Saturday nights in muscle cars back in the days when they'd go "tooling 4th" as they called it. He smiled when he thought about how happy his father must have been during those days. The way he talked about it made Zak feel like he was right there beside him the whole way. The destruction of the Camaro was more than about the car. He'd managed to eliminate the thin threads his father had to a cherished life now lost forever. He'd hold the heaviness, feel the weight of his guilt all throughout his training and maybe, just maybe, the hard physical work would pound it out of him. Maybe.

He heard a noise behind him. Turning, he saw Amy Dobson.

"Hello, Zak."

"Amy—I'm not in the mood—"

"Come on, Zak, it's been, what—nearly three years since we last spoke?"

"We spoke this afternoon, Amy."

"I mean, since we really talked. Can't you give me just five minutes of your time?" She held her fingers out, measuring, showing him how small five minutes would look, as if it was something she could hold. Her charm bracelet jingled and glinted in the night air. He'd made a lot of good decisions this afternoon and realizations about his future. He wasn't going to drink, he was going to go to bed early. He was going to head back to face his future and the biggest challenge he'd ever faced.

"Five minutes, Amy," he said as he held up his splayed fingers. Walking to his truck, he unlocked the passenger door, let Amy climb up inside, then walked around the front and sat behind the wheel. Night dew had formed droplets of water on the windshield, blurring car lights as they passed by.

Her scent came to him like it always did, at first itching his nose, then enveloping him in a familiar aura he'd lost himself in so many times over the years. The elixir of her just sitting beside him made his heart beat faster. His head cleared, pushing away the cobwebs of all the hurt and guilt he'd been feeling. A lightness came upon him. Was this how it was when a person was addicted to drugs? Did the anticipation of something that would take his mind off his problems give the addict a bit of clarity before the plunge downward?

And would this be a plunge downward? Was this good for him or bad for him? This was no celebration. The whole trip had become something entirely different than a celebration. It was like a tearing away of something, cutting the cord of something, eliminating his road back. Somehow, he knew that the man who would return after his BUD/S experience wouldn't be the same one he started the training with.

He dared a glance over to her. She slowly turned her eyes up to his. He could see the need in her face and her recognition that he'd also missed their times together. But, she didn't move, and neither did he.

"You once asked me why we never talked," she said carefully. Her eyes twinkled, and she moistened her lips. "Maybe it's about time we did. Just talk."

Zak saw she was trying to hide the smile forming on her left side, in spite of her efforts. That little twitch of her mouth spoke volumes.

"Is that what you want, Amy?"

"I wanted you to know that I'm proud of you, Zak. And I want to be here for you when you come home."

"What does that mean?"

"I'll wait for you."

"You? You never waited for anything in your life, Amy. I can't ask you to do that."

"I know you can't make any commitments, but I've changed. And what hasn't changed, I want to. I want to become the girl you come home to."

"No, that's not how it works. I can't offer you anything. Anything at all, Amy. I may never come back here. If I wash out of BUD/S, I might get sent off to the fleet and be gone for a year. I can't have you holding onto me. I just don't need that. It feels dishonest. I don't want to do that anymore. Do you understand?"

"Then trust me to wait for you? Trust me?"

Zak placed his palm against her cheek. One tear streamed down her face. “No, Amy. I can’t ask that of you. I don’t know where my head will be. I just have to focus on what’s ahead. Please don’t change anything for me. I’m not worth it. Really, I’m not.” He could see it had finally sunk in. “Amy, we’re going in two separate directions. We have two separate paths to follow.”

She removed his hand from her face and held it in her lap. “Okay, Zak. Then let’s just say goodbye nicely. Just one more time together and then we both go our separate ways. No strings. No agreements or commitments. Let’s just part friends, good friends with a past we enjoyed together, okay? Can you do that?”

He did trust her, and it overrode his better judgment. Touching Amy had been a huge mistake. Now as her forefinger traced up and down his palm to his wrist and back again, the back of his hand against the fabric of her dress, feeling her thigh underneath, he could feel his resolve melting. He’d done so many things without thinking, it was new to be thinking carefully about whether or not to be with Amy one last time. She wanted it, he knew that. But damn, he wanted it too. Could he justify it as a way to say goodbye? Was it taking something from her to have a pleasurable encounter and then part? Was there dishonor in this, or was it a natural cycle, a final farewell to their relationship?

He smiled and cocked his head. "I think we've said more words tonight than we ever have had in the past."

She matched his grin. "I guess maybe we're growing up, Zak. I'm ready for a good old-fashioned grownup good-bye. How about you?"

"I think I can do that." He leaned over and kissed her. Amy let him lead and when she didn't pull him to her he wasn't sure at first if she really wanted him or not. But as her lips parted and she accepted him, as their kiss deepened, he could feel her fire burning, waiting to envelop both of them.

Her fingertips touched his face as they parted. Her brown eyes were honest, as tears continued to roll down her cheeks. "Thank you." She brushed back her cheeks and sighed. "You know where I'd like to go?"

"I think I do." Zak smiled back at her, turning to start the truck.

"You have a—" Amy looked over the seat to the small king cab seat behind them and found the familiar quilt folded there. "You still have it," she said as her face lit up.

Zak shrugged his shoulders, bringing his arm around her shoulders. "Part of my truck, I guess." Looking down the road he realized for the first time since he'd been home, he was relaxed and actually looking forward to the next few minutes with her.

CHAPTER 6

OAK TREES ARCHED overhead just like they always did, but Amy saw in their shadows a greeting, as if they were welcoming her home. She'd been to the golf course many times during the daytime over the past couple of years, even recently, but this was their favorite spot. She loved the smell of the fresh cut lawn, the sound of the night birds, how the stars twinkled so brightly, away from nearby harsh lighting.

Zak even parked in the spot he always parked before, at the end of the first row, turning off the motor. Headlights illuminated the course in the distance, rising and falling in swales and hills dancing in the shadows.

"You sure about this?" he asked her.

Amy knew the answer, squeezing his hand. "Yes. Completely." But she still felt a little scared even though her heart was beating with anticipation.

For the first time ever, she wanted him to know

how much she'd missed him. What if it felt different? What if that luxurious chemistry they had was gone? What if they didn't have that spark, that feedburner of passion usually enveloping them? Would it still be okay?

He led her out from his side of the truck. They walked hand in hand, his left arm cradling the comforter. Frogs from the numerous creeks nearby abruptly stopped as they walked closer to their hiding places. She heard an owl overhead.

"Sure hope the sprinklers are turned off," Zak chuckled in reference to one of the times they'd been sprayed with water in the middle of having sex. She'd forgotten about that time, and it brought a smile to her face.

Zak lay the blanket down and sat. Amy took up her place next to him.

"This is the last thing in the world I thought I'd be doing tonight," Zak said.

"It's like, well," Amy hesitated, but continued, "I've thought about what it would be like to be with you one more time. I've thought so much about it, I kind of don't know how to act."

"Come here."

His kiss put her right back where she belonged. He smelled like the man she knew growing up. The feel of his cheek against hers, the taste on his lips was all what she'd remembered, dreamt about.

His hand slipped up under the hem of her dress as he stroked her backside. Amy leaned into him as he lay back, allowing her to ride his thigh. His fingers snagged her panties and slipped them down one side while she helped with the other, pushing herself against the length of his upper leg when she was free of her undergarment. She unbuttoned his jeans, and her fingers found him just as she always had. Squeezing his package she helped him ease his pants down over his hips with her other hand. He pushed her back against the blanket, hiking up her dress.

He dug into his pockets, fumbling a little and produced a foil packet. She took it from him, opened it and sheathed it over him. "I always loved this part," she whispered to him.

"Are we sure what we're doing here?" he asked.

"Ask me if I'm ever sure about anything, Zak. Are you?"

She felt and tasted some nervousness from him as they kissed. Before long, the heat came up between them and she was gasping for air. She noticed his breathing had shortened. His hands were smoothing over her breasts, her shoulders, her back and up the long ridge of her thigh.

He pressed himself against her opening and waited. Bending down to kiss her again, he said, "Amy, you know this is goodbye, right? I just want to be sure you are okay with us this way."

She smiled as he pressed, beginning to breach her opening, agreeing with him. "Why, what were you thinking?" She raised her knee, allowing him to slide inside. Looking into each other's eyes, he entered fully to the hilt. His thumbs smoothed over her cheeks. He dipped his head down as their lips barely touched for a couple of tender, soft nibbles. She grabbed the back of his neck, pulling him down and deepening his kiss. She arched, first to accept him fully and then releasing as their familiar rhythm began to pulse. His hot breath in her ear, the kisses he covered her neck with, the way he lifted her buttocks up and hiked her knees above him urgently telling her of his need ignited the fire in her soul.

He let out a small groan as his breath hitched. She pressed her chest against his, feeling the strength of his heart beating against hers, loving the feel that her arms could not fully encircle him. Her hands moved up and down the bulging muscles of his back. She held his hips as he undulated into her, pressing himself up and deep inside her.

Her natural instincts were to be urgent with him, but she let the rhythm build between them, long and slow, each coming together and parting approaching that oneness they used to feel as they made love. She never wanted it to end.

Already her body was spasming to his penetration, her muscles milking him. The familiar tingling sensation began spreading all over her body. Her spine became warm and liquid. Her knees hugged his sides as her legs crossed over his back. His rough kiss matched the urgent cry coming from deep inside his chest as he stilled, arched and she felt the familiar pulsing of his buried cock.

"Oh, Zak. Not yet."

"I can't help it, Amy. Ah! So sorry."

She found herself laughing lightly, snuggling with him as he kissed her chest, laughing too. "Oh, I remember this. I remember how wonderful I felt afterwards," she whispered to the stars.

"I do too. I remember it all. It comes back to me in dreams all the time."

"Really?" She looked at him askance. She felt him lurch and then sharply inhale. She lowered one leg to the side, but kept the other one crossing his rear.

"Well, not every time, but a lot of times. Those were good days, Amy. Crazy, but good days. I spent a lot of time being angry at you."

"I remember. I liked making you jealous."

"But I couldn't stay away."

"Yeah. And I was glad. I didn't want you to." She remembered how intensely she had felt. "You scared me. How I felt about you scared me. Like it was way too soon."

"It was too soon. Hell, we were just kids." His thumbs caressed her cheeks again. He kissed her tenderly. "Amy, you know what I mean about it being too soon?"

"Correct," she said as she pinched his nose. "Playing grownups, but not having a clue what it was all about."

She inhaled, as something hurt inside her heart. She turned her head to the right to distract herself, watching the smooth green of the course round the top of a small hill, the blades of grass shining in the moonlight. She knew she was on borrowed time.

"You okay?"

"Of course, never better." She giggled, hoping it would cheer her up more than it did.

"What's so funny?"

"I was just thinking that whenever I see a golf course, I think of these times we had. I think of you."

"Obviously you haven't taken it up."

"Never. I'd bust a gut. Honest. I couldn't do it."

Zak rolled to his back, hiking up his jeans and stared up to the stars. His hands were threaded across his chest. She folded her dress against her thigh and assumed the same position. It was a nice feeling having his warm body along the length of hers. There was something clean and honest about the way she felt, unlike before.

She could tell he'd fallen asleep so she turned carefully and watched him for a few minutes before he opened his eyes again. She wondered what he was thinking and dreaming of, if she was part of that vision.

"Sleep. I won't be getting much of it very soon now."

"Part of the training?"

"After the initial few weeks, we have Hell Week. We get like forty-five minutes sleep in five, six days."

"I know you'll make it, Zak."

"Less than ten percent chance. I doubled up on my PT before coming up here, but I've missed a couple of days."

"I believe in you, Zak. I always have."

"Thanks. I'm ready. Ready to start my life."

The comment shouldn't have hurt her, but it did. He was ready to start his life, and she wasn't really a part of it. But an agreement was an agreement, and they'd decided it would be no strings, no long goodbyes. Just a send-off.

The comforter was getting damp in the night air and despite her trying not to, she shivered. Zak immediately leapt to action, pulling one corner over her shoulder, holding it down with his long arm. She felt comfortable leaning against him, listening to the sounds of his breathing. She never wanted the moment to be over, but after several minutes she felt Zak stiffen. He uncrossed and stretched his long legs, squeezed her shoulder and said, "You ready?"

Was she ready? Hell no. But it was what she'd agreed. She'd done all the begging she would do. He was going to go off and challenge himself to do something no human had a right to think they could do. That meant that despite how she felt, she'd be strong, show him her strong side. But inside she wanted to beg him to never leave her side.

She knew the only possibility she'd get him back was if she looked like she was strong enough to let him go.

CHAPTER 7

ZAK'S FOCUS ABRUPTLY shifted the first time he hit the cold water during the early phases of the BUD/S training. His swim time was good, but his running time sucked, landing him in the bottom third of the class during several initial runs. He deemed this to be unacceptable.

At night, all he could do was take a quick shower, stretch out a bit and then hit the sack. He tried not to be noticed by the instructors. Tried not to even make eye contact with others, since that one could be gone the next morning. As he looked over the class of recruits, which had dwindled down to less than half, he couldn't tell anymore who would make it and who wouldn't. He didn't even know if he'd make it or not. The only thing he thought about was not quitting.

A friend of his had to be medically rolled due to shin splints. Another recruit shattered his shoulder when one of the telephone poles came down on him.

He was forced to DOR and not allowed to return with that type of injury. The helmets lined up as the colors changed through all the phases of the training.

He'd developed a swim buddy who helped his times as they swam drag for each other and then one day, Dan just wasn't there anymore. Only thing left was his red helmet with their class number on it in white and Dan's last name: Snyder.

After BUD/S, he relaxed. The instructors still gave him trash talk, but they looked at the recruits differently. He didn't know what exactly they were looking for, so Zak decided it wasn't any of his business, he'd just stay quiet and do his job. It pissed him off when he saw a foreign trainee receive special favors from the instructors. He caught himself harboring malicious thoughts, reeling them in after hearing some of the other guys complaining too. He couldn't afford to be indignant. This wasn't the time for that.

Eventually his aloof attitude got noticed, and for the first time he felt they were looking to pick a scab. A couple of the other recruits started referring to him as the Gentleman Frog, as if he was from a privileged background.

"You got a problem hanging with the rest of us in the slime pool?" One of the recruits asked him one day. Several of the instructors looked up.

Zak had left a space between himself and the African American recruit for Charlie, who normally took that spot. He was being watched by the instructor table.

"Thought Charlie was gonna sit there. Just leaving his spot."

Recruit Carter smiled, showing a gold tooth in the front. "You see Charlie anywhere?" He motioned with his fork.

Zak scanned the room and didn't see the frizzy-haired kid he thought looked like a weasel. He shook his head.

Carter stared at the seat next to him like it had a blood stain on the bench and then back up to Zak.

Zak decided to make his comment loud enough for the instructors to hear too. "Carter, you want to cuddle, I'll cuddle with you for a bit, keep your ass warm, but that's as far as it goes," Several recruits began laughing. Carter had a piece of bread thrown at him, and the tension was broken.

Carter became one of his circle of close friends.

"I like you, white boy. You don't stick your nose where it don't belong," Carter said. "You got a past?"

"Doesn't everybody?" Zak answered.

"Oh, that they do. I'm actually lucky to be here." Carter looked out over the inlet as they sat in the sand, eating ice cream.

"Me too," Zak admitted.

"You got trouble with The Man back home?"

"Who? You mean my dad?"

"Fuck no. The Law. You have trouble with the law?"

Zak smiled and licked his ice cream.

"Oh yeah, that. That memory. I wanna know about that," Carter barked, punching him in the arm.

"Just the Chief's daughter. Lovely daughter."

"Oh snap, froglet! I'd be dead if I tried that. I'm guessing her and her dad's white?"

"Yes."

"Hell, I wouldn't even try one of the black Chiefs in my home town in Louisiana. I thought you had some past." He wiped his fingers clean. "What'd you do?"

"Just pranks. Pumpkins in the pool. Jell-O in the other school's fountain."

"What the hell you talkin' about? You get arrested for throwing pumpkins and shit? I never heard about no Jell-O bandit. You bad. You a bad dude!"

Ever after that day, Zak's nickname was changed to Jell-O. Carter never let him forget he wasn't a real bad-ass, and Zak didn't want to touch what was in Carter's background. He was a fellow recruit.

He worried about what he would do to start paying his dad back, since he'd only been able to save about one thousand dollars. He didn't do much dating, and kept himself on a strict budget so he could save as much as possible, but he never could get ahead.

As the weeks went by he was so exhausted he couldn't remember even his own past, let alone anyone else's. He'd throw himself in bed at night, see another empty bed occasionally and not run to hear the story, but wait until someone told him. It just happened. People stayed. People left. That was the way it was. He had too much work to think about it anymore. He was in it until he felt like quitting, and each day didn't become that day.

Only Easy Day Was Yesterday was a suitable motto for this kind of training. He knew it would never get easier, just easier to deal with. That's why he was here.

OVER THE COURSE of the next few weeks, the team bonded into a cohesive unit. Zak always deferred to others to lead, but when asked, stepped up to the plate and did his job. He never again sought out the anonymity of being a loner and he began to settle into a routine so that by the time the thirty recruits graduated, he felt like he'd die for any one of them.

His folks came down for the Trident ceremony. Over their weekend stay, he showed them what he could of Coronado. He took them to some of his favorite watering holes and noticed at every turn his dad didn't order alcohol.

"He's trying very hard, Zak," his mother told him one time while his dad was in the head. "Going to meetings, doing some light workouts. Doesn't stay down at the shop as much as he used to, and of course isn't always tinkering with that car." She stared down at her French fries.

"What did the insurance come up with?"

"Peanuts, really. He had it insured as an antique, but that didn't give him the real value to him, you know, didn't compensate for all the time he put in, and the labor he traded to fix it up. He got a check, but not enough to buy something else he felt like tackling, and way short of the real value of the car. You know how that goes. You learn from your mistakes."

"Not fair."

"Well, let's just say we'd do it differently another time, except that there won't be a next time. That was that." She looked at him hard. "Perhaps this was a good thing. Never seen him so determined to get back into shape. He's a different man when he's not drinking, Zak. I think he wants you to be proud of him."

Jack Chambers approached. "We done? Nice sunny day, good day for walking around." He put his hand on his wife's neck and gave her a peck on the cheek. It hadn't been very long ago when his dad would have preferred to stay in a darkened bar for hours on end.

Zak chose to bring up the subject of money one last time before his parents left. "Dad, I'm saving to pay you back."

His dad stared down at his feet and didn't say anything.

"Sorry to say, I've only managed to save about a grand. But it's yours. I'm giving you a check before you go."

"Nah, not necessary, Zak." Still, his dad wouldn't look at him. "Not like you have a real job, anyway. Doesn't seem right taking that from you."

Real job?

He had to say something, even if it upset his dad. "This is a real job. It's the hardest fuckin' thing I've ever done."

"I didn't mean that. I just think you need to put the past aside. You're never going to be able to pay it all back, so just quit trying. I've given up. So should you."

"But I owe you, Dad. I want to make it right."

"Forget it, Zak. You saved me from the folly of my past, in a way. Your mom will tell you I was one pissed off guy. She reminds me every day maybe I loved that car too much. Now. If you ever want to borrow another one, just for the record, the answer is no."

Before his parents left, his mother asked him if he'd had any communication with Amy. Zak told her the truth: no.

"She came by the house one day, brought me some flowers, and asked about you. I let her in. Told her you'd just made it through BUD/S and were off for your other training. We had tea. She thanked me."

"I hope you were okay with that. I haven't talked to her since the night before I left. We agreed to leave it that way, Mom."

"She looks different. She's moving to San Francisco, she said. She told me to say hi and to call her if you felt like it." His mom smiled.

"What?"

"She said she had stopped herself several times from dialing your number, because that's what you'd agreed."

"We did. What's so danged funny?"

"She said talking to me was breaking the rules a bit, but then she said you two always did break a few rules along the road."

"That's true. That's certainly true." Zak was thinking those were the best parts of their relationship.

"So I guess I'm breaking a few of my own. I told you to stay away from the Amys of the world. Now I'm not so sure about that. I think she really cares for you."

AMY DIDN'T CALL him, and he wasn't going to start that up again. He needed to focus on his training. After his parents left, he tore into his studies, preparing for the underwater diving school in Florida, some jump schools, and his stint at Quantico. After that, there was talk of them doing some jungle training south of the border or back up to Alaska. He didn't care what it was. He was all in for whatever the Navy was going to shove at him.

He was proud of himself for staying unattached, because he saw how hard it was on the married guys, especially the married ones with kids at home. It changed their focus, he thought. How could it not? Right now, he knew the only time he'd be able to get more than casual with a woman was if she allowed him to have his primary loyalty to his country and to his fighting brothers. Nothing could come between him and that bond. He was grateful he didn't have to choose.

CHAPTER 8

AMY BEGAN TRAINING in San Francisco selling high-end condominiums for a large developer. The job came with wonderful perks. She got a one bedroom unit overlooking Ferry Plaza and the Bay Bridge, which included access to the exclusive gym, conference rooms for meetings with clients and a secure garage to park in.

One of her favorite walks was down the Piers, wandering through shops and boutique grocery stores where they sold hand-milled soaps, fresh-pressed olive oils and vegetables straight from the farms up north. It was an upscale farmer's market, not unlike what she was used to in Santa Rosa. Several vendors she recognized from there, including her favorite egg lady, where she bought blue and green eggs once a week.

She studied for and passed her real estate exam in the months that followed. Her father worried she was living in the City, but even he ventured to visit on a couple of occasions. One time he brought someone with him.

Marlene was a redhead with green eyes, and Amy could tell her father was totally smitten with her. She was lively, like Amy had always been. About ten years younger than her dad, she brought out some of the parts of his personality Amy hadn't seen for years. It was as if he was growing younger before her eyes. Marlene had all sorts of plans to come down and go shopping with Amy, and the idea made Amy a little uncomfortable. But as they were talking, she found herself agreeing to a future date to do just that. Her dad seemed to be delighted the two of them got along so well.

Before they left, her father ventured a private discussion with Amy. "I'm still concerned about you living down here where there are so many places you could get into trouble."

"I don't go to those places."

"But you can't avoid them. They're all around."

"Dad, you have to let go. You have to let me live my life."

"I just get so nervous thinking about you being alone here, too far away from my protection."

She kissed him. "That's sweet, Dad, but I don't need that protection now. I'm fine. This is about the safest place I could live. Honest. We have a security guard downstairs. No one comes in or up the elevators without key cards, and access to the garage is restricted."

"I know. But things can be stolen."

"Why? When there are so many other places much easier to get into? Why would they bother to rob or cause a problem here where the security is so tight?"

"I know. Probably just my active imagination." They hugged one more time, waiting for Marlene.

"She's nice, Dad. I like her."

"I do too, Amy." He stared down the hallway as Marlene's compact frame came barreling around the corner and toward them. "She's good for me," he whispered, then embraced Marlene and planted a kiss on her forehead.

"Thanks, Amy," said Marlene, her face blushing from the kiss. "I'll call you and we'll set that shopping date."

"You bet. Midweek is best for me, since I work heaviest on the weekends."

"Good for me, too. Bye."

She watched them head to the elevators, closed the tall solid mahogany door to her unit, leaned against it, and sighed. She picked up the remnants of their plates, taking them to the kitchen, and returned to her living room. Hand on her hips, she surveyed the view of the bay. She could see the smooth waters of the inlet from

San Francisco to Oakland. The island to the left. The busy Ferry Plaza and Pier was teaming with tourists, even on a weekday.

The San Francisco side of the bay was still bright white, buildings looking like a bunch of folded paper cups of various sizes, anchored by tall dark spires. There was a rhythm, a pulse here. A sort of order to the way life went. She wasn't yet a part of it fully, but was stepping closer to an experience outside her control. She was partially fearful, but mostly, she was ready to join her next great adventure.

Was this how Zak felt? She wondered if he ever thought about her. On a nice clear day like today, this was something she'd like to share with him some time.

SEVERAL MONTHS LATER her Saturday was shattered by a stream of bright red lights and piercing sirens as paramedic vans and police cars, even a fire engine, zoomed past her glass Model Home office on the ground floor. Crowds of people began spilling out from buildings nearby, heading towards the Pier. News crews arrived and attempted to get parking.

One lone figure in disheveled green clothes, came running from the crowd that had gathered, and abruptly turned in front of her office. With his hands tucked into his jacket he lost his balance and tripped over her sandwich sign, toppling it. When he picked it up, the man's hands were bloodied, and left a bloody print on the sign as he righted it. His wild hair was pushed off his high forehead. His light chocolate skin and large brown eyes framed lips that showed a purple cast to them. He stared into the glass at Amy, his eyes full and round. He yanked on the doors, which were securely locked, waiting for her to release the button. Amy knew letting him in would be a horrible mistake.

He shook both handles, attempting to jiggle the glass, yelling something in a dialect she didn't understand, tugging and pulling on the doors in panic. He shoved against the doors with his shoulder, and although the glass bent slightly, they remained intact and didn't shatter.

Amy dialed 911, and then decided to call building security. She pushed the red button and heard a small alarm go off somewhere upstairs. The man stormed off to the left, barreling down the street, leaving a bloody print on the glass in front of her.

For several seconds Amy stared at the bloody print, frozen in place. Lights continued to flash outside, noises were escalating. She heard no shots fired and no other signs of violence or struggle. No blasts. But her eyes fixated on the red handprint with one bloody drip trailing down over the smooth clean surface of the door.

Doors behind her opened and she started, whipping around to find one building security guard entering through the rear entrance behind her, calling her name. When he reached the lobby, she noticed he was unarmed.

"I—I'm okay, but there was a guy out there with blood on his hands." Her voice was shrill. She could barely speak. Amy saw another security guard running toward the doors and stop just short, seeing the blood on the handles.

"I'll buzz him through," said the other guard as he pressed the entry button.

Amy pushed with her shoulder, letting in the second guard. "Bring in the sandwich sign," she called to him. "Don't touch where he did."

The guard reached low, bringing the sign inside the lobby, setting it down gently on the granite tile. They let the doors lock into place. A large crowd was gathering in the street over by the plaza.

"What happened?" asked Amy. "Does anyone know?"

One of the guards had been monitoring chatter on his radio. "I guess there's been a shooting at the Plaza."

"Listen," said the second guard, "I've got to help Kwon over at the Building One desk. The occupants are bound to start calling and coming home soon. You okay here?"

"Sure. You both can go. I'm safe here. Not going

anywhere. I'll call the police so they can check out the blood. I'll make sure you get copied. I can let myself up to my floor through the back. I'm closing this place down."

After they left, Amy turned on her laptop and read about the shooting just being reported in the local news. Someone had shot at a military man and his wife who were taking a stroll down the Pier. His rifle had jammed after the first spray of rounds, which also caught several bystanders in the crowd. The Marine was killed by the shooter, while an accomplice stabbed the wife several times. She'd been taken to the hospital, and was now reported in critical condition.

Observers said that one assailant was dropped at the scene by one of the man's buddies, also a Marine, who was wearing a firearm. The second one got away.

Amy's stomach clenched as she realized she'd seen the face of one of the killers. She tried to remember everything about the assailant, recalling what he was wearing, what the shape of his face was.

She called San Francisco P.D. and reported what she had seen and agreed to wait until someone came by to take her statement. She shut down the lights, but remained back at her desk, following all the rushing back and forth of crowds, ready to bolt to the back if she saw someone coming toward the door. Several pedestrians walked past the doors, pointing to the blood on the handles. That certainly deterred someone from wanting to come inside the Sales Office.

News reports came in over the two hours she waited. Feeling somewhat like a fish in a glass bowl, she moved her computer and things to the kitchen area and set up at the table there, out of view of the public. Her heart was beating furiously. She knew the doors were secure but would not hold up against a bomb blast, and some on the news were reporting the backpack found had some small explosive devices in it that had remained unused.

Her cell phone rang and she jumped several inches from her chair. She thought about her dad, and cursed herself for not thinking to call him. She knew he'd be frantic with worry. She answered her phone.

"This is Detective Lombardi, San Francisco P.D. Looking for Amy Dobson."

"This is she."

"You're at the MegaOne complex still?"

"Yes."

"You reported seeing a man you think might be a suspect?"

"I don't know. His hands were bloody. He tried to come in the building, but I didn't buzz him through."

"You got a good look at him, ma'am?"

"Yes. He looked right at me."

"Okay, we're gonna send a couple guys over there

and a sketch artist. Where can we find you?"

"Could you meet me at my condo? I'm up on the tenth floor. I'm getting the creeps staying down here—"

"Sorry, no. I think we need meet you there. I'll try not to make you wait longer than need be. Are you injured in any way?"

"No. And I have security I can call if I get nervous." She gave them the address of the corner Sales Office.

"We got someone over in your other lobby interviewing people. Geez, you were right there, only five blocks away." He put his hand over the phone and barked out instructions. "Okay, stay in touch with your security team and don't move. Keep your cell by you and keep it charged. We'll be over as soon as we can."

After Amy hung up, she plugged her cell into the wall socket, thanking her lucky stars for the strong WiFi signal throughout the entire building. She next called the security station and left a message she was still in the Sales Office waiting for the police. Then she called her dad.

Her father had just been told about the event in San Francisco.

"I saw him, Dad. I think I saw one of the guys."

"Hold tight, Amy, I'm coming down."

"No, don't. I'm fine. The building is very safe. The police are on their way to interview me. I don't want you down here. There are so many people all over the place, and I just—"

She finally broke down. Tears started streaming down her cheeks. She realized she'd been jumping at the sound of every siren, every flashing light coming into the lobby area. Her body was on overload.

"That's it, Amy. I'll be down in an hour. Don't go anywhere until I see you."

It didn't do any good to ask her dad to not come. She hung up the phone, sat in the dark, waiting. Her neck hurt. Her toes were cramped in the high heels she'd been wearing, so she kicked them off. She got herself a bottled water and gulped it half down before spilling it on herself. Her hands shook. Another loud peal of a rescue vehicle made her jump again.

She went into the small guest bathroom off the hallway and sat on the closed lid of the toilet and put her head in her hands. It felt good to be in the semi-darkness of that tiny room, somewhat muffled by all the noises around her. She finished the water and then stood, examining herself in the mirror. She could see the worry lines form in the middle of her forehead, her eyes were red from crying and her hair was a mess. She looked as old and tired as she felt.

A knock on the glass doors caught her attention. Two men were waiting for her, both plainclothes. She buzzed them through after she saw their badges.

"So you're Amy Dobson?" the taller one said as the

doors clicked into place behind him.

"Yes."

"I'm Detective Scarpelli, and this is Mears, our sketch artist. Can we ask you a couple of questions?"

"Sure."

"Our photographer is around here somewhere, but he's a little busy."

"Can you tell me what happened?"

"Well, we're trying to put all that together. Unfortunately, we got one dead and several injured. Beyond what you hear in the news, I can't really give you anything, sorry."

"I know."

"So tell me what you saw?"

"He was a light chocolate brown-skinned man with curly hair, not real long, but curly."

"Approximately when was this?"

"Right after the sirens and things started zooming by—like within a minute after I heard the first one."

"About three-ten, then?"

"Something like that. I wasn't looking at my watch. Maybe the security guards would have a time."

"Okay, so his hair, you said it was curly?"

"Yes. Black."

"Like an Afro?"

"No, long and wavy. Maybe four inches long, just coming out all over the place. Like Garfunkle?"

"The singer?"

"Sorry, yeah. My mom always—"

"Hey, I got 'em in my family too. Hippies."

"Well, she wasn't a hippie, she just liked folk music. Anyway. Coming out like that." She gestured holding her palms all around her head.

The sketch artist began to draw. "Shape of the face?"

"Long. Thin nose, tapered. Big round brown or blackish brown eyes. His lips looked kind of purple? I know it doesn't make sense, so maybe it was the light?" she squinted.

Behind them there was tapping on the glass.

She saw a photographer taking pictures of the handles and the lobby through the glass. Another had roped off a triangle with yellow tape, keeping people away from the door.

"You wanna let him in?"

Amy buzzed the photographer and two other officers inside. They began taking pictures of the sandwich sign. Someone outside was investigating the outside glass door.

The sketch artist drew up a shape, hair, eyes. "Like this?" he said as he held up his tablet.

"Yes. Except deep, like dark colored marks under his eyes, like this," she showed them where her under eyes were puffy and red. "Darker brown, a little purple."

"Would you say he looked African, like East African, or African-American?"

"He didn't look African-American. He looked like he was from Somalia or Ethiopia. And he was thin. Very skinny. Like he wasn't from here, you know?"

After a few more questions and getting the names of the security guards, the two detectives left. Before the crime scene guys left, they took pictures of the entire space, including the hallway to the upper floor elevators outside the back door.

"We'll probably have someone posted here overnight. You have another one of these?" he said as he lifted the sign.

"Yes."

"Okay, good. Someone will be over to clean up and take down the tape. You going to be open tomorrow?"

"I—I wasn't sure I should."

"Up to you. Anything suspicious, you let me know, okay?"

"Sure."

"You got their cards too?" he said thumbing over his shoulder, indicating the two detectives who had questioned her.

"Yes."

"You call if you find anything, anything at all, okay? No matter how small."

"You—you think I should open this office tomorrow? I mean, was this a terrorist attack or what?"

"That's the thing. We don't know. All this is under investigation. More than likely it was a couple of lone wolves, just doing their thing."

Amy wasn't sure she was hearing this correctly. *Doing their thing?* Someone had been murdered. How could the world just go on its way? She must have been staring with her mouth open because the officer touched her on the shoulder, smiling.

"Look, the crime scene isn't here, so you're probably safe. You weren't the target, so why would anyone want to come back here? They were looking for big targets, crowds, in all likelihood."

"Except that he knows I saw him."

"He probably won't even remember where he ran. He was probably scared out of his mind. I mean, you think this building would be a target? With all this security?"

She recalled the conversation she'd had with her dad about it. Easier targets. Now those arguments seemed hollow.

"If it makes you feel any better, some of the shops in the Plaza are going to be open. Yes, it was a murder. But that doesn't stop life from going on. People have jobs, go to work, you know."

As the door buzzed shut behind him and he slipped

under the tape outside, carting the sandwich sign wrapped in a large plastic tarp, she wondered why she hadn't heard from the building owner and developer. Or from security. No one at the complex seemed to be concerned about what had just happened to her.

She was glad her father was on his way.

CHAPTER 9

Zak and Carter were shooting darts at the Scupper. Several of the other guys joined in. They'd just gotten their orders to report to SEAL Team 3 and were given four days leave, but most of their group decided to stay around the San Diego area and get more familiar with the surroundings. Zak knew some of the guys from Team 3 hung out there regularly.

Fredo and Coop sauntered into the bar. They were most distinguishable by the fact that Coop looked nearly twice the size of Fredo. But the two were the best of friends, as they had been over the past nearly seven years together on the teams.

"Ohhh, lookie dis. We got us some tadpoles here, Coop," Fredo said shuffling over to their table. Zak had his arm extended back, ready to throw his dart, but hesitated. Fredo shook his head. "You get too distracted, my little tadpole. Never take your eye off the target."

Sure as shit, when Zak returned to focusing on the dartboard, his aim was off and the brass marker hit the wall, way off the target.

"Thought you qualified expert, Jell-O" Fredo grinned. He had a gold tooth for one of his canines.

Zak lowered his shoulders and frowned at Carter, who shrugged back in return. Several others of their group snickered.

"You like Jell-O shots?" Coop asked.

"No, sir. I don't drink."

"Smart man," returned Cooper as he looked down on the other newbies. "Fredo, they're making them younger and younger, and they're short now too."

"Another Smurf crew for sure. Thas okay. Good things come in smaller packages, right there my tadpoles?" Fredo was glad-handing all of them, slapping backs and acknowledging each one of the new guys. Coop followed as Zak hit his second and third dart, the third one right in the center.

"Look at that! A barn dart!" Coop barked. "Thought you was gonna dust them all."

"Focus. And yes, I qualified Expert," said Zak softly.

"So how'd you get the tag then, Jell-O Man?"

Zak tried to shrug it off.

"Oh come on, white boy. Tell the man," Carter shouted. "You guys gonna love this."

"I can hardly wait." Fredo came over to Zak and sniffed. "You smell like Chrome, man, that teen after shave. You don't smell like Jell-O. So what gives?"

Zak could feel his ears getting red. He figured he'd get it over with. "I pulled a prank when I was in high school. We put cherry Jell-O in the other high school's fountain. It foamed all over the place. Turned the whole quad red."

No one said anything for a few seconds. Finally Fredo turned to Carter. "That's it? Carter, what the hell you talking about?"

"No, my man!" Carter ran to Zak's side and placed his arm around his shoulder. "He got *arrested* for doing that prank. Arrested by the father of the girl he was stickin."

"Oh I get it. Daddy didn't like you and his little one hanging out, so he sort of threw the book at you?" Coop said.

Zak nodded.

Fredo gave a disgusted look by scrunching up his unibrow. "That's not funny. Carter, you got some sick sense of humor if you think that's funny. We got things way better than that and you better be ready, man. That shit," he said as he pointed to Zak, "That shit is boy scout stuff."

"I think Carter has the stories you really want to hear. Mine are just, well, probably tame," answered

Zak.

"You can be as tame as you like as long as you got my six, Zak. You don't have to be outrageous to be a good team guy. You don't have to drink, don't have to do half the shit the other guys do. Just keep it clean."

"Yessir."

"Alright. So you guys are all invited over to my place tomorrow for a barbeque. You'll be on good behavior, 'cause our wives will be there. We'll invite some local girls, friends of the ladies, and such, but you be respectful. We got a few days for you to recover, but nothing stupid, and no fuckin' pranks at my house. I got two kids," Cooper boasted.

"You guys can bring your girls, if you want," said Fredo. "If they're decent type. No hookers or strippers. We got the ladies and the kids to think about."

The tadpoles grinned.

Zak's cell phone chirped. Looking down at the number, he saw it was Amy. His gut turned over as he looked at the monitor a second time.

No question. Amy was reaching out to him, and for some reason, he knew it wasn't good news.

"Excuse me for a sec." Zak ran outside and took the call on the patio which was much quieter than the inside of the bar. "Amy? That you?"

"Zak! Oh my God, Zak. I'm so glad I got hold of you."

"What's going on?"

"There's been a shooting."

Zak plugged his other ear so he could hear. His heart began to race, and his gut felt hollow. "You okay, Amy? Are you hurt in any way?"

"No, Zak, but it's like a zoo down here."

"Where did this happen? Where are you?"

"I'm in San Francisco, at my job—"

"Are you safe? Are you in a safe place right now?"

"Yes. Behind locked doors. Already talked to the police."

"So this happened at work?"

"Well not exactly. A gunman, I guess they're saying two gunmen, shot some people at the pier close to my office."

"They catch the guys?"

"No. Well, yes. One was shot, but the other one—"

"So they haven't captured everyone yet? You've got to get out of there, Amy."

"I know. I'm waiting for my Dad. I probably have to wait for the police again too. But Zak, *I saw the gunman who got away!*"

"You saw him?"

"Yes, he tried to get in the building where I work, but the doors were locked. But he knows I saw him, Zak. That's what's got me so scared. I mean I was lucky he didn't get in, but I saw his face, saw the look on his face, and he knows I would recognize him. I'm afraid he'll come back."

"You have to get out of there."

"This might sound ridiculous, but the police said I should just hold the open house like I always do on weekends. I mean—"

"That's stupid, Amy. No. You don't do that."

"It's my job. That's what I do. This just happened, so I haven't heard from the building owner yet. I'm sure he'd want to hear all about it and will probably contact me tomorrow. But I just wanted you to know."

"I'm so sorry, Amy. I didn't hear anything about this down here."

"You're back in San Diego. Not at a training site?"

"No, we just finished one set of trainings and are getting ready to do our workup."

Zak needed to make a decision and quick. He knew what would happen if he went near Amy. His overarching motivation was to help Amy feel safe, help comfort her, but he didn't want to take advantage of her fear. It was a thin line he was walking. He knew she was terrified and had nowhere else to turn, except her father, who might not be exactly what she needed right now. He felt obligated to protect her, yet knew he'd promised himself he wouldn't get entangled.

Damn. She was going to let him make the first move.

"I have a few days, Amy. You want me to come up there? Would that help?"

He heard her relax as she let out air she'd been holding. "Could you do that, Zak? I'd be so grateful." He was still shaken from the news that Amy had been so close to danger—and she was an innocent, not trained to be part of this type of action. He knew she must be working hard to hold it all together and it worried him.

"Let me see what I can do. Gotta check in with our Team liaison. I'm new to all this. If he says no, then I'll have to stay here, but I'm willing to check. The Navy owns my ass first. I'll call you back, tonight if I can." He wasn't sure how this would go over with the liaison, but he had to try.

"Thank you, Zak."

"Are you staying in San Francisco, or going home with your dad?"

"I think I have to stay here for the investigation. I just don't know. He'll want to take me home, I know. But I don't think I can. He should be here any minute."

"Okay, then. Try to get some sleep. Good that your dad's coming. I know better than to have you give him my best. Probably better you not tell him, but that's up to you."

"Not to worry. I can handle Dad. Just get up here as soon as you can. I miss you."

That was the part of the conversation that made him stumble. He'd opened the door to something bigger. Was this an honorable thing to do or a mistake? Could he trust himself?

He decided that if the Navy would let him go, he'd be there for Amy. It was the right thing to do. But not if it affected his career.

CHAPTER 10

AMY HOPED ZAK would be coming up. She knew it wasn't a sure thing, but took some solace in the fact that at least she'd talked to him. It settled her nerves just a little. She took a shower, letting the warm water sluice down her body, trying to put the visions of the sirens, the blood, and the killer's face out of her mind. It wasn't working.

She put on some comfortable clothes she could fall asleep in and waited for her father's text.

True to his word, Chief Allister Dobson arrived an hour plus minutes later. As usual, he pulled up to the garage gate. Amy took the elevator down and ran through the abandoned garage to where her father was parked outside the security curtain. She used her key to raise and then lower the gate after her father entered. She directed him to a spot next to her car.

Dobson took firm hold of Amy as she rushed to his arms. She felt the stiffness and tension in his frame.

"Thanks, Dad," she whispered to his ear.

He seemed hesitant to let go of her, as she struggled to pull away. "Anything new?" he asked quickly. "I figured you'd call me if there was. I've been listening to the reports on the way down."

"I haven't had the nerve to watch anything except the initial reports. Waiting for you to come, I guess."

"Apparently they still haven't caught the other guy. You say you saw him?" Dobson said as they made their way to the elevators. "Who talked to you?"

Amy shrugged. "I have their cards. You can call them if you want."

"I'll do that later."

The whir of the elevator ended in an abrupt jerk as they reached the tenth floor. Amy jumped nervously and noticed her dad study her, with his eyes narrowed and a furrow between his brow.

"You okay, Amy?"

She started to tear up, grateful she was leading him down the hallway to her door so he wouldn't see her state. "I'm holding up. Just not what I'm used to."

The door closed behind her father. "No one should have to get used to this. This is what we do every day. Just can't contain all the nuts of the world. I wish it was different, but everywhere has the same problems. No one is really safe anymore. Not really."

Amy knew that now. She felt like she'd been awakened from a deep sleep. Her world of picnics, parties, hookups and shopping suddenly felt very small and meaningless. "I guess I've been living in a bubble, Dad. I just never knew how close I could be to something—"

"Now you know why I was so afraid of you living here in San Francisco. Amy, you've got to come home." Her dad looked disheveled in his dark rain slicker with two layers of shirts underneath, not the usual crisp uniform she was so used to seeing him in. He looked smaller and older than she'd remembered him.

"No, Dad. I have to stay here for now. And do you think things are really safer in Sonoma County? Really? I mean can you honestly say this type of thing wouldn't happen there too?"

Dobson angled his head. "But there at least I can keep an eye on you."

"But you protect and serve the whole community. It's your job. You can't spend your time 24/7 protecting me."

"But if you lived at home—"

"Don't you think I have to start living my own life? I mean when will it ever be safe enough?" She took his hands, drawing him over to the couch. "Sit. Can I make you something?"

"No I'm fine." Amy left him sitting in the middle of her living room as she got him some icewater. He was searching the room, looking at furniture and pictures, and then focused on the sliding glass door to the outside with views of the San Francisco skyline at night. She handed him the water, taking a seat at an adjacent chair.

"This is home now, Dad."

He took a sip and shook his head. Searching the walls and then focusing on her face, he answered her. "I don't see it. You've made a nice place here. I can understand why you like it. Exciting to be on your own. I get that. But these are strange times, Amy. I can't even begin to tell you what we have coming in every day, alerts and information from the FBI. The whole social media thing has gotten way out of hand. We got the military asking all their service members to stay off social media, like we've been telling our own guys and gals for more than a decade now."

"Maybe it's a good thing people are more aware of their surroundings, like I've become. Although I wish it wasn't this way. I just never thought these things would happen here."

"Still the safest place around. But that doesn't mean you have to live in the middle of it. This is a nice neighborhood, and still you're not immune."

Night sounds from the city began to drain back into the background as Amy's nerves began to chill. She checked her phone, expecting either an update from building security or from Zak. It was close to nine-thirty.

"So tell me what happened, exactly," her dad asked finally. Over the next few minutes she told him about the man and her interaction with the police.

Eventually, she was talked out. The stress of the day had taken a toll on her body. "You're staying over, right, Dad? That couch makes up."

"I'll be fine. I can sleep anywhere."

"Except you're going to sleep here, in my living room. And then I'll make you coffee and breakfast in the morning. Maybe then you can check with some of your friends down at SFPD."

"Not much I can do tonight. You should check with building security before you turn in, Amy," Dobson added.

Amy did so, and was told no further incidences were recorded anywhere in the complex. She informed them she would not be holding the office open on Sunday and asked them if they'd heard from the building owners. They indicated they had not. She told them she'd been cooperating with police.

She left a message for the building management offices, who usually did not work weekends, informing them of the closed sales office.

After getting her dad situated with a blanket and pillow, she closed the door to her bedroom and climbed into bed. Her body ached. Laying her head against the pillow, she noticed her neck hurt, and her jaw felt like she'd been chewing down on something hard all day. Just before she closed her eyes, her phone beeped.

The monitor flashed a message:

'Taking an early flight to SFO. See you tomorrow. Zak.'

She texted back a smilie face, then added a heart emoticon. She'd just fallen to sleep when she heard the ping of her phone again. Zak had sent a heart as well.

CHAPTER 11

ZAK RACED THROUGH the San Francisco terminal, down the escalators and out past the baggage claim. He hiked the black nylon duffel on his shoulders and exited to the taxi stand, got in line and gave directions to the cab coordinator. Checking the driver's name badge swinging from the passenger window sunscreen, he noticed the gentleman's name was Addis.

"Why you want to go back down there?" Addis said as his eyes wildly searched him over the top of the driver's seat. "You hear about the news?"

"Yes. Is it still a mess there?"

"Oh, no. All quiet now. But I've been telling people to go someplace else. Pier 39, Fisherman's Wharf. Some other place. Not there."

"I'm meeting someone there."

The cabbie grunted. He swerved into the fast lane and joined the slow ribbon of steel heading into the City, several charms and a necklace hooked over the rear view mirror, flapping in the breeze of his open window. He spoke on the radio in a dialect Zak didn't understand.

He'd texted Amy that he'd landed and was on his way. It was past nine o'clock, much later than he'd expected. Now he was stuck in traffic.

"Plane was late. So much traffic," he said to the cabbie.

Addis rolled his head and then barked back, "No! Worse earlier. This is much better. Always like this on the weekend except real early. Worse on the work days. Sunshine, clouds, shootings—everyone wants to come to San Francisco today. Nuts. All peoples are nuts."

Zak was inclined to agree.

"So no word on the other shooter?"

Addis laughed. "He look like me!" He continued to chuckle, his eyes getting wide, giving a grin showing off all his stark white teeth. "But trust me, I don't know the guy. From the pictures they have, I don't know anything about him. Looks like one of thousands of peoples who live here."

Zak watched the slowly moving landscape and other passengers in vehicles. This highway had the same numbers of Mercedes as the San Diego area had. Traffic was just as bad, too.

"They're saying he was a terrorist," Zak said.

"Who knows? Somebody unhoppy. All sorts of

peoples unhoppy all the time. Too many." After a pause, the cabbie looked in his rear view mirror at Zak. "You police man?"

"No."

"What you do here?"

"I'm not part of the investigation. Here to visit a friend, that's all. Visiting a—a—girlfriend."

"Okay. Well, do her a favor and take her away from this place. No place for a woman here right now."

Zak was dropped off at the front of the address Amy gave him, and he walked into the Building One lobby, after being buzzed inside by the guard behind the desk. He texted her that he had arrived.

"I'm here to see Amy Dobson. She's expecting me."

Before the guard could call up to her apartment, the back door opened, and Amy came running out. Her light brown hair was down, trailing after her. She wore faded blue jeans that hugged her impossibly thin hips, and an oversized white sweatshirt hung off one shoulder. Her fresh face sparked all kinds of good things, kicking his heart into gear as he felt adrenalin spread all over his body. Clearly, that familiar chemistry was there again. Big time.

He felt her crush into him, as his arms wrapped around her, squeezing and lifting her feet up off the floor. "So happy to see you're okay, Amy," he whispered.

"Thank you so much for coming, Zak."

They parted and he could see from the redness in her eyes where she'd been crying. "You okay?"

She slipped her arm around his waist as she waved to the guards and then took him through the doors to the hallway leading to the elevators. "Dad came last night and spent the night on my couch. He's down at the station right now, getting some information. Supposed to call me later on. I've just been here, waiting."

The elevator doors opened. Zak drew her into his arms as the elevator rose. "You must have been scared to death. What did the police tell you last night?"

"Not much of anything. Just that I should be available to them if they catch the guy. I'm apparently one of the only ones to get a good look at him. That's my artist sketch they're putting all over the news."

"Of course, you have to cooperate. I'm sure they know what they're doing."

Zak followed, holding Amy's hand as she led him to her front door. When he stepped through the tall doorway, he was stunned to see the panoramic view coming from her sliding glass door to the outside. The San Francisco Bay, the water, the Bay Bridge and glittering buildings nearby looked like a picture perfect post card of everything beautiful about the city.

Amy walked up behind him, leaning into his back,

wrapping her arms around his front. “You like?”

“My God, Amy. It’s unbelievable. What a view. I don’t think I’ve seen anything like it before.”

“Yeah. I thought it was special too.” She stood next to him, admiring the picture before them. She hadn’t let go of his hand.

“I don’t blame you,” he said, turning toward her. “This is you. This is perfect for you here.”

Her eyes smiled before her lips did. She stepped closer to him, putting her hands up to his neck as he laced his fingers at her lower back. “So good to see you again, Zak. Thank you so much for coming.”

“Of course. Thanks for—” His lips were over hers so fast he wasn’t able to finish. The traveling, the frantic phone call from last night, all his training and all the events of yesterday pushed back into the woods of his mind. It was as if they began right where they’d left off before all the drama. Before the paths they’d taken. The life they’d started separately suddenly seemed to merge into one.

He felt himself falling again down a slope he didn’t want to recover from.

Amy’s cell phone went off. Then it rang a second time. Amy was still returning his kisses.

“Sweetheart. Might be your Dad. The police.” Zak separated them and smiled. He kissed her nose.

Amy ran to the phone. “Dad? What did you find

out?"

Zak watched the slow long look she gave him, starting from his eyes, his chin and then his chest, down below his beltline, to his shoes and then slowly back up again. She angled her head in the opposite direction with a satisfied smile.

She was nodding. "So all that's good, right?"

Zak walked to the sliding glass door and out on the deck. Sirens didn't sound the same as they did in Sonoma County. They echoed and reverberated off the tall buildings. There was more traffic, and he was surprised to hear sounds of people talking as well as the sounds of the boats out on the water. A wind had picked up and was making whitecaps out on the blue bay.

"No, Dad. That's not necessary. I'm okay. You go on back up to Santa Rosa. I'm sure you have a lot to do up there. I'm available by phone anytime. And I'm secure here for now."

There was a pause. Zak could hear her father trying to work his way into coming over.

"Dad. Zak came up. He's here." She paused again. "Because I called him and asked him to. After I called you. He's not staying long. I promise I'll be safe."

Some of the old stiffness returned to Zak's back and shoulders. Dobson would be not happy with this development.

"No. This isn't Zak inserting himself into my life. This is me asking for his help. This is my life, Dad. You do understand that, don't you?"

He could tell Dobson was irritated. He heard a slight edge to Amy's voice.

"No, Dad. My decision is final. He's here, and he's going to stay here for a day or two. That's all. I'll be in touch." She sighed and added, "Yes, I'll tell him." Zak heard the phone shut off.

Amy joined him at last. She slipped her arm into the crook of his elbow and leaned against him. He was going to let her tell him the message from her father. It was her story to tell. Her life. Right now, Zak was feeling like a fifth wheel, second guessing his decision to come up to San Francisco.

"No real news. But Dad said to remind you of the request he made of you to leave me alone. He said you promised."

"I did."

"But that was before all of this. Before you went off to your training. Before a lot of things that have happened since."

"Yup. He might be right, Amy."

She turned toward him, leaning back to get a good view of his entire face. "You think so, Zak?"

Zak slowly focused on her eyes, her lips, remembering the vision of her standing on the deck in the late morning sunshine. The woman he saw was different in some way. Stronger. More determined. She waited for him to respond, didn't cut him off. She *talked* to him. It didn't feel like she was pushing herself at him anymore, while he was having to spend all his time resisting her. That had been their game all growing up. Now he wasn't fighting her, he was fighting with himself.

"No. He's not right, Amy. I don't know what's out there in the future, but being here, right now, seems pretty great to me. Seems like the place I need to be."

The path to her bedroom seemed to take forever, but Zak wasn't complaining. It was the first time he'd been with her in a place of her own. It wasn't the front of his pickup or on a blanket on some golf course lawn somewhere or even at a friend's place for a stolen hour or two.

Amy faced her bed, which was shaded in the long shadows of the morning, the sun having gone to the other side of the building. Zak was standing right behind her, his palms smoothing down the backsides of her thighs as she removed her sweatshirt and turned around in her bra. His fingers gently pushed the straps off her shoulders as he held her face under her jawline and placed a sweet kiss there. His lips found the place under her ear.

She unbuttoned his shirt slowly, placing fingers

against his tanned flesh, kissing him as more of his chest was revealed to her. Slowly they finished disrobing. He let her first place the condom on him, and then they slipped under her cool sheets.

Zak kissed her chest, down to her belly button and then went lower, kissing her at the top of her sex. His intense gaze focused on his fingers, now massaging her labia, pushing a finger or two inside her opening, then his thumb as he looked up at her before he bent to kiss her there.

She arched at the touch of his tongue in such an intimate spot, at the feel of his probing fingers. Her lips began to swell and she felt her pulse quicken. The sounds of their limbs shifting over the cotton sheets punctuated by the sounds of his kisses sent her into euphoria. It was all real. She could hear the sounds of the boats and the fog horns, the traffic and the bells and chimes of the city as he tasted her, as she heard his soft groan and then watched as this muscled warrior traveled up to lay against her body. They fit so perfectly together.

It was like her dream every night, what it would feel like to have Zak here with her, making love to her in her own bed on a lazy Sunday morning, as if there wasn't anything else in the world to worry about, to concern herself with. The feel of his muscled shoulders and arms was delicious as her hands smoothed up and down. The way his knees separated her thighs, pressing his groin to her core as she rose up, set her heart on fire. With her head forward, they kissed again. She would have said something, wanted to say something, but hesitated.

He spoke first. "Thank you for asking me to come to San Francisco. I wanted to see you. I should have called before—"

He rooted to find her opening as her fingers covered his mouth, and she kissed him again.

"Shhh. You're here now. It's perfect now, Zak. Truly perfect."

"Yes," was all he said as he slid inside her. He watched her face as she stared back at him through watery eyes. She closed her eyes and held her breath, feeling her breasts press against his chest as his cock filled her fully. He kissed her lids like he was begging her attention. Back and forth, their movements were long and unhurried. She studied his stubbled chin, the way his clear eyes washed her with passion, the hair falling over his forehead, the way the muscles in his back rippled as she felt the power of him.

Her body was falling in slow motion as they moved in time together. He brought her to her stomach. She placed a pillow under her abdomen as he mounted her from behind. She loved the feel of his heavy breathing at the sides of her face as he kissed her neck, elevated her hips with his hands and plunged in deep. She splayed her knees, needing more of him, not ever being able to get enough.

Slowly her orgasm built as they lay on their sides, her knee over his hip. She threw her head back as she exploded, shattering into spasms that shook her whole body. He held her hips with his hands until, side by side, she felt him pulse into her.

An hour later, they were still entangled together on the bed, hot sweat now dried. A cool breeze drifted from the living room door left open.

CHAPTER 12

HASSAN SHAVED OFF most of his hair, but not his chin hair. The face that stared back at him from the cracked mirror did not look like the face on his passport. His parents even would not recognize him. If he were a woman, he could use makeup and trace his eyes, change their shape and wear something to color his lips. But this would have to do for now.

He'd hoped to receive confirmation a gift would be waiting for his parents in Aden, but nothing had come. He'd tried several numbers given to him, but no one was answering.

The news reports listed his younger brother's picture which was undoubtedly going to lead to him, since the two shared a flat in East Oakland. He doubted the baker where they worked would reveal much, if anything. Besides, all of his contacts happened at the coffee house, not at his place of employment.

He'd cleaned up at the bus terminal, washing his

hands and face in the restroom filled with sleepers. The place was not a stranger to bloody handprints either. He wetted down his hair and put up his hoodie, making it over to the home of his friend, where he told him a fake story about how he'd been robbed and needed a place to crash for the night. He knew his friend worked late nights at a restaurant, so when he went to work, Hassan went on a search of things he could take with him. That's when he discovered the clippers.

His friend didn't have anything in his kitchen, except for a few pickled grains he could take. He knew he couldn't trust the man. He didn't own a television, but that wouldn't stop him from seeing Hassan's face plastered on TVs all over the city. He knew the ferries and busses had cameras, as well as some of the busy street corners. He was better off staying off the street until he could properly disguise himself.

Hassan's cell rang. After their customary greeting the voice was terse and angry.

"You dimwit."

"Did the money get sent?"

"No. You haven't finished the job."

"Sorry? The statement was made."

"Yes. But you were seen. You'll be caught."

"No. I will take my own life first. First I want to be sure my parents got the money."

"You must not be caught."

"I vow I will not be caught alive. What must I do?"

"You have to eliminate the woman who saw you."

"How do I do this?"

"You remember where you saw her. The newspaper says she worked at one of the building near the Ferry Terminal. You know it?"

"I—I don't remember very well. I could retrace my steps. But wouldn't that be risky? And the door was locked. How would I get inside the door of her office?"

"Not my problem, Hassan."

"But we have sacrificed our brother already, please."

"I'm telling you it isn't good enough. You have to make it look like they can't get away. It's the statement. You find her, you take care of it. You both go with God."

Hassan's stomach clenched. He knew he had to leave soon. Morning would bring his friend back home, and it would be too dangerous to trust him.

"You still have the devices?"

"Yes, I have three of them left."

"Good. So you find a way inside that building, you find her. I will make arrangements for the money transfer."

"But how will I know?"

"How do I know you'll do your duty?"

Hassan wanted to protest, but he knew it was a losing argument.

"You make a statement. If you get the girl, your parents get the money. No other way, Hassan. Either way, you'll be looking down from Paradise. You'll be in the garden, my friend."

After he hung up, he checked his canvas bag. The three little IEDs were tightly wrapped in plastic, then put into boxes with bubble wrap to make sure they didn't detonate before he wanted them to. He'd hold one, clutching the bag, and holding the woman by the hair, and he'd send them all away. He replayed the scene over and over in his mind. It was going to be the only thing he thought about. No reason to store up provisions, food or things to seek comfort. All this would be over in a day, maybe less. He'd have his reward, and the things of this earth—all the anger and the pain, the despair of his life—would be gone forever. It was a fair tradeoff.

CHAPTER 13

ZAK WOKE UP all of a sudden and wasn't quite sure where he was. Then he remembered their long lovemaking. He felt her warm body against him, felt the sheets tangled around his legs. Her light brown hair was all over the pillow next to him as he cradled her into his chest. How he wished he could just stay inside all day and play, stay in her arms, love her over and over again.

His forefinger rubbed along the arch of her ear, and he felt her squeeze his arm as she came to with a smile. She rolled over to face him.

"Hi," she said, looking all pink and radiant and more beautiful than he'd ever seen her. He knew a lot of things had changed, and he was seeing her colored in the light coming from his own eyes, a light that cast a rosy shadow over her and everything she was right now. This wasn't something that had ever happened to him before. He knew that he would protect her if it was the last thing he ever did.

"Amy, we have to make a plan."

"Okay, sailor. First you kiss me here," she said as she pointed to her bare right breast.

"Gladly. I intend to do much more than that, but I mean a plan about this guy, the shooter and what the police are working on."

She sat up and covered her chest with the sheet. Zak fingered the sheet down until she was sitting topless. "I like it better this way."

She leaned over and removed the sheet from his thigh and rear. "And I like it better that way."

He whipped the sheet off both of them, grabbed her and pulled her down onto the mattress again. So much for talking about a plan. Time to execute something important, something he didn't have to think about first.

AMY HEATED UP some soup and made a small salad.

"You hear from your building owner yet, Amy?" Zak asked.

"No. I don't think they'll be in until tomorrow, but it's odd. I mean, aren't they contacted when something like this happens? Wouldn't they have precautions? I just feel like I have no guidance.

"Maybe call security?" he asked.

Zak overheard Amy's conversation with the guys at

the front desk. None of them had been contacted further by the police, but they'd been pestered by news media, and several camera crews had been rushed out from the lobby after sneaking to talk to residents going and coming.

"So can't you guys get them to leave? Do they have the right to just barge in here? This is private property."

She listened further.

"Well, give the police a call, then. I think the safety of the residents is primary. And what about the owners? Any word from them?"

She shrugged, indicating to Zak the owners hadn't made contact yet.

"Who are these people?" Zak asked after she'd hung up.

"I thought they were local people, but I guess not. Overseas investors, I'm thinking. The MegaOne Group is a California corporation, but that doesn't mean all the owners live here."

"So what else did the guards have to say? Is there some protocol in place now, with all this going on? They have to have an emergency plan. It's law."

"I guess it depends on what you call an emergency."

"So how would someone sneak into the building if they wanted to?" Zak could see the suggestion was unsettling to her. "Where could you go that's safe, Amy?"

"I have no idea. My place would be safe."

"What if they knew where you lived?"

"How would he—you're not really thinking he'd come here, are you?"

"Well, let's think about it. You're living in the middle of several blocks of people who work, live and play all around you. Lots of strangers. Lots of places to hide."

"But he'd have to know what apartment I lived in. That's not posted anywhere."

"Who would know?"

"The guards. They wouldn't let anyone who didn't live here—"

Zak tilted his head to the left. "The guards? How effective do you think they'd be against terrorists? Tell me honestly, do they look like they have any military training, Amy? Honestly?"

"Well, no."

"Exactly. So what do you think?"

"It's a big assumption. You assume he'd go to the trouble to find me, where I live. I just don't think the world works that way. Maybe in the movies. But in real life? Do you honestly think he'd be stupid enough to come back here, knowing I could recognize him?"

"We're not talking about fantasyland, Amy. This is

the real world. So humor me, where would you go if you couldn't come here?"

"There's a theater. A public kitchen. Some conference rooms."

"Okay, the kitchen would have knives and things. Good. A conference room?"

Zak shook his head. "No. You ever try to beat someone up with a wastebasket or a phone?"

"I'm not trying to beat someone up. Besides, I'll have you here."

"You own a gun?"

"Fuck no."

Zak was actually sorry she didn't.

"Illegal in San Francisco."

"Which is why the shooting happened here, my guess."

"Did you bring one, Zak?"

"No. I left all that behind. Not sure that was so smart."

Amy took their dishes to the sink. She turned around. "I guess the gym on the ninth floor, just below us, would be safe. He'd need a key card to get in." She showed him the ring with her two key cards on it. "I keep one here at all times, the other one goes with me everywhere."

"So he'd steal one."

"The gym has some places to hide, maybe. Some

hand weights and equipment, maybe. Ropes. What do you think?"

Zak stood up and gave her a hug. "That's my girl."

The security desk called and asked Amy to come down to pick up a form the owners had faxed into the guard station and wanted her to fill out. At about the same time, Zak got a call on his cell from San Diego. He began updating his liaison on the situation and confirming he arrived safely as Amy grabbed her card and held her finger up.

"Wait, I'll go with you," said Zak as he cradled the phone.

"No. We have no reception in the elevators. I'll be right back."

Amy was out the door before he had time to protest. He finished his call and sat back. He knew he'd just screwed up letting her leave.

CHAPTER 14

AMY HADN'T EVEN bothered to put her shoes on. She was running down the hallway in the flip-flops she kept by the front door. She almost turned around to go back to the apartment, but changed her mind as the elevator doors opened.

She flipped the key card back and forth in her palm. The conversation with Zak was troubling, but she knew why he wanted to have it. His brief time in the military made him wary of all sorts of dangerous situations. That was a good thing. One couldn't be too careful, she thought.

Zak's being present had a levitating mood on her spirit. She was sure he was as into her as she was into him. This morning and early afternoon had opened up a new phase in their relationship, something she wanted to explore fully. Sure, the passion and the fire was still there, but now there was something else. Something—

She heard noises on the other side of the doors leading to the guard station in the lobby. Just as she opened the door, she heard a scream. A woman was jammed in the glass doorway of the building, halfway inside, halfway outside. She'd dropped her purse and her eyes were wide as she looked in panic at Amy's face. She screamed again.

Then Amy noticed that at her side was a man, the same man she'd seen in the doors yesterday, wearing the same green khaki clothes, although his appearance had changed. But there was no mistaking the murderous stare he fixed on Amy as he held something up to the woman's neck. A wide ribbon of dark red blood was trailing down her neck, over the man's hand, onto her shirt, and spilling onto the floor. Her legs were pumping back and forth, slipping in the red goo as she struggled to stand up.

The lone security guard was on the phone before the man dropped the woman on the floor with a loud thud, ran over to him and yanked the phone from the guard with his bloody hands. Another man rattled the glass doors and began to shout.

Amy turned and ran. Luckily, the elevator was still at the bottom floor and as she pushed the button, she noted the stairs and swore under her breath, instead wishing she'd made that choice. As the doors closed, she gasped in relief.

She tried to text Zak, but her lack of cell reception made that impossible. The elevator stopped on the fifth floor, with a couple wanting to get inside.

"Call 911. There's a break-in down at the security office," she shouted to the older couple who jumped at her words.

As the elevator headed to her floor, she heard the security alarm system sound, asking residents to evacuate the building. It took forever for the elevator to make it to the tenth, and she ran down the hall to her door, pounding against it.

"Zak!" she shouted. No one answered. She inserted her card and stormed into the room. Zak wasn't anywhere. His duffel bag still sat at the foot of the bed. Dishes were still in the sink. She called out for him several more times, even going out onto the deck. Adrenaline was pumping through her so fast, she thought her heart would burst.

Out on the balcony, she dialed him. The line was busy.

She continued to call but knew the rapid busy signal was probably generated from multiple people trying to call out. At the kitchen she stopped. The hook that hosted her key cards was now empty. She had one. That meant Zak had the other. He'd taken the card and gone after her.

"Fuck!" she screamed. Outside she heard a siren.

She dialed 911 and got another busy signal.

All of a sudden she remembered their conversation this afternoon. Opening the door, she glanced down the empty passageway with the door to the exit stairs four doors down. Several residents were beginning to come out of their rooms. She carefully closed her door, leaving her flip-flops in the hall. She didn't want them slowing her down or making slapping noises while she ran.

Barefoot, she slipped past a cluster of residents waiting for the elevator. She quietly opened the heavy metal door to the stairwell getting the attention of a couple other residents who began to follow her. She quietly ran down the metal grids until she got to the entrance of Floor 9. The doorway was closed, but unlocked. She could hear other residents heading down the stairs from below and someone running up, pushing past other people moving opposite.

She poked her head over the railing, hoping perhaps it was Zak, and came face to face with the shooter, staring up at her from two landings below. Immediately she ran through the Floor Nine entrance, nearly toppling as she banged against the walls. She passed utility and equipment room signs, as well as a unisex bathroom, until she found the glass doors of the gym. Quickly scanning her key card, she went inside the cool studio dotted with weight equipment and matting. As the glass closed behind her she heard the stairwell door burst open, followed by footsteps.

Amy chose to run into the men's rest room, thinking he'd not expect that. She stood on the black seat of the toilet, trying to keep the metal stall opening from swinging back and forth, and held her breath. She was gripping the key card so tight it nearly cut into her palm, so she quickly inserted it inside her bra.

Listening for every sound, she heard someone swipe the key card and walk inside the gym. Their deliberate steps were calm, unhurried.

"I have captured you. It is of no use to run," the man shouted. She could hear him chatter prayers while he searched. "Your days of living a filthy life in a filthy country are over forever. It is no use holding out for a chance at what you call redemption. This is your fate."

Amy heard chanting as the man began to sing a prayer, repeating a stanza several times over and over again. That's when she realized he wasn't going to come after her, but was going to do something else instead.

She tried to recall what the news reports had said. The first shooter had with him several small explosive devices which had been undetonated, indicating he'd been stopped before they could achieve their original goals.

She looked at the metal walls of the lavatory stall

and hoped it could save something of her—enough so she might survive a blast. She put her head below her outstretched arms, resting her chin on her knees as she attempted to squat and balance on the flange of the toilet, and held her breath.

She thought about her dad and mentally told him he was right, telling him she was sorry she hadn't listened. She thought about Zak, his kisses, the way he'd loved her body for hours throughout the middle of the day.

If there ever was a perfect time to die, let it be on a day like today. A beautiful day, full of love. Loving someone who loves me back completely.

She felt the hot tears form at the tops of her cheeks at the injustice of it all, knowing Zak would do what he could to avenge her. She prayed that he didn't wind up being too bitter and angry, that he keep working for the good and decent people of the world.

She took one last, long breath and then heard the sound of a key card on glass, the doors pushed open, and a struggle on the mats in the other room. Something metal hit the ground. Someone grunted.

Amy jumped off the toilet, picking up a wooden plunger she found sitting on the granite-tiled floor next to a waste basket. As she rounded the corner she saw Zak wrestling with the shooter as they rolled over the mats in a life and death struggle. Running up to the clutch of arms and legs, teeth and blood from bites and scratches, she raised the plunger and with all her might forced it down on the shaved head of the shooter, breaking the wooden stick in splinters.

Zak looked up at her stunned, his eyes round with fear. He grabbed the sharp stump end in her hands, and stabbed the shooter in the chest, forcing the wood through a crunching of ribs and bone. Blood spurted up like a fountain, covering them all. Zak pointed to the corner.

"IED."

The little metal tube was still rolling until it hit the outer wall, near a large plate glass window. In slow motion, Amy felt the tug on her arm as Zak pulled her through the glass doors and began running down the hall. A second or two later, a huge explosion blew out the glass doors, sending large shattered plate glass like a wave over the whole floor.

Zak tackled her, covering her completely and they slid to the furthest corner away from the gym doors just as another larger explosion sent a fireball that ignited the carpet and the walls and caused the metal light fixtures to melt and drop like candy syrup.

As things began to pop, explode and drop all around them like a mechanical rain, she listened for signs of life coming from the body shielding her. Smoke in the air made her cough. Sprinklers began hissing and attempting to shoot water in uneven sprays over everything. She was lying on her stomach and something was beneath her, pressing against her abdomen. And then it moved. One of Zak's arms was slowly trying to move to the side as another arm held her forehead from pressing into the floor. She felt his warm breath in her ear and heard the delicious sound of his voice, "Are you okay, baby?"

"Yes. How about you?"

He groaned and said through parched lips, "I think I broke a couple of ribs, but I'll live."

She started to lift herself up onto her elbows, as Zak sat up, pulling her with him. "Does that hurt, sweetheart? Can you sit?"

Turning her body, Amy saw his roughed up face, including a couple of head wounds. His blue eyes sparkled back at her, dancing in the light of the small fires surrounding them. She gingerly kissed his cut lips as water streamed down his face.

"Amy, I think this is what you'd call explosive chemistry," his voice husky.

She laughed, hugging him until he seized up again, knees coming up to his chest when she squeezed too hard.

"Sorry. Sorry, Zak. I forgot."

"Sure you did, kid. You've always been the one to get me into trouble. Look at this place. You think they'll fire you?"

She laughed again. "Ask me if I care."

"Anything hurt?"

"My head," she reached behind and felt a knot Zak found as well." Her hands were covered in cuts, and she was beginning to show signs of bruising. Zak helped her up to standing position.

Another light fixture crashed to the ground, and she started. She could hear sirens and the blare of large rescue vehicles and possibly fire trucks sounding a long ways down below. Wind whipped through the hallway tunnel, blowing fabric, and pieces of miniblinds that bundled up looking like metallic bunches of grapes.

Zak had a trickle of blood falling down below his ear. His lips were cut and chapped, and he squinted. A large purple welt was forming on the right side of his forehead.

"The shooter?" she asked.

"Oh, they'll find bits and pieces of him all over this floor, probably scrape some of him off the side of the building too when the window washers come." Zak coughed. "We should get out of here. Can you walk?"

She tried a step, her arms around his waist. "I'm good."

"Let's get out of Dodge," he whispered, leading her toward the stairwell entrance. He pushed her behind him as they walked past the nonexistent doors to the gym and found the windows had completely blown out, the force of the blast overturning equipment. The mirror-covered walls covered in blood spray looked like a contemporary painting. Several rags of clothing remnants soaked in deep red puddles against the walls. There was a large crater blasted in the center of the room with splinters of flooring scattered everywhere like toothpicks.

Opening the stairwell door, they could hear heavy boots running up the steps, carrying equipment. "Anybody up there injured?"

"We're fine. Not sure about anyone else, but I think your shooter has become one with the source," Zak barked.

CHAPTER 15

THE OYSTER BAR at the Ferry Plaza he had on good authority was a good place to have a special occasion. His new LPO for SEAL Team 3, Kyle Lansdowne, had told Zak all about it, told him to say his goodbyes and then get his butt back to San Diego for the workup.

"You don't want to start out on this team as a slacker. We don't really get time off, so while it's nice to get all cozy with the girlfriend and get her head on straight, we've got a mission to work up for."

"Roger that, sir."

"We can't always come home. Most of us miss holidays, anniversaries, kid's birthdays, and even our kid's births on a regular basis. That's just the way it is. Don't cry over it."

"I get you, sir."

"But damn, I gotta say for a little tadpole, a newbie frog, you sure handled yourself well, sailor. Way to get that little punk to give it up and not take any more people with him."

"Thank you, sir."

"Mighty proud. And your lady, I hear tell she held up quite well. You got a keeper there, son."

"I think so too, sir."

"So what the fuck you waiting around for? Ask the girl to marry you, and get her little ass down to San Diego where you can keep an eye on her."

"I intend to, sir."

"I'm gonna ask you first thing when I see you next. Don't complain and cry on my shoulder telling me you screwed all night long and forgot to ask her, okay? Make an honest frog princess outta her, son."

"I get your message loud and clear, Chief Petty Officer Lansdowne."

Amy was returning from the ladies room, so he signed off and took a sip of his beer. She sat next to him. Except for the fact that the two of them looked like they'd gotten into a fight, Zak thought they made a pretty good looking couple as he stared across the bar to the large wavy mirror. The waiter brought them six barbequed oysters from Marin County. The hot spicy tomato flavor wafted up in the steam that blew in their faces as they hovered over them.

"Those look wonderful." Amy's eyes were bright, her face illuminated by soft candlelight.

Zak squeezed a lemon wedge over the hot mixture. He held one shell up to Amy's mouth. "Yours. These are supposed to be the best in the bay."

Amy swallowed the mixture, shutting her eyes as a little part of the sauce dribbled out the right side of her lips. Zak kissed it away.

"Your turn," she said and held up another shell, tipping it so the hot oyster mixture slid onto his tongue.

"Hog Island is famous to SEAL Team 3, or at least to our LPO."

"LPO? What does that mean?"

"Leading Petty Officer. He's like in charge of our platoon. You'll get to meet him soon, I hope. Maybe there will be time before we deploy, but for sure when I get back."

"So what are your dates?" She asked, taking another oyster.

"Well, that kinda depends on you, Amy."

"On me?"

"When I come home next time, I'd like to ask your father permission to marry you, if you'll have me."

Her smile started slow, and for a second Zak panicked. But when her lips turned up and she winked at him, he relaxed. He'd been nervous all day, knowing he wanted to ask her, and not knowing exactly how to do it, until Kyle told him about this place. And it seemed fitting to do it here, near where all the violence had happened, where their lives had changed forever.

"If you can't answer, I'd totally understand. You don't even know about the community, and it's not an easy life. Hell, I'm just getting used to it myself, getting to know all the guys. But these are special guys, unlike anyone else I've ever met. I think you'd fit right in, if you're willing."

"Of course I'm willing. You sure, though?"

"Completely. You wanted to be the girl I came back to. I want that too."

She looped her arm through his and leaned into him, rubbing her chest against his elbow. "So did you ever think of a Plan B? I mean, what if I said no?"

"Well, I was going to go look for a golf course."

ABOUT THE AUTHOR

NYT and USA Today best-selling author Sharon Hamilton's award-winning Navy SEAL Brotherhood series have been a fan favorite from the day the first one was released. They've earned her the coveted Amazon author ranking of #1 in Romantic Suspense, Military Romance and Contemporary Romance categories, as well as in Gothic Romance for her Vampires of Tuscany and Guardian Angels. Her characters follow a sometimes rocky road to redemption through passion and true love.

Now that he's out of the Navy, Sharon can share with her readers that her son spent a decade as a Navy SEAL, and he's the inspiration for her books.

Her Golden Vampires of Tuscany are not like any vamps you've read about before, since they don't go to ground and can walk around in the full light of the sun.

Her Guardian Angels struggle with the human charges they are sent to save, often escaping their vanilla world of Heaven for the brief human one. You won't find any of these beings in any Sunday school class.

She lives in Sonoma County, California with her husband and her Doberman, Tucker. A lifelong organic gardener, when she's not writing, she's getting *verra verra* dirty in the mud, or wandering Farmers Markets looking for new Heirloom varieties of vegetables and flowers. She and her husband plan to cure their wanderlust (or make it worse) by traveling in their Diesel Class A Pusher, Romance Rider. Starting with this book, all her writing will be done on the road.

She loves hearing from her fans:
Sharonhamilton2001@gmail.com

Her website is:
sharonhamiltonauthor.com

Find out more about Sharon, her upcoming releases, appearances and news from her newsletter, **AND receive a free book** when you sign up for Sharon's newsletter.

Facebook:
facebook.com/SharonHamiltonAuthor

Twitter:
twitter.com/sharonlhamilton

Pinterest:
pinterest.com/AuthorSharonH

Google Plus:
plus.google.com/u/1/+SharonHamiltonAuthor/posts

BookBub:
bookbub.com/authors/sharon-hamilton

Youtube:
youtube.com/channel/UCDInkxXFpXp_4Vnq08ZxMBQ

Soundcloud:
soundcloud.com/sharon-hamilton-1

Sharon Hamilton's Rockin' Romance Readers:
facebook.com/groups/sealteamromance

Sharon Hamilton's Goodreads Group:
goodreads.com/group/show/199125-sharon-hamilton-readers-group

Visit Sharon's Online Store:
sharon-hamilton-author.myshopify.com

Join Sharon's Review Teams:

eBook Reviews:
sharonhamiltonassistant@gmail.com

Audio Reviews:
sharonhamiltonassistant@gmail.com

***Life** is one fool thing after another.*

***Love** is two fool things after each other.*

REVIEWS

PRAISE FOR THE GOLDEN VAMPIRES OF TUSCANY SERIES

"Well to say the least I was thoroughly surprise. I have read many Vampire books, from Ann Rice to Kym Grosso and few other Authors, so yes I do like Vampires, not the super scary ones from the old days, but the new ones are far more interesting far more human then one can remember. I found Honeymoon Bite a totally engrossing book, I was not able to put it down, page after page I found delight, love, understanding, well that is until the bad bad Vamp started being really bad. But seeing someone love another person so much that they would do anything to protect them, well that had me going, then well there was more and for a while I thought it was the end of a beautiful love story that spanned not only time but, spanned Italy and California. Won't divulge how it ended, but I did shed a few tears after screaming but Sharon Hamilton did not let me down, she took me on amazing trip that I loved, look forward to reading another Vampire book of hers."

"An excellent paranormal romance that was exciting,

romantic, entertaining and very satisfying to read. It had me anticipating what would happen next many times over, so much so I could not put it down and even finished it up in a day. The vampires in this book were different from your average vampire, but I enjoy different variations and changes to the same old stuff. It made for a more unpredictable read and more adventurous to explore! Vampire lovers, any paranormal readers and even those who love the romance genre will enjoy Honeymoon Bite."

"This is the first non-Seal book of this author's I have read and I loved it. There is a cast-like hierarchy in this vampire community with humans at the very bottom and Golden vampires at the top. Lionel is a dark vampire who are servants of the Goldens. Phoebe is a Golden who has not decided if she will remain human or accept the turning to become a vampire. Either way she and Lionel can never be together since it is forbidden.

I enjoyed this story and I am looking forward to the next installment."

"A hauntingly romantic read. Old love lost and new love found. Family, heart, intrigue and vampires. Grabbed my attention and couldn't put down. Would definitely recommend."

PRAISE FOR THE SEAL BROTHERHOOD SERIES

"Fans of Navy SEAL romance, I found a new author to feed your addiction. Finely written and loaded delicious with moments, Sharon Hamilton's storytelling satisfies like a thick bar of chocolate." —Marliss Melton, bestselling author of the *Team Twelve* Navy SEALs series

"Sharon Hamilton does an EXCELLENT job of fitting all the characters into a brotherhood of SEALS that may not be real but sure makes you feel that you have entered the circle and security of their world. The stories intertwine with each book before…and each book after and THAT is what makes Sharon Hamilton's SEAL Brotherhood Series so very interesting. You won't want to put down ANY of her books and they will keep you reading into the night when you should be sleeping. Start with this book…and you will not want to stop until you've read the whole series and then…you will be waiting for Sharon to write the next one." (5 Star Review)

"Kyle and Christy explode all over the pages in this first book, *[Accidental SEAL]*, in a whole new series of SEALs. If the twist and turns don't get your heart jumping, then maybe the suspense will. This is a must read for those that are looking for love and adventure with a little sloppy love thrown in for good measure." (5 Star Review)

PRAISE FOR THE BAD BOYS OF SEAL TEAM 3 SERIES

"I love reading this series! Once you start these books, you can hardly put them down. The mix of romance and suspense keeps you turning the pages one right after another! Can't wait until the next book!" (5 Star Review)

"I love all of Sharon's Seal books, but *[SEAL's Code]* may just be her best to date. Danny and Luci's journey is filled with a wonderful insight into the Native American life. It is a love story that will fill you with warmth and contentment. You will enjoy Danny's journey to become a SEAL and his reasons for it. Good job Sharon!" (5 Star Review)

PRAISE FOR THE BAND OF BACHELORS SERIES

"*[Lucas]* was the first book in the Band of Bachelors series and it was a phenomenal start. I loved how we got to see the other SEALs we all love and we got a look at Lucas and Marcy. They had an instant attraction, and their love was very intense. This book had it all, suspense, steamy romance, humor, everything you want in a riveting, outstanding read. I can't wait to read the next book in this series." (5 Star Review)

PRAISE FOR THE TRUE BLUE SEALS SERIES

"Keep the tissues box nearby as you read *True Blue SEALs: Zak* by Sharon Hamilton. I imagine more than I wish to that the circumstances surrounding Zak and Amy are all too real for returning military personnel and their families. Ms. Hamilton has put us right in the middle of struggles and successes that these two high school sweethearts endure. I have read several of Sharon Hamilton's military romances but will say this is the most emotionally intense of the ones that I have read. This is a well-written, realistic story with authentic characters that will have you rooting for them and proud of those who serve to keep us safe. This is an author who writes amazing stories that you love and cry with the characters. Fans of Jessica Scott and Marliss Melton will want to add Sharon Hamilton to their list of realistic military romance writers." (5 Star Review)

"Dear FATHER IN HEAVEN,

If I may respectfully say so sometimes you are a strange God. Though you love all mankind,

It seems you have special predilections too.

You seem to love those men who can stand up alone who face impossible odds, Who challenge every bully and every tyrant ~

Those men who know the heat and loneliness of Calvary. Possibly you cherish men of this stamp because you recognize the mark of your only son in them.

Since this unique group of men known as the SEALs know Calvary and suffering, teach them now the mystery of the resurrection ~ that they are indestructible, that they will live forever because of their deep faith in you.

And when they do come to heaven, may I respectfully warn you, Dear Father, they also know how to celebrate. So please be ready for them when they insert under your pearly gates.

Bless them, their devoted Families and their Country on this glorious occasion.

We ask this through the merits of your Son, Christ Jesus the Lord, Amen."

By Reverend E.J. McMalhon S.J. LCDR, CHC, USN
Awards Ceremony SEAL Team One
1975 At NAB, Coronado

CPSIA information can be obtained
at www.ICGtesting.com
Printed in the USA
BVHW042132110619
550785BV00009B/120/P